1/13

19.95

Don.

# RIGHTEOUS RESCUE

*Heroism that healed a hurting nation*

John L. Rothdiener

WestBow
PRESS
A DIVISION OF THOMAS NELSON

WestBow Press books may be ordered through booksellers or by contacting:

WestBow Press
A Division of Thomas Nelson
1663 Liberty Drive
Bloomington, IN 47403
www.westbowpress.com
1-(866) 928-1240

Because of the dynamic nature of the Internet, any Web addresses or links contained in this book may have changed since publication and may no longer be valid. The views expressed in this work are solely those of the author and do not necessarily reflect the views of the publisher, and the publisher hereby disclaims any responsibility for them.

Scripture taken from the King James Version

Scripture taken from the New King James Version. Copyright 1979, 1980, 1982 by Thomas Nelson, inc. Used by permission. All rights reserved.

Scripture taken from the HOLY BIBLE, NEW INTERNATIONAL VERSION®. Copyright © 1973, 1978, 1984 Biblica. Used by permission of Zondervan. All rights reserved.

ISBN: 978-1-4497-0385-1 (sc)
ISBN: 978-1-4497-0384-4 (dj)
ISBN: 978-1-4497-0386-8 (e)

Library of Congress Control Number: 2010936770

Printed in the United States of America

WestBow Press rev. date:9/8/2010

# Dedication

---

*For those who have loved ones who did not return*
*home from the Vietnam War. God bless you.*
*May the memories of your loved ones give*
*you comfort. Our prayers are with you.*
*"You are not forgotten."*

*Freedom is never more than one generation away from extinction. We didn't pass it to our children in the bloodstream. It must be fought for, protected, and handed on for them to do the same, or one day we will spend our sunset years telling our children and our children's children what it was once like in the United States where men were free.*

—*President Ronald Reagan*

# Acknowledgements

---

*Special thanks to James, who saved my life in basic training at
Fort Bliss, Texas, in 1967, when he introduced me to Jesus.
Until we meet again.*
*Thanks to my wife, Joy, and Burton & Sylvia Murdock, whose
combined effort made "Righteous Rescue" all that it could be.
And thanks to my granddaughter, Kaylie, whose image graces the
front cover.*

# Contents

PROLOGUE     xv

Chapter 1:    The Forgotten Battle    1

Chapter 2:    The Prison Guard    11

Chapter 3:    Days of the "Weak"    16

Chapter 4:    The Plan Begins    34

Chapter 5:    Recruiting the Prisoners    43

Chapter 6:    Decisions    55

Chapter 7:    The Escape    71

Chapter 8:    The Rough Road    80

Chapter 9:    The Evil Tyrant    88

Chapter 10:    The Embassy    100

Chapter 11:    First Day of Freedom    112

Chapter 12:    Headed Home    119

Chapter 13:    America    127

Chapter 14:    Meeting the President    140

Chapter 15:    The Reunions    149

Chapter 16:    Welcoming the Heroes    164

Chapter 17:    The Award Ceremony    175

Chapter 18:    The Wall    193

Chapter 19:    Honor Due    200

Chapter 20:    Life Again    212

# Cast of Characters

## Prisoners of War

**Sunday**, Specialist Anthony Williams; United States Army medic; rescued by Captain McCarter; spiritual leader of the group of POWs; dreamed of becoming a doctor and missionary in a third world country

**Monday**, Captain James McCarter; United States Army helicopter pilot; highest ranking prisoner; close friend to Specialist Anthony Williams

**Tuesday**, Sergeant Brent Pfingston; captured when supply depot was overrun by Viet Cong; fascinated with cars

**Wednesday**, Specialist Thomas Traber; helicopter gunner; from small town in Kansas; desired to be a helicopter mechanic; captured by Viet Cong when helicopter crashed; lone survivor of ten captured GIs

**Thursday**, Specialist Robert Freeman; psychologist; specialized in neurotic disorders caused by stress of war; diehard baseball fan; captured when ambushed taking patient, Specialist Ronald Lomack to hospital in Saigon

**Friday**, Specialist Ronald Lomack; dairy farmer from Missouri; traumatized in battle; paranoid; strong willed and defiant; seeks revenge

**Saturday**, Corporal Daniel "Danny" Sparks; alias Le Huu Trang; Vietnamese prison guard; spy for General Yo

## Other Characters

**Le Huu Trang**, young guard at POW camp; speaks fluent English; alias Corporal Daniel "Danny" Sparks and Saturday; spy for General Yo; married to Linh; father of three

**Samuel Jefferson**, operated orphanage in Vietnam; formerly served in United States Army Special Forces; befriended Le and his wife Linh

**Corporal Daniel (Danny) Sparks**, known as Saturday; captured by Communist soldiers; General Yo's first prisoner; name lived on for forty years

**Wendy McCarter**, wife of Captain James McCarter; mother of two children—Braden and Kaylie

**Abigail Williams**, married Anthony Williams in 1970; pregnant when husband left for Vietnam

**Linh**, supportive Vietnamese wife of Le Huu Trang; volunteer at orphanage; mother of three children

**General Yo**, sadistic Communist general; operated POW prison; hated Americans; tortured prisoners

**Corporal Nancee Quinn,** young marine; assisted Le to America and helped ease him into society

**Nathan Alexander**, President of the United States; Vietnam War Veteran

**Norman Kingman**, Brigadier General; Chaplain of the United States Army

**Captain Richard (Goldie) Jensen**, close friend to Captain McCarter; rescued by McCarter

**Lieutenant Jason Rader,** Army Intelligence; debriefed Vietnamese prison guard

*He will make your righteousness shine like the dawn,*
*the justice of your cause like the noonday sun*
*Psalm 37:6*

PROLOGUE

# *Arlington, Virginia*

---

Arlington National Cemetery—this beautiful, hallowed ground is a military cemetery and the final resting place of many of the nation's brave heroes. Scores of men and women whose lives were cut short defending America's freedom rest here. Others died after years of torment, still haunted by the horror of war. The famous are buried among the unknown at this sacred memorial.

It was a crisp autumn day; a slight chill lingered in the air. The leaves displayed a wide array of hues—reds, oranges, yellows, greens, and browns.

A frequent visitor, a man of Vietnamese descent, sat on a blanket spread across an ornamental concrete bench. He sat directly in front of the gravesites where five courageous American servicemen were laid to rest. They were extraordinary heroes who fought for freedom and their country in a way most could never imagine.

At first glance, one would think he seemed out of place. His tan-yellowish skin, high cheekbones, and large, dark-almond eyes are common Vietnamese characteristics. However, his face revealed something atypical. Perhaps it was the seriousness in his eyes, or the way he stared at the graves; it was as if he were lost sometime—somewhere in the past.

Since his wife died a few years ago, this had become an almost daily routine. He arrived early in the morning and sometimes stayed until sunset. All for one reason—to pay his respects to the bravest souls he ever knew. He was driven by the need to let the world know who these men were and what they had done.

To an observer, he looked as if he was guarding the five

gravesites as he studied the headstones and then drifted off, deep in thought.

He believed everyone should know the incredible story of these men. Therefore, he continued to type the narrative on his laptop for the world to see. Finally, the truth of their courage and fortitude would be revealed. Their lives would touch the hearts of many.

Curious people stopped and questioned him. He took advantage of every opportunity to share the story of the courageous soldiers. Occasionally, school-aged children placed a wreath on a nearby grave, paying their respect to a fallen soldier. Other times, youngsters gathered around him, listening with interest as he spoke passionately about the unbelievable lives of these men.

He was the only one who could tell the account accurately. He knew the whole truth, because he had been a vital part of their lives many years ago.

Their story began in 1970 in Vietnam, a war-torn country in Southeast Asia, where a controversial war was raging. It was a dark part of United States history. The nation was polarized. Violent protests were frequent. Newspapers and television programs covered the daily events and reported the bloody results.

A great cloud of disagreement surrounded the conflict. The protesters, news reporters, and politicians were the ones who screamed the loudest, but real life was about the patriots who fought the war. Whether or not they believed in the war was irrelevant. Thousands of brave, young, American soldiers put their lives on the line for their country.

Many young people today know little about the Vietnam Conflict. What was the purpose? Who was involved? Some adults still wonder why it happened. To many Americans the war was perplexing.

It was difficult to explain how the man on the bench felt about it, since he was not alive during that complicated period of American history. Yet sometimes he wondered, "Did the South

Vietnamese people deserve their freedom from the oppressive force of the North? Yes, they did. Are they free? No."

His writing may be hard to believe. In fact, if he had not experienced it himself, he would not have believed it. However, it did happen. "They" were his proof—those men whose remains lay deep in the graves where he sat day after day.

# ONE

# The Forgotten Battle

---

Vietnam; August, 1970

Colonel Lawrence Moore entered the crowded mess hall where over one hundred men stood awaiting his orders.

"Atten-hut," the sergeant major yelled.

Every man immediately snapped to attention, eyes fixed on the colonel.

"At ease, men," the colonel ordered.

The air filled with tension. "I'm going to make this short. Intel reports that the enemy has dug in at a province about ten miles from here. Our job is to seek out and destroy all the Cong in this region. The choppers will drop you near the villages. Men, sweep the area carefully. We do not want the enemy getting any closer to this base. If they do, we will be within mortar distance. I don't have to tell you twice—shoot first; ask questions later. Do you understand?"

The men in unison chorused a hearty, "Yes, sir!"

"Let's get a move on. You have ten minutes to be on those choppers. Hit the dirt." The colonel hastily left the room, and the men sprang into action.

Captain James McCarter joined a fellow pilot as they hurried to their barracks.

"This doesn't sound like it's going to be a good day," he murmured.

"I'm with you, James. It's not the way I wanted to spend my

weekend," Captain Richard "Goldie" Jenson replied quietly. "I hate it when the colonel says that."

"Says what?"

"Shoot first; ask questions later. You and I both know when the press gets hold of something like that, there's going to be big trouble for us. They haven't got a clue what it's like to be in a battle and face an enemy you cannot see. They ought to be here a while! The VC's idea of a good day is to burn our eyes out or cut off a limb. They are heartless, and we all know it."

With resolve in his tone, James stated, "I hear you. We do what we must in order to survive. We'll face the consequences later."

"Did you hear the scuttlebutt about Captain Santiago?"

"Do you mean the fire incident and the children?"

"Yes. How was he supposed to know the huts he ordered his men to burn had kids in them? All he saw was the Cong firing from inside. It's unfortunate it was captured on film. The next thing you know, he was burned at the stake by the top brass. They had a perfect scapegoat. How sad! They should have defended him to the last man."

Nearing their quarters, James quickly questioned the other pilot, "What was the latest you heard?"

"All I know is his life is ruined. Too bad. He was a good man. Even if he gets off, the press has made it impossible for him to go home. They call him 'baby killer.' His wife and family get hate mail and threats almost every day."

The men reached the barracks, each deep in thought. "We'll just have to do everything by the book," James replied.

"I don't think it's possible, James. You can't always fight a war by the book. Not this war especially."

The pilots wished each other well.

"I'll see you when it's over," James declared, and punched his friend lightly on the shoulder.

The men ran to their bunks, and hurriedly grabbed their

gear—anything they might need in battle, mostly guns, and ammo.

They also snatched keepsakes from home: photos of a loved one—a wife, girlfriend, or child. Some held pictures of their mothers. One of them clutched a cross necklace, kissed it, and gently placed it around his neck. A couple of the GIs looked in the mirror, precisely combing their hair, so they looked their best as if they were getting ready for prom.

Anxiously, they rushed to the choppers, which were ready for takeoff.

"Move it, move it," the sergeant blared through the deafening sound of the rotors.

The sergeant in command gave Captain McCarter the thumbs-up, which indicated all men were present and accounted for.

The captain returned the signal as the last soldier jumped aboard. His helicopter rose quickly, followed by eleven additional choppers. Gunners positioned themselves on both sides of the aircraft as they headed to their assigned destination. They were ready for action.

The men were silent. Experience told them that mental preparation was vital in winning a battle. They all knew what was at stake. Some took the few quiet moments to pray and ask God for guidance and safety. Others reflected on their loved ones at home. Every man knew the danger of the mission. The hope was that all men would return alive and uninjured.

Approaching the first village, they noticed a battle looming on the ground.

The enemy fired at them, so the gunners quickly returned fire. They knew anything below was fair game. The gunners reasoned correctly that the women and children had taken shelter inside the huts around the perimeter.

The center of the village became the focus of their fire, where the Cong stood, firing at the choppers. The firefight continued nonstop, back and forth.

Three choppers landed in the first village. The other nine continued north to villages a couple of miles away. When the aircraft landed, the soldiers jumped out, firing wherever they saw the enemy. The choppers would take off again with the gunners aboard, still shooting. They circled, waited, and watched for the precise time to pick up the soldiers on the ground. If all went well, every one of them would return safely.

In the first village, the firing from the helicopters ceased when the Cong centered their attention on the immediate problem— the GIs approaching on the ground.

Captain McCarter circled overhead and waited for the smoke bomb that would signal the "all clear." Less than ten minutes later, the white smoke poured out of the first village signaling for the pick-up.

McCarter saw smoke rising in the distance. Obviously, a major battle was taking place in one of the other villages. The black smoke was not a good sign.

McCarter and the two other choppers prepared to land and pick up the ground troops.

Suddenly, an urgent voice blared through the radio, "Red Dog! Red Dog! We need back up now. Red Dog, come in."

"Goldie, this is Red Dog," McCarter replied.

"James, we need help, fast! We've been downed. The VC overran the village. We're surrounded." Goldie's frantic voice verified the urgency of the situation.

"We're on our way, Goldie. Hang on."

McCarter relayed the message to the other two pilots. "Choppers are down in the next village. This one is secure. We need to make the pick-up here later." The choppers immediately escalated skyward.

"Gunners, be ready," McCarter shouted. "There is trouble ahead."

As they approached the village, McCarter could see dozens of Cong swarming from the jungle. There seemed to be no end to them. On the ground, there was chaos everywhere. Three helicopters lay crippled in the center of the village—one flipped on its side.

Some of the GIs had taken refuge in the huts. However, they quickly realized that at any moment the American choppers would attack the village and fire at the Vietnamese dwellings, not knowing they were inside them. Other men were injured and stranded in the downed aircraft.

The dark smoke billowed into the sky making McCarter's visibility difficult. A number of choppers fired at the VC below. The GIs on the ground fought intensely for survival. McCarter knew time was running out for the soldiers.

The enemy persisted aggressively.

The remaining choppers from the other villages swiftly arrived to assist them.

Another pilot's voice boomed through the radio, "Who has room to pick up?"

McCarter's voice echoed, "Our three choppers are empty. Gary, you and the other gunships concentrate on the outskirts of the village by giving us firepower. We are going down now for survivors."

The remaining aircraft fired in the area of the downed units, carefully avoiding their own men, while the others landed to pick up survivors. The barrage of firepower from the gunners ravaged the jungle and obliterated the enemy soldiers.

The sole thought the GIs on the ground had at this point was survival. They would do everything in their power to protect not only themselves, but also their comrades. The scene was frenzied and the situation extremely bleak.

Anxiously, James radioed the ground troops. "Goldie, do you have any casualties?"

"James, it's a blood bath. There are no civilians here, just VC. We walked right into a trap. Smith's helicopter is in flames. Davidson's and mine are disabled. Only my two gunners are left. The rest of the men have taken refuge in the huts. I don't know their condition. My gunners are wounded, but somehow still keep shooting."

"Goldie, we can't be on the ground long. We can only take survivors at this point."

"Got it."

Immediately, McCarter shouted into the radio, "We need fire, we need fire."

"Read you loud and clear," another pilot's voice sounded as his gunners opened fire on the enemy below.

McCarter's unit and two others landed close to the downed aircraft. The rest circled the village, shooting in all directions. The survivors from the crippled choppers, and those in the huts ran to their rescuers. They fired at the enemy while hurrying to safety.

James caught a glimpse of Goldie crawling out of his downed helicopter.

⟶•⟶•⟶•⟶

The two men had a long, intriguing history. James chuckled the day he saw photos of Goldie as a child, showing his golden, curly locks. He understood why he received the nickname that he carried most of his life. Now a captain in the army, Goldie's hair is short, but still honey-colored.

The friends served together at basic training, then air school. They always helped each other through trials and lonely times away from their families. The comrades learned to depend on each other when times were rough. They laughed together when the opportunity arose.

Goldie confided in James when he received word that his wife gave birth to a stillborn son. He would never hold the infant he dreamed of having. His baby, his own flesh and blood, would never have a chance at life. He would never be able to watch his son take his first steps, or toss a football to him. Goldie felt completely helpless during those days. It devastated him to be in

Vietnam, while his lovely, young wife was alone in Dallas, Texas, going through the pain of losing their baby. He was across the world from her. Both were lonely and heartbroken. James was available to listen to him during that dark time, even though he had no answers. He knew more than anything Goldie just needed his friendship.

---

Goldie assisted his wounded gunner as the men piled into James' chopper.

He instantly knew what hit him when a bullet ripped into his leg. Goldie grasped his leg in agony and fell toward the aircraft.

"There's only room for one more. We are already over our weight limit," a soldier in the chopper yelled. "One of you will have to catch another ride," he shouted to Goldie and his injured gunner. The helicopter pilot knew too much weight in the chopper could make it crash, killing everyone on board. Goldie realized the GI was just doing his job.

The pilot's leg wound made it difficult for him to make it to another aircraft. Still, he ordered his wounded gunner on board, stumbled to his feet, and hobbled toward another unit.

"Goldie!" James called as he opened the door and jumped out of the pilot's seat.

He turned to face his trusted friend and confidant. James put his arm around his waist for support and gently lifted Goldie into his seat. "Get out of here. Fast! The Spooks are on their way," McCarter yelled.

When Goldie realized James was willing to make the ultimate sacrifice for him, he was speechless.

"I'll hitch a ride on one of the others."

Goldie and James looked at each other for a few seconds, both unable to speak. They were interrupted by gunfire when a couple of rounds of VC bullets suddenly hit the chopper.

James hastily drew his pistol as he turned and downed the

three enemy soldiers firing at his chopper. "Get out of here. Now!" James yelled and waved him off.

He turned and ran toward another chopper as the injured Goldie piloted James' helicopter into the dark, smoky sky.

The battle scene on the ground below was surreal; the VC invaded the village like an army of fire ants. Flames shot from the downed choppers. Chaos reigned everywhere. Thick, black smoke and fire made it difficult for anyone to see what was happening. VC bodies were strewn throughout the village.

The GIs realized the AC-47 gunships would be on site within minutes. Their six thousand rounds-per-minute guns would obliterate this village and everything in it. They had to evacuate quickly.

The last time anyone saw Captain James McCarter, a number of VC were chasing him toward the opposite side of the village. He fired the final rounds in his pistol. A couple more attackers fell to the ground. The helicopter gunners opened fire at the remaining Cong as McCarter disappeared into the cloud of dark smoke. The last chopper lifted off and returned to base without him.

On the return flight, Goldie saw the Spooks in the distance, headed toward the village. Comforted by their sight, he knew they would finish the fight swiftly. In a matter of seconds, there would be nothing left in the village; the enemy and everything in its path eliminated.

It was not until all the aircraft returned to base that they discovered Captain James McCarter had never made it to the other choppers.

On the ground, James saw the two remaining choppers lift through the black smoke. Knowing he was in trouble, he ran for his life. His pistol was out of ammo, so he dropped it on the ground. He passed a downed chopper, grabbed an M-16 from it, and noticed movement inside. An apparent head wound had knocked a soldier out, and he was just regaining consciousness.

"Can you move?" McCarter hollered over the bedlam.

The dazed, wounded soldier looked behind McCarter and saw the VC approaching in the distance. "If I can't, we're both dead." He stumbled out of the chopper, holding onto McCarter for support. Together, they sprinted as fast as they could.

"The Spooks will be arriving any second. We need to get out of here. Everything in its path will be shredded," the captain yelled as he fired his M-16 at the nearing enemy.

The two soldiers used the smoke to their advantage; it provided cover for escape. They quickly disappeared into the jungle.

Seconds later, the AC-47 military aircraft, known as the Spooks, dropped a number of bombs and riddled the village and jungle with lead. The village lay in smoldering ruins.

The men ran through the jungle until they collapsed, exhausted. They had no choice, but to take a much-needed breather.

McCarter noticed the soldier's injury was severe. He reached into the young man's backpack and pulled out a handful of bandages. As he dressed his head wounds, he discovered the man was a medic in the United States Army, Specialist Anthony Williams.

McCarter and Williams immediately hit it off. They realized right away they had one major thing in common—their Christian faith. While on the run from the VC, they frequently took time to pray for safety, their fellow comrades, and their families back home.

McCarter prayed many times for his friend, Goldie—for healing of his wounds and for his salvation. Goldie did not believe in God, at least not a personal one. He felt if there were a God, he certainly would be too busy for a person like him. "Maybe later in life my faith will be stronger," he told James on more than one occasion.

The men traveled cautiously for two days through the hostile country, always on the lookout for the enemy. They were weary, but fear and anxiety kept them pressing on. They assumed that if they kept heading south they would eventually run into some "friendlies."

Late afternoon on the third day, a few Vietnamese children spotted the two soldiers. When the terrified children ran off, the two friends realized they soon would likely meet their fate.

Within hours, hundreds of VC surrounded them. The GIs knew fighting was out of the question, only certain death would occur. They surrendered reluctantly, knowing they would face hardship and torture, perhaps even death. However, at that moment it was impossible to imagine the extent of brutality ahead.

Words cannot describe the evil treatment they endured. It began immediately following their capture, and never ended for the captives. How any human being could force such inhumanities on another person is unexplainable.

Two
# The Prison Guard

---

Vietnam; 2010

For four years, Le worked as a guard at a prisoner of war camp, deep in the Vietnam jungle, just east of Laos. The disgusting, heartless acts he witnessed during that time were more than most people could bear, but all part of his daily routine.

Le Huu Trang entered the world, February 13, 1985, in a small village in the jungle of Vietnam. He was the only boy out of four children. His parents worked in the rice paddies; a common routine in Vietnam.

The dog tags around Le's neck identify him as "Daniel Sparks," a corporal in the United States Army. Corporal Sparks survived in the prisoners' minds as an American POW for forty years. In reality, Sparks was the young Vietnamese guard named Le. After dark, he was also known as "Saturday" to the prisoners in the cells.

How could a twenty-five year old Vietnamese be an American POW for forty years? The answer goes back to that horrific war in Southeast Asia.

The real Corporal Sparks died in General Yo's prison camp years before. The exact date was unknown. There was no body, just scorched bones, with those of twenty-six other brave young men. General Yo burned the bodies hoping to destroy the evidence. He had a personal vendetta with each of these men because they were from America. His hatred ran deep against all Americans.

As a North Vietnamese soldier, General Yo was known for

his destructive, cold-hearted techniques of warfare. He made his presence known by capturing, torturing, and killing South Vietnamese soldiers in the most inhumane way possible.

When bombs from an American plane leveled his village, killing his entire family, his focus became clear. All American soldiers he captured would be victims of his gruesome revenge and hatred.

To keep the prisoners hidden, they were relocated a number of times over the course of forty years, and ended up on Yo's personal property. Most Vietnamese officials were unaware that these men were in captivity in their country. They were Yo's "secret project."

Thirty-three prisoners began the imprisonment. Only six remain. All the others died in captivity from wounds, torture, or suicide. Sadly, not one died of natural causes. Every death devastated the comrades who survived.

The last attempted escape was a trap. Evidently, the guards listened to the men's conversations and were prepared for the breakout. The failure resulted in the tragic deaths by torture of seven fellow prisoners.

General Yo recruited Le because of his knowledge of the English language. The Vietnamese guard took pride in learning what many believe to be the International language. He studied each word and understood its meaning. With clarity, he enunciated each word. His job was to listen to the prisoners' conversations and report to General Yo anything that would interest him.

Le wondered what information Yo expected to get from them. Why the endless beatings and interrogations? They knew absolutely nothing of value to him.

Undoubtedly, it all went back to the bloody attack on the village when the evil tyrant's family was killed.

All who remain are six men who refer to each other by the days of the week. For personal safety, the prisoners' cell names are Sunday, Monday, Tuesday, Wednesday, Thursday, and Friday. Le was Saturday.

However, Le knew the real name of each one.

--->--->--->---

Years of maltreatment emaciated the prisoners' bodies. What was left of their teeth had yellowed and decayed. Their bodies were afflicted with open sores, unable to heal. Their feet callused, due to not wearing shoes for as long as they can remember. Their eyes were sunken. Their hair was almost gone from lice and mange. All that remained were dirty shells of what used to be strong human beings. They literally resembled walking skeletons with sunburned, scarred, dry skin covering their weakened bones.

Their two meals a day were always the same—a handful of rice, usually mixed with dirt and insects. Sometimes they received rotten fruit or potatoes as a special treat.

Bathing was not a part of their life, but a monthly lime-wash while they were fully clothed was routine. Designed to keep them tolerable for the entire month, it did not work. Their stench became unbearable, especially toward the end of the month. The last time they had new clothing was almost a year ago.

There is an old saying, "Home is where you lay your head." Their home was a cell, which was nothing but a wooden cage with a dirt floor, just big enough to sit up or lie down, uncomfortably.

The treatment of the prisoners by General Yo and his guards was merciless. They starved the men for days, sometimes weeks. Beatings were frequent. At times, they were whipped until they could no longer walk; sometimes they were beaten to death. One of the worst punishments was what the prisoners called, "The hole." It was a small, dark, hot building, which served as a cell. There was just enough room for a man to stoop. He was unable to sit or stand for hours, sometimes for days, and usually cried out in agony.

--->--->--->---

Not only did the prisoners take new names, but they also

created a silent way to communicate with each other to keep anonymity. They developed a unique system of communication similar to Morse code by tapping their feet or hands on the wall of the adjoining cells. It was vital their captors did not know who was tapping. They soon learned what various "taps" meant. Their contact could not be stopped. Their favorite topic of conversation was always the same—home!

The prisoners had one day a week to talk about whatever they chose. It wasn't actually "talking" because no one heard any of these men speak aloud for years. They might scream, or cry out in pain from torture, but never talk, even whisper. Their captors never permitted speaking aloud except during interrogations.

When they returned, exhausted from working in the rice field, digging holes, or some other meaningless drudgery for twelve hours or more, they sat in their dark, dingy cells and watched the same rat night after night, begging for food. Many times, the men were tempted to grab the rodent and eat it. However, they never did, maybe because they considered the rat their friend. The cockroaches and other bugs were a different story—they were fair game.

When night descended, the men sat in their cages and listened to the tapping. Tap, tap, tap. They seldom asked a question. While one man tapped, the rest of the men listened without a sound. In the dark hours, their tapping gave them a sense of closeness with each other.

At the end of each brutal day, they eagerly looked forward to that special time of voiceless communication. Maybe, because when nightfall arrived, they knew they survived one more day. Perhaps, because needed rest would soon overtake them. Sleep was the one time when all seemed okay, unless the nightmares took over as they often did.

The tapping was significant because they talked about what used to be. It was their time to reflect about happy times in their lives, when all was good. It was the only time that each man lost himself in the past, forgetting all the present misery. He could forget the loneliness, the pain, and even the torture, briefly.

It did not matter if the memories were his, or a fellow prisoner's, because they all became part of each other's lives. The fragmented assortment of one another's memories became intertwined. As time passed, their own recollections faded, but others in the group helped them remember their special times.

---

Five words came to the forefront as Le listened to the conversations; they were significant words. Life…Hope… Faith…Love…Responsibility.

Life meant just being able to survive one more day. It could have a positive or negative connotation.

Hope had waned that the American people and their military comrades still remembered them.

Faith once was in God, but that time passed many years ago for most of the men. They felt their unanswered prayers meant that God had given up on them. Some of them wondered if God really ever existed. Did even He abandon them?

Love was the most difficult word to understand. For forty years, they were separated from their parents, wives, children, brothers, and sisters. There was no evidence of love anymore. Was it still an emotion they were capable of feeling?

Responsibility was another complicated concept. What responsibilities could there be? All they had was each other, in a sense that was their only responsibility.

Their hope, faith, love, and responsibility were in their past lives. The words held no meaning for their present or future lives.

# THREE

# Days of the "Weak"

The imprisoned men rarely talked about the last forty, miserable years. It may have been self-preservation, a way to keep their sanity, or possibly simply a survival instinct. Each day was the same as the previous one. None remembered a "good" day.

They never forgot the countless beatings and abuse they suffered at the hands of their captors. The excruciating pain—both physical and emotional, was a daily reminder.

Each week on their day to tap, they looked forward to sharing their recollections of home. It was all they had left; faded memories of past lives, when life was joyful, simple, and contented. Maybe that is what kept them alive.

The men never talked about the days of their capture.

However, Le knew about them. He was aware of exactly what happened that hot summer in the humid jungle in Vietnam. In fact, he knew all about the men's lives—past and present.

## *Sunday*

Specialist Anthony Williams, a man of strong convictions, was nicknamed "Sunday," mainly because of his tendency to preach. Sunday became the day he shared his life experiences.

During the early years of captivity, it seemed like preaching, but not anymore. As time passed, the prisoners rarely, if ever, talked about their faith. God seemed distant, far-off—maybe, non-existent.

There was a time when all of these men prayed daily. They

were not all "religious," but some wanted to play the odds, just in case there might be a God out there somewhere. If so, they surely could use His help. They reasoned that maybe He wouldn't forget them as others did.

Williams, a vibrant black man, handsome and physically fit, was a conscientious objector. He was taught that all human life was to be treasured, not taken. His father, a Protestant preacher, raised him to believe in the sanctity of human life. He had a conviction that all life was sacred—young or old.

As a youngster, Anthony dreamed of becoming a doctor in a third world country. He also had a heart for missions. Many countries would allow doctors to serve, but not missionaries. This way he could get into the country and fulfill both dreams.

When drafted at eighteen, his plans changed dramatically. Williams left his upstate New York home to serve in the United States Army. He was a proud soldier; putting his hopes and dreams on hold while serving his country.

Almost immediately, the young soldier experienced the horror of war. At only nineteen, the army shipped him to Vietnam where the war was raging. He left behind his young, pregnant wife, and lifelong desire to become a doctor.

---

On Sunday's turn to talk, he shared the few remaining memories he had of his wife, Abigail, his high school sweetheart. He married her a month after high school graduation. They were happy newlyweds, on top of the world, when he received his draft notice right before Christmas.

Through the years, he often thought about his bride. He no longer remembered her face; the image was not clear in his mind.

What was Abigail like today? Did she remarry and find love in the arms of another? Does her smile still brighten a room? Her beautiful, dark eyes or the funny snort in her laugh was all things he loved about her. They laughed together at the simplest things, sometimes to the point of embarrassing themselves. They enjoyed life to the fullest!

He recalled how Abigail could not control her laughter when she saw somebody fall. One incident was imprinted indelibly in his mind. They had just arrived at church on a frigid, snowy, January morning. Sunday was dressed in his powder-blue leisure suit. He carefully stepped out of the car and headed over to his wife's side to open her door. The last thing she saw was his step off the icy curb as he disappeared downward.

Laughing hysterically, she barely noticed his head appearing next to her window as he used the door handle to pull himself up. His suit was torn, wet, and dirty. Abigail laughed uncontrollably as she fell to the floorboard, tears running down her cheeks.

When Anthony finally made it into the car, he glanced over to see that tears had smeared her makeup all over her face. That set them both into another wild bout of laughter. They were a sight to see, and never did make it to church that day. They went home and cleaned themselves up.

That was the day they conceived their precious baby.

———✦——✦——✦———

Every day Sunday wondered about his baby. Did I have a son or daughter? He or she would be forty-years-old. Has life treated him or her well? Did my child learn about God and His sovereign power? He prayed for his son or daughter daily.

Sunday and Abigail had a short relationship; but it was happy and fulfilling. She taught him to be a better person—how to live, love, and laugh.

Forty years later, still in the enemy's prison, his dreams were no more than faded memories. Occasionally, one popped up in the back of his mind, almost as if it belonged to someone else.

Death seemed to be all that awaited him. At times, he yearned for it, knowing it would be his only escape to freedom. Life's finality was something he did not fear.

# Monday

"Monday's" real name was Captain James McCarter. He was the high-ranking soldier—a United States Army helicopter pilot.

It was difficult to imagine what he looked like when he was young, fit, and muscular. Undoubtedly, he was a good-looking man with dark hair, deep-blue eyes, and stood over six feet tall. Now, he was just an empty shell; his skin and bones hung loosely on his gaunt frame.

Scenic Colorado Springs, Colorado, was the captain's birthplace. He lived what he believed was the perfect life, with his loving wife, and two adorable children—a son named Braden and a daughter, Kaylie. They were an ideal family; the kind many people envy.

The captain's wife, Wendy, was a stay-at-home mom as most mothers were during that time in America. James owned a thriving insurance agency, which his father had started.

Often when he walked into his comfortable home after a hard day at the office, he broke out singing the classic sixties hit, *Wendy*. His wife smiled, ran to him, and wrapped her arms around him in a loving embrace. They had a special love; it was a fairy-tale kind of romance. They were soul mates, their lives mapped out, far into the future. James was a caring, involved father, and respected husband.

He enjoyed flying his twin-engine plane, and used it for both business and pleasure flights. On occasional weekends, he flew his family across the majestic Rockies. They stared silently in awe at the magnificent, deep-purple mountains, knowing they were seeing one of God's most beautiful creations.

Special surprises delighted Wendy, so James looked for ways to astonish her. One day they flew to the other side of the mountain range, just the two of them, for a romantic picnic. The moment was perfect as they toasted each other with sparkling apple juice. He had slipped champagne glasses in the picnic basket when she wasn't looking. That day they both wondered if life could be any better, or their love any stronger.

Church involvement was important to James and Wendy. Their Christian faith was a priority. James was a deacon in the church. He and some of his friends regularly visited schools, hospitals, and nursing homes giving away small Bibles. Every Sunday they eagerly attended their local church to worship, and often later visited with friends.

As a POW, James occasionally commented that he wished he had focused on the sermons more diligently. When the dark times came, he realized that many truths from the Bible, the things he did not pay careful attention to, could have helped sustain him.

James received his pilot's license his senior year in high school. Flying was the main reason he joined the Army Reserves following graduation. He took up gliding, which quickly became his favorite hobby. The freedom he felt as he soared through the vivid, azure Colorado skies in total silence, exhilarated him, and helped him feel closer to God.

Life as the loving couple knew it ended abruptly when he received the dreaded letter from the government. His reserve unit received a notification to report for active duty. The time had come to pay the United States Army back for his extensive training in the reserves.

Words cannot adequately describe how difficult it was for James to leave his beloved family. He resolved to be strong for them as they said their goodbyes. However, when Braden clutched his leg crying, "Daddy, don't go," his heart shattered into a million pieces.

"I love you, Daddy," were the last words spoken to him by his daughter, Kaylie, as tears streamed down her cheeks.

About to depart, he took a calming breath, bent down, and held his children tight as they cried in his arms.

Then he rose to face his sweetheart, Wendy. Through muffled sobs she cried, "You come back to me; you are the love of my life. Promise me, you'll take care of yourself. I will pray for you every day."

James' voice cracked. "God will protect me." He assured his family of his love.

"I will return in a year," he pledged. As he turned to walk away, his blue eyes moist, he waved a final goodbye.

He walked with his unit to the waiting airplane, and the tears started flowing freely. As they boarded the flight that would take them to active duty, he was not the only soldier with wet eyes. Each had his own reasons for deep contemplation as the plane winged upward into the unknown.

✦ ✦ ✦

The haunting memory of that final goodbye to his family still lingered in his mind. Not a day went by that the men didn't wonder about the loved ones they left behind, four long, hard, decades ago. Many times James wished he had spent more time with his family. People usually do when they lose someone they love.

Monday tried to recall memories to share about his wife, Wendy, in her rose garden. He envisioned her profile, while pregnant with their first child, leaning slightly to trim one of her rose bushes. He was always awestruck by her beauty; her golden hair glistened in the sun. How he wished he could stroke her soft hair again!

At first, he distinctly remembered the fragrance of the roses. In later years, the stench of the prison camp overpowered it—the vomit, diarrhea, filth, and death itself, were the only odors he knew.

Monday and his comrades were mere skeletons; they resembled the walking dead, each awaiting his demise. They no longer had the strength to attempt an escape, and guards watched for any possible suicide attempts.

---

The day of his capture, James received a letter from his wife, which reported his father was critically ill. It was priceless to him, a rare, tangible possession from Wendy. That day he read it repeatedly. He thought he could even smell the faint scent of his wife's favorite perfume on the stationery

On that horrifying day, the captors ripped the letter from James' hands and maliciously burned it in front of him. That was typical of the enemy's cruel tactics.

James watched with misty eyes, his face showing torment, dread, grief, and even fear.

After the capture, there was complete silence, no more communication from home. He never knew what happened to his father, but thought about him every day.

The leader of the captors was a North Vietnamese Army Officer, named General Yo. He used any kind of mental or physical torture he could think of—the crueler the act, the better.

During an interrogation, Yo ripped James' wedding ring off his finger. It was the ultimate act of mental brutality. It nearly killed James.

One of the things Yo often did in his sadistic way, was to concoct stories about the men's families—news that something terrible had happened to a child or wife—horrible things to cause mental anguish. His vile deeds were detestable.

Lies or truth, James never knew which they were. He gave up trying to sort it out, and tried not to dwell on it. He would focus on the first twenty-three years of his life, which he knew were real.

---

Personal faith in God was a priority to both McCarter and

Williams, and the main reason the two men formed a close bond from the beginning.

Monday was the high-ranking military leader, but Sunday was the spiritual leader. Together, they helped each other make it through another agonizing day.

The other four GIs appeared to lose all hope and faith. They sometimes wondered why they even existed in such misery and horror.

Sunday and Monday appeared to have accepted their fate, perhaps because they did not fear death. Yet, their faith had changed. They did not talk about spiritual matters as they once did, tapping on the walls in the darkness of their lonely cells. They realized they were still there for each other, and the only encouragement they ever received. They were resolved to the outcome.

The other four men had only their fractured recollections to keep them alive. No faith in God, or hope in America. They merely existed, perhaps for only one more day.

## Tuesday

Sergeant Brent Pfingston, from Indianapolis, Indiana, was the prisoner called "Tuesday." He was the shortest of the group. Before the capture, his comrades kidded him about it. Sometimes he'd mention how much he weighed before the military. He stated, "I was a little overweight, but not too much—just some left over baby fat." The army routine quickly turned his baby fat into muscle. He was not overly athletic, but certainly no longer "plump," as he called it.

After four decades, he was frail and thin, looking much older than his years. Captivity left its scars on him as it had the rest of the prisoners. His body evidenced harsh abuse. Any muscle he once had was long gone.

Brent, also drafted into the U.S. Army, felt deeply honored

to serve his country. He was proud to be in the army and even prouder to be an American.

The Vietcong brutally attacked the supply depot where Pfingston worked. Sadly, it was just a couple of days before his scheduled return home to his family.

He was one of the fortunate ones—he survived. At least, that is what he thought at the time. However, he soon believed the lucky ones were those who died in battle.

When deployed, he left five sisters, his mother, and father. He does not recall what they looked like. He often tried to capture their pictures in his mind, but after forty years of horrific beatings, those memories were gone.

Many times, he sarcastically asked the question, "Why do they torture a supply sergeant? What possible information can I give them? How many squares are in a roll of toilet paper?"

On Brent's day to tap, he often talked about the Indianapolis 500, especially his favorite racecar driver, A.J. Foyt. Before the army, he worked part-time at the famous Indianapolis Race Track. He met many of the well-known racers of the time: Foyt, Andretti, Unser, even the great British driver, Graham Hill. What a thrill it was to sit in some of their cars!

Since he was the oldest of the siblings, he felt protective of his sisters and took his "big brother" job seriously. Fortunately, for his older sisters, he left for army basic training before he could scrutinize their dates.

During his conversations on his day, Tuesday often commented that he wondered what happened to his sisters. He would tap, "I hope they married good men."

When Brent was in high school, like a typical teenager, he often turned up the volume of the speakers on his car radio to booming music. He would listen to his favorites: The Beach Boys, Jan & Dean and their "car" songs like, "*Hey, Little Cobra*" and "*409.*" He loved cars and continually talked about what car had the biggest and best engine, as if any of the men really cared.

However, they all let him tap about his cars because it was his turn to talk, and those cars were his love.

Very seldom did he converse about relationships. Occasionally, he would lose himself and talk about his dating days in his '67 Camaro. He said it was not a good car to take to a drive-in movie. It had bucket seats and a very small back seat, which meant he could not get close enough to his date.

He never talked about his faith, in God that is. He had faith in certain engines and race drivers, and even cars, but he never mentioned trusting in a Higher Power.

Only Sunday and Monday ended their days with a prayer. Eventually, it became a silent prayer as the years dragged by. Usually their prayers were for others, mostly their families.

How religious the others were before captivity was not clear, judging by the wild lives they lived and the stories they told. There is an expression, "There are no atheists in foxholes." There was even more truth to that in a POW camp, at least in the beginning of confinement.

## Wednesday

Wednesday's real name was Thomas Traber. Before enlisting in the army, he worked as a mechanic in a small town in central Kansas.

Thomas joined the army fresh out of high school. He could hardly wait to enlist because he desired further education, desperately wanting to be a helicopter mechanic. After basic training, he arrived at helicopter mechanic school. He only enjoyed three short weeks of instruction before his company deployed to Vietnam.

Somehow, he became a gunner. "The man in the doorway," the other GIs called him. He was working with helicopters, but not repairing them as he hoped. The gunners had a difficult job. They operated the guns on each side of the aircraft and were indispensable in fighting the war. Sometimes they would see where they were firing, other times they fired blindly into the jungle, hoping to hit an enemy target.

His job was essential. It was his job as "The man in the doorway," to get his fellow soldiers on and off the chopper as quickly as possible. The men were vulnerable when they were getting off the chopper, but even more at risk when they were getting on, with their backs exposed to the enemy. Traber believed it gave new meaning to the term "watch my back." There was no way to know how many people he killed in his military career. He tried not to think about it.

One day, on a routine mission, Traber's helicopter crashed in the jungle. All ten soldiers aboard were captured by the Cong. Years later, he was the lone survivor of that group.

Wednesday frequently tapped about his fishing trips to Wilson Lake. Every weekend, during the hot summer months, he would go to the lake to rest, relax, and have fun with his friends. One of his friends owned a speedboat. Water skiing, fishing, drinking beer, and eating cheeseburgers were all part of the excitement. Many times in captivity he would comment, "Oh, to smell a burger on the grill one more time."

As a youth, Wednesday had several small jobs to raise spending money. One of his favorites was mowing the yard for a senator in Kansas, an influential politician. He often talked about one summer in particular, when he was fifteen. The senator relaxed on his back porch and watched him mow the large grassy area. The Kansas sun was hot and the wind made it stifling. Sometimes it was difficult to breathe.

Often the senator brought out a couple glasses of lemonade and waved Thomas over for a break. They both enjoyed the lengthy conversations about life in Kansas. He had utmost respect for the politician. Wounded in World War II, he still limped from his injury. The senator told him once how it happened, but Wednesday no longer remembered the details. All he recalled was a kind, gentle, man who cared about a young boy. He often wondered what became of him.

One day Le put that senator's name into his computer and ran a search. Wednesday would be surprised to learn he ran for President of the United States. He would be proud of the fact that as a youth he was close to one of America's most influential politicians. Le could not share that news with him, although he wished he could.

The two favorite topics for all the prisoners were Thanksgiving and Christmas. Le could repeat hundreds of stories about those days. The memories of those special holidays seemed embedded in the prisoners' minds, more than any other times.

## *Thursday*

Specialist Robert Freeman, known as "Thursday," was an only child of divorced parents. His red hair once made him stand out in a crowd. Years later, he had very little hair left, and it was dingy gray. Mange and lice took over his once-full head of auburn hair long ago.

Raised in Cooperstown, New York, home of "The Baseball Hall of Fame," Thursday became obsessed with baseball as a young boy. Robert, a die-hard New York fan, believed if the Yankees did not make it to the World Series, there was always the Mets. His philosophy about New York and baseball was interesting. If they play each other at the Series, it was no contest. It would be the Yankees all the way. If neither team made it, then it really was not a World Series after all—at least not one he would be watching. He felt strongly that the Yankees were the team of the century.

He talked about two specific World Series. He remembered the Series in 1961 as the most exciting one ever. His only regret was how it turned out. Yankee, Ralph Terry, pitched to Pittsburgh's Bill Mazeroski. The result was a game winning home run. Pittsburgh played well and deserved their win that day.

However, his favorite was the 1969 "Miracle Mets." He talked endlessly about that series and boasted, "Tom Seaver was one of the greatest pitchers of all time. Players like him are one in a million."

Robert's father, a prominent New York City lawyer, had many famous clients. None was more important than the New York Yankees organization. This gave him the privilege of having season box seats just a few rows behind the team's owners.

One of the biggest highlights in Robert's life was the day he witnessed Roger Maris break Babe Ruth's home run record. What an experience for a young boy—a memory of a lifetime that no one can take away—not even General Yo.

After that legendary game, his dad proudly took Robert to meet the man who broke the remarkable record. To his amazement, the giant of a man kindly shook his hand and signed a baseball for him.

When he left for war, the ball was still protected in a special case at home.

The thing Robert remembered most about Maris was his humility. He did not boast about his exploits. He just thanked the lad for watching the game and told him next time he would take him down to meet all the great ballplayers. Maris did not realize that to most people, at that moment in history, "he" was the greatest ballplayer in the world.

Robert tailored certain characteristics of his life after that baseball legend. He always tried to be kind, considerate, polite, and true to his word, just like his hero.

The past forty years in this hole they called "home," he has done that. Whenever he could help a fellow prisoner he would, no questions asked, no expectations in return.

Thursday's dream in life was to become a psychologist. He was fulfilling that goal by going to college when drafted into the army.

As a soldier, he worked with a medical unit as a psychologist, treating neurotic disorders caused by the stress of war. His job was to determine if certain men, after being in battle, were mentally fit to fight again. He had cases when the stress of war was too much resulting in the men taking their own life or lives of others.

It was called "Post Traumatic Stress Disorder," or "PTSD." During the Vietnam War, it was "Post Vietnam Syndrome." Unfortunately, the illness has been around as long as there have been wars. In Civil War days, it was called "Soldier's Heart." During the First World War, it was known as "Combat Fatigue." During World War II, it was "Gross Stress Reaction." Whatever the name it was the same thing—severe emotional problems caused by a traumatic event in one's life, such as the horror of war.

While on duty, Thursday headed to a base with a man suffering from PTSD. The soldier's name was Specialist Ronald Lomack—a medic in the Army. Ronald had recently been active in a vicious battle. He saw three of his comrades torn apart by a VC explosive.

The Cong designed a technique to stretch a line with mines or grenades attached to it across a path, or through the jungle. When GIs combed an area, they frequently hit the line with their feet and exploded the bomb.

Lomack walked behind some comrades the day they tripped one of the lines. Three men died instantly, but Ronald lived, the images fixed in his mind. When he returned to camp, they could not quiet him—such a gruesome, horrific experience affected him immensely. He tried to get it out of his mind, but the experience haunted him day and night.

One day Lomack was out of control, distraught, yelling at everyone, and throwing things around. Crazed, he took his M-16, walked to the front of the headquarters, and fired haphazardly. Shots scattered everywhere. Fortunately, everyone was at the mess hall eating lunch so nobody was hurt. This action caused him immediate admittance into the hospital where Thursday had the responsibility of evaluating him.

While moving to the larger hospital facility, Lomack and Freeman were traveling in a caravan. The VC attacked and captured them, along with several other soldiers. Through the years, all the others in that attack died. Freeman and his patient were the only ones still alive.

That other prisoner is "Friday." Consequently, Specialist Ronald Lomack had forty years of evaluation because Freeman felt compelled to help him, whenever and wherever he could, including in the miserable prison cells. However, tapping was not as beneficial as face-to-face counseling would have been.

## *Friday*

Specialist Ronald Lomack tried to get a deferment from the military on the basis that his family farm in Missouri needed his help. The army denied his request and he received his draft notice shortly after.

The farm had been in the family for three generations. His three younger brothers took over the responsibilities on the farm when he left to serve his country

Lomack attended a small schoolhouse near his home. Ronald's graduation class consisted of nine students—six girls, and three boys. Obviously, the senior prom was fun for the boys, but not as much for the girls. He commented about what good friends his schoolmates were. Eleven of them started out in first grade. Most of them remained close through the years.

Tragedy marred Ronald's young life. A dreadful farm accident killed his best friend, Ken, who was only twelve-years-old. While baling hay, he hit a stump and fell off the tractor. The baler crushed him.

The heartbreaking incident happened only a month after Ken's sister, two years older than he, drowned in a swimming accident. She hit her head on a rock while diving into a shallow lake.

He tapped about Ken's attractive sister and told how much he missed her. He and all of his friends had a secret crush on her. He wondered if she knew how much he cared about her.

In his senior year, another friend in his class died in a tragic car accident. The police report said the cause was reckless driving. Ronald wasn't sure about that. It raised many questions in his mind. A couple of days later, he went to the scene to investigate and discovered what really happened. Tim had hit a deer. A piece of the car's headlight still clung to the animal's hide, which lay decomposed in the nearby forest. Ronald deduced that his friend managed to control the car until he hit a ditch, then went airborne and eventually crashed through a large hay barn. The car and barn had caught fire. The officers believed Tim was conscious when he burned to death in the car, alone and terrified. What a horrible way to die!

His friend's death haunted him. In his nightmares, he heard screeching tires, glass shattering, and Tim screaming, as his car burst into flames. Ronald dwelt on that thought and it sometimes terrified him.

Frequently following the crash, Ronald visited the accident scene. He sat silently and reflected on life and death. At his young age, death had stung him far too many times. He wondered if he should stop caring because it hurt too much when he lost someone he loved.

At times, he looked upward and cried out in pain, "Why God, why? Why did you take three people that I loved with my whole heart? How could a loving God allow this to happen?" He raised his clenched fist toward heaven in a fit of rage. Filled with torment he yelled, "Where were you God; why didn't you help?" Sometimes he even cursed God.

---

Friday often tapped about those he lost. If there were any tears left they would have flowed, but there weren't any—empty, dry, hollow eyes were all that remained—and a heart filled with sorrow.

Unlike the other prisoners, Ronald talked about his

imprisonment. Clearly, the hatred he felt towards the enemy consumed him. Bitterness does that to a person.

That was why Ronald suffered more than the others did at the hands of his evil captors. They sensed his hatred and bitterness, and he paid for it through extra beatings and cruel abuse.

The other prisoners mellowed out somewhat. Not in a cowardly way, but almost as if they had no feelings left—no emotions or expectations. Definitely, no hope for freedom existed in any of the men.

When ordered to do a lowly task, the other captives said nothing. There were no dirty looks or muttering under their breath. They just went ahead as told; like dead men going through the motions.

They would never acknowledge their captor's superiority by saying, "okay," or "yes." Certainly, they never would answer, "Yes, sir." All the soldiers refused to do that; they would rather die first.

More than anything else, General Yo wanted them to feel subservient to him. After years of torture, he finally gave up. Just seeing them suffer was enough for him. He continually sought new and more bizarre methods of inflicting pain on his prisoners.

Friday was different from the others. When he received an order, he would insult the guards, using vulgar language. Even though he knew it would result in an immediate beating, he felt justified. He hated them and wanted to be sure that they knew it.

Once he insulted General Yo in front of the guards. Yo beat him non-stop for almost an hour with a bamboo stick, and then stabbed his foot with it. The result was a badly broken foot and open wounds that bled profusely.

Sunday doctored him the best he could, but Friday had a lifelong limp from many broken bones that never healed correctly. Medical care was non-existent in the prison.

In recent years, General Yo eased up on the beatings. He knew the men would not survive in their weakened conditions, unless he did. He wanted them to continue to suffer. Death would be a means of escape and put an end to their suffering, so he preferred them to feel miserable, to grovel in subjugation.

## *Saturday*

"Saturday" was the remaining prisoner, also known as Corporal Daniel Sparks. In reality, Saturday was a Vietnamese soldier named Le Huu Trang. Most people called him Le. The real Daniel Sparks died forty years ago. Le was a spy within the group, a mole, planted by General Yo. In other words, he was a spy within the "weak."

# FOUR

# The Plan Begins

Le's life began to change one rainy day while off duty. He met some Americans who had established an orphanage in a nearby village. He often heard about the children's home from his wife, Linh, who volunteered there. When she heard of a need, she eagerly jumped in to help whatever way she could. She lived up to her name, "Linh," which in Vietnamese meant "Gentle Spirit." At times, she helped in the kitchen, or with cleaning. Mostly, she loved working with the orphans. Her heart broke for them, knowing most of the children came from deplorable backgrounds.

While working with the Americans, she sensed an emptiness in her life. She realized they had something she desired. Through talking with the staff, and reading the Bible they had given her, she discovered it was Jesus. Her quest led her to discover a personal relationship with Christ.

She came home in the evening and told her husband about how different the Americans at the orphanage were. She told him about the remarkable compassion they showed the orphans; a trait she had rarely seen among her own people. She saw them display love to the unlovable. She admired that.

The orphanage housed twenty-five children ranging from ages three to fifteen. All were needy children—rejected by parents and society. Some were abandoned on the orphanage steps because they were an inconvenience, or as in the case of many of the girls, simply not wanted. The orphanage became the only home many of these youngsters ever knew.

The well-built, rough-looking, black man in charge of the orphanage was one of the kindest people Le had ever met. Samuel Jefferson came from New Orleans, Louisiana. The locals respected him as he worked among them caring for the needs of the children. Everyone just called him, "Sam."

Le was not a Christian, but enjoyed spending time with Sam whenever he had the opportunity. Le spoke fluent English, so the two men would talk for hours. They chatted about their families, each other's cultural traditions, and life in general.

Almost every time they conversed, Sam would tell him about a special friend he had met named "Jesus." He told him how Jesus Christ changed his life. Le could see the compassion the Americans had for the children in the orphanage. He also witnessed these qualities mirrored in the children.

He noticed a drastic change in his wife Linh, after her conversion.

Occasionally, Sam talked about his life before he met Jesus. He told Le how he was a man filled with hate, willing to fight anyone who gave him the opportunity. It would only take an action, a word, or even a look to set him off. Fighting was his way to "fix" things that he didn't like.

Sam served in the United States Army Special Forces. It seemed the right fit for him because of his background and fighting instinct. He was in many firefights and battled numerous enemies. Sam never talked about the men he killed, but the number was high. One of the young men at the orphanage told Le he heard rumors that Sam killed over a hundred men in close-combat fighting in Iraq and Afghanistan.

Le found it hard to believe that such a gentle person, who compassionately cared for orphans, could have been a man filled with such hatred. It piqued his curiosity about the One Sam called, "Jesus."

Often the two men would get into lengthy conversations about God. Sam talked about the role Jesus played in his life. It always left Le with many questions. He was confused and hungry to know more. How could Jesus change a person that much? When they talked about spiritual matters, Sam would explain how Jesus loved the unlovely. He defended the lowly. He stood up to the authorities when something was wrong, or he saw someone treated unfairly.

Le realized that Christians, like Sam, had something he wanted for his own life. Soon he came to know Jesus in a personal way.

Le often asked Sam questions about America; what was it really like? Were people friendly? Could citizens own their own business? He only heard stories, and they weren't always favorable. He wondered if America was really their enemy as he was taught to believe.

Sam told him what freedom in America was like. With passion he spoke, "In the United States you have the opportunity to become wealthy, no matter what class you come from. You can fulfill your dreams if you work hard. I came from the bottom, the slums of New Orleans. Now, I have college degrees in economics and theology. I'm not rich, but I am content."

Le sat spellbound as Sam continued, "America is the land of unlimited opportunity and prosperity. There is freedom of religion and speech. It is a democracy where you vote for the officials you want to serve you. Your opinions matter, regardless of your heritage. Even though America has many problems, it's still the greatest country on earth."

Le imagined what Sam's homeland must be like. Sometimes in the stillness of the night, he would dream about it. He pictured it in his mind. He hoped his family could someday visit the land Sam loved. The American planted a desire, which would only grow stronger with time.

Freedom is a difficult concept to grasp for someone who never experienced it. The freedom Sam talked about seemed unbelievable, unattainable. Yet, Le could only take him at his word. And continue to dream.

His word—that was the trait Le respected most about Sam.

He always spoke the truth. When he said he would do something, he did it. He followed words with actions.

Le observed the American stand nose-to-nose against Communist soldiers and officials. He never backed down. Le wondered why the government tolerated him. Maybe they feared him. Perhaps it is the reason they turned their backs on many things he did; actions that others in the oppressed land could not get away with.

Sam walked the talk. He was available to assist the local people when they needed help. He often was the first on the scene after a storm. He repaired roofs, rebuilt homes, and aided where needed. He tended to physical ailments of the people: brought medical supplies, bandaged wounds, and even helped bring a baby into the world.

Le and his wife respected Sam and the other Americans. They watched closely day-after-day, and Sam never wavered in his compassion, loyalty, or values.

One day Le asked him, "Why do you do what you do? After all, there is no money involved, no material things, really there's only hardship—both physical and mental anguish. I know how difficult it is to keep an orphanage going with the Communist Government always watching and threatening you. Why do you endure that? What's really in it for you?"

Sam's reply was simple. It was always the same. "It just seems like the right thing to do."

Le's upbringing in Vietnam drilled into him Communist doctrine. It taught that only Mao Tse Tung, the former leader of China and the Communist movement, and Ho Chi Minh, who he referred to as "Uncle Ho" were right and never to be questioned.

However, since Le became a Christian he could see the control his leaders had over their subjects. He questioned the cruelty. He had a gnawing realization that it was wrong to treat others with such brutal, atrocious tactics.

Le heard about freedom, but never understood what it

meant. In the military, he saw what appeared to be freedom, but also witnessed hatred and controlling power. Many times, he observed his fellow soldiers beat innocent people simply because that person disagreed, or hesitated too long before following an order.

The last four years, Le listened to the prisoners talk about their past lives and the freedoms they once enjoyed. Over time, he realized he was not free, and this life was not for him anymore. He loathed the brutality and the harshness of the helpless, tortured prisoners. In his heart, he knew it was wrong, but what could he do?

The Vietnamese citizens did not have the freedom of full access to the Internet. The Vietnamese Government filtered it tightly. Propaganda was rampant; and news was controlled. Thanks to Sam, Le learned how he could get around many of the Internet limitations.

A few months earlier, Le completed an Internet search on each of the six prisoners. He explored the "Vietnam Veterans Memorial Wall" site. Many names had personal messages posted by friends or family. Williams and McCarter had web sites designated in their honor. One site read, "Until they all come home." Another said, "Remember to pray for our POWs."

It piqued his interest. Le expanded his search secretly, and researched what happened to some of the prisoners' family members through the years. Of course, he never mentioned it to any of the captives. If his superiors found out he knew the information they would have him and his family imprisoned or killed.

Through the years, Le frequently asked the other guards what the prisoners did to deserve such demeaning treatment. In return, the reply would always be the same, "They are Americans who fought in the Vietnam War. They killed our babies and women. They are the enemy." It was the rehearsed answer the authorities gave and never wavered.

As Le studied the conflict, he found out differently. Accounts of soldiers who went into villages and dug wells, built orphanages, or flew sick or pregnant Vietnamese to hospitals for needed medical care were documented. He was shocked! That is not what he was raised to believe.

One night, "Saturday" (Le) tapped this question, "Were you ever in a position where you had to kill innocent people?"

The prisoners agreed that innocent people were not deliberately killed. Sometimes Vietcong hid in villages among civilians, and possibly the shooting caught women and children in the crossfire. They were always distraught when that occurred. At times, it was difficult to identify the enemy. The men insisted they never intentionally killed the innocent.

Le realized by this time, the only crime the men had committed was being American. General Yo found them guilty, gave them a life sentence, and imprisoned them simply because they came from the United States of America. Le was keenly aware of the treaties Vietnam and the United States had signed freeing all POWs. He knew something had to be done.

On a rare occasion, Le would catch a glimpse of the six prisoners working together, never uttering a word, staring at the ground as they dug or hoed. Their faces showed only a blank, expressionless stare—all visible signs of any emotion erased from their lives.

One night as they walked back to their cells, the captain quickly glanced at Le. Their eyes met briefly. Monday noticed something out of the ordinary on Le's face. It resembled pity. Le smiled at the prisoners on other occasions after he made sure no one was watching. This time was different. That strange look confused Monday. He wondered if he saw a glimpse of compassion on the guard's face. What did it mean?

Monday would never forget what happened next. Le nodded to him, looked around to make sure no one was watching, and unmistakably smiled. Monday walked by, his eyes locked on the guard.

Le never knew why he voiced those three words to Monday, but they came out clearly, "I'm sorry, GI."

Monday's eyes grew wide as he stared back at the man who quietly spoke to him.

Then Le repeated, "I'm sorry, GI."

Was it a joke, or another method of Yo's torture? Out of fear, Monday quickly lowered his gaze to the ground. As he turned away, he looked one last time at the guard. There was no mistake. His eyes showed compassion. Why? What did that look mean? What did those words imply? Was it a trap?

That night when Monday returned to his cell, Le listened for tapping about what happened. Would Monday mention the unexpected exchange that took place that afternoon?

It was never brought up.

Confused, Le went home after his shift, and talked to his wife, Linh. They chatted about the situation: the men, their conditions, and Le's role. He related how his heart and mind were tormented by the continued persecution of the helpless men.

As he laid his head on the pillow that night to get some much-needed rest, he noticed the smell of fresh sheets. The laundry had been washed and hung outside to dry in the gentle breeze. He took deep breaths trying to capture the fresh scent, and make it last forever. The fragrance triggered another thought of the soldiers in their humiliating, disgusting cells, and the rank smells they dealt with every moment of their lives. When was the last time they smelled fresh sheets? They didn't even have sheets—only smelly, bare, dirt floors, and a torn, filthy, old blanket.

As these thoughts raced through his mind, Le turned over in bed and faced Linh, "I must help them. I am their only hope."

"Yes, I agree. We are in this together my dear," she whispered. "But what can we do?"

They talked until dawn about the prisoners. For days, these thoughts haunted them, monopolizing every conversation when they were together.

Finally, they could not bear it anymore. Le made a life-changing decision. He had to help free the prisoners, no matter the cost. As for him and his family, only God knew what would become of them. He must take the risk.

In total agreement, Le and his wife began to work on the plan. They knew they had to right a terrible wrong. They both recognized that Le was the only person who was in the position to help. Together they would find a way to gain freedom for the suffering prisoners.

Le immediately began investigating different ideas and theories. Linh thought of ways she could assist their effort. They brainstormed each possibility, weighed the advantages and disadvantages, determined to find the correct solution.

Le knew it was not an option to report the tyrant, General Yo, to the Vietnamese authorities. He was uncertain how they would react. After all, the Vietnamese Government had signed several peace treaties with the United States, and had agreed to help locate all the POWs and MIAs. If he turned Yo in, the Vietnamese authorities probably would not believe him, or be forced to eliminate the POWS. Either way, he and the prisoners would surely lose their lives.

After much thought and discussion with Linh, he reached a conclusion. He decided the only possible solution would be to help the POWs disappear. But how? And when?

Le was well aware of the risks. The stakes were enormous. Everything in the plan must synchronize perfectly. One small mistake and all would fail. The consequences would be devastating, no escape. Death for the prisoners would be a better option.

Le and his wife thought about their three children and his parents. They discussed what could happen to them. Would their possible suffering be worth the freedom of these men? It was not the time to quit. They would be in God's hands.

Everywhere Le went, he kept his eyes, and ears open for an escape route or help of some kind. He knew he could not accomplish this mission alone. He needed assistance. Was he facing an impossible task? Was his goal attainable?

One day, Le realized he had exhausted all possibilities. He could not think of any way to achieve their objective. Desperate for help, Linh mentioned Sam's name. Yes, Sam. Why hadn't they thought of him before? Maybe he was the answer they sought.

The more Le contemplated his wife's suggestion, the more apprehensive he became. Could Sam be trusted totally? How much should they tell him?

There was another vital consideration. Who would believe that just a few miles away, hidden deep in the jungle, lived six American POWs left from the Vietnam War? How could they have survived in those harsh conditions for forty years? Why would a Vietnamese prison guard want to help them?

He knew Sam's knowledge, and military expertise could prove beneficial. That is, if he was willing to take the risk, and help him with the dangerous mission. The more he considered it, the more he realized that Sam was the only option.

When Le discovered that Sam and his staff were ordered to leave the country—he knew it was his moment of opportunity. He needed to move fast. The first step was that Le had to convince the prisoners to trust him—a huge challenge. Only then could he prepare for the escape.

Le believed with his whole heart that within the next few days the prisoners would walk to freedom, or die trying.

# FIVE

# Recruiting the Prisoners

It was Monday. Actually, it was Thursday, but the prisoners lost track of time years ago. To them it was Monday, which meant it was Monday's turn to tap.

The men rarely talked about the day of their capture. All they discussed were past occurrences, reminiscing about happy times, events that took place before their capture forty years ago.

As usual, that night Monday talked about his wife and family. He tapped about the time his daughter Kaylie, fell, and badly gashed her head. They could not stop the bleeding. Wendy and James rushed a disoriented, frightened Kaylie to the hospital, praying the entire way. If anything would happen to her, James would never forgive himself. He felt responsible and believed it was his job to protect his family.

"I wonder what kind of woman my Kaylie grew up to be," Monday tapped. "She was always smiling, fun-loving, and beautiful. She enjoyed making new friends."

Le envisioned a smile on Monday's face as he spoke about his little girl.

"One day when we were Christmas shopping at a mall in Denver, Kaylie spotted a helpless young man with a coarse beard, dressed in wrinkled army fatigues, and an old, worn U.S. Army hat. He sat slumped in a wheelchair. She asked if she could give the man some money because he looked lonely and poor.

"I remember thinking; this man is obviously taking advantage of people. Reluctantly, I gave my trusting daughter a dollar to give him. I was considering the best way to explain to my innocent child that sometimes people take advantage of others. They are willing to do anything to make a buck.

"Then something happened I will never forget. The man smiled at her when she handed him the bill. Then a tear trickled slowly down his cheek. It appeared the man was moved because one sweet, blond-haired little girl showed him compassion."

Monday continued tapping his story. "As I stood watching the scene, a woman walked up beside me and told me the man's story. When drafted, he had a wife and young daughter. Six months into his tour of duty in Vietnam, he was severely wounded. He came home paralyzed. Some doctors believed he might be able to walk again, but he had given up all hope. When he returned to the states, his wife left him, taking their little girl. She said she could not handle his problem—it was too big for her. They meant the world to him, especially his daughter. He never saw them again. How he missed them! Every day he went to that spot and sat helplessly in his wheelchair, not wanting, or not being able to walk. He no longer cared."

Monday shared his heartfelt thoughts. "Words cannot explain what I felt at that moment. I stared at the veteran in the wheelchair. He did what his country asked of him. He paid a high price and returned home to face rejection, not only by the American people, but also by his own wife.

"That was too much for me," Monday said. "I opened my wallet and pulled every bill I had out of it, walked up to the man, and handed it to him."

The tapping stopped briefly as Monday reflected on the life-changing event.

He continued, "As the disabled veteran slowly took the money from my hand, he looked directly into my eyes for a long moment. I saw raw pain and loneliness. I looked down at my daughter. She had a huge smile on her face as she tenderly touched my arm."

Monday began to tap again. "Then, Kaylie turned to that dirty, rugged man, leaned over his wheelchair, and gave him a hug and soft kiss on his rough face. Then she did another amazing thing. She said, 'Jesus loves you.'"

Even though tapping relayed the story, the prisoners could feel the emotion as they pictured the episode vividly in their minds.

"I watched, absorbed by the scene before me. Tears flowed freely from my eyes. That simple act of love by my daughter brought me, as well as many onlookers to tears. What a lesson I learned that day! Compassion for someone less fortunate should never be withheld because of pre-existing ideas or stereotypes. Children look through eyes uncolored by prejudice. I remembered how Jesus reached out to people in need, like the woman at the well, and I vowed to do the same from that moment on."

Silence reigned in the cells as everyone pondered what Monday said.

Le listened to the heartbreaking story with the others. He decided to tap a question that had been heavy on his heart. "Did you ever see this man again?"

There was complete stillness. No one, nothing, not even a rat made a sound.

Finally the tapping resumed, "It's funny you should ask that. A few days later, I contacted a client in Denver who owned a cabinet shop, and asked him if he could use a disabled veteran. I knew the owner of the business was a Korean War vet. I didn't have to ask twice. Not only did he hire him, but he gave him his upstairs loft at the factory to live in, complete with a convenient elevator."

Monday continued telling more captivating stories about his wife and children.

It was getting late and Le knew it was time to cut in. That was something they rarely did unless they had a question. He knew he had to make his move before the prisoners fell asleep. For security reasons, nobody ever knew who asked questions, but on this rare occasion, Le identified himself.

He needed them to know they could trust him. Certainly, if the escape was ever going to work he had to gain their confidence.

He tapped, "Saturday here…do you ever feel like leaving this place?"

There was absolute silence for a full thirty seconds. Then came, tap, tap, tap. Of course, Le did not know who it was.

"Leave? How?"

"Escape," Le replied.

"Are you crazy? We would be killed!"

"After they tortured us," another added.

"I know how to do it," Le responded.

"This conversation is over," one of them insisted.

"No, hear me out. I know how to get away. All of us."

Dead quiet! Nobody answered. Probably out of fear that the guards would overhear, and all would suffer the consequences. Why now would anyone bring up the idea of an escape? They had been there so long!

Le pressed on. He had gone this far. He knew this was his opportunity. "I have figured out a way to get out of here. I mean all of us. We can do it. But only if we all are in agreement."

A hush came over the cells. For what seemed like an eternity, there were no sounds. Nothing.

He decided to continue down the path he established. "I want to see my family again. I want to experience freedom." As Le tapped on the wall, he realized that he was not only talking about the prisoners, but also himself. He desired to experience freedom for the first time in his life.

He thought of Sam and the other Americans at the orphanage. He recalled a Bible verse Sam had once shared with him. Le tapped, "Jesus said, you can be free."

"The only way Jesus can free us is through death. If we try to escape, we will face certain death. You are right; we will be free with Jesus in Heaven," someone tapped back.

"Why are we afraid? What do we have to lose?" Le asked boldly.

"I don't fear death. I fear another beating. I fear being whipped to the point that I won't be able to walk again. I fear that I will be left to die in pain and misery. That's what I fear."

"Don't we have to at least try?" Le asked.

"We have tried many times. All we got in return is more beatings. Almost thirty men are dead; many because they tried to escape."

"I agree," another soldier replied. "We will not face death when we are caught, that's too easy. We will face more beatings. I can't take anymore of those."

That ended all communication for the night. Nothing more was said.

Le was disappointed that the prisoners were not open to his plan, but he also understood. As he reflected on the details of the night, he realized he did not know who or how many men talked. Perhaps, they were afraid to say anything. Could there be a couple silent men who agree? Or even just one?

＊＊＊

The next day Le traded duty with another guard. He planned on working straight through the night. He knew time was running out, and he had to make the prisoners understand before it was too late. He felt his best chance was to convince their leader, the captain, also known as Monday. Then perhaps Monday could persuade the others to join him.

As Le helped get the prisoners to their jobs, he inconspicuously stayed close to Monday. Occasionally, Monday looked at Le, still surprised by the three words the guard voiced to him. He glanced back at Le and saw him flash a smile. Monday, confused by the guard's bizarre behavior didn't know what to think.

As the blazing sun beat down on them, the other guard stationed with Le motioned that he needed a break. This gave Le the opening he wanted.

Noticing the sweat pouring off Monday's brow, Le offered him a drink from his water bottle.

Monday looked at the Vietnamese guard with skepticism.

Le nodded his head, "Go ahead."

Monday's canteen was filled with dirty water from the river. Cautiously, he reached for the guard's canteen. At first he hesitated to drink, but then took a big swallow. He glanced at Le, watching for his reaction. Then he swigged the rest of the cool, clean water down, almost to the last drop. Finally, he realized what he did and abruptly stopped. Water ran down his chin. He noticed the nearly empty bottle. He apprehensively handed it back to the guard.

Without wavering, Le raised the bottle to his lips and finished the last few swallows.

That act of kindness baffled Monday. He wondered about the bizarre behavior of the guard.

The rustle of the nearby brush gave warning that the other guard was returning. Le hurriedly nodded to Monday, and whispered, "It's a beautiful day to be alive."

He stared directly into his eyes.

Shocked, Monday realized those were the nicest words he had heard in forty years, or maybe the cruelest, depending on how he looked at it.

Monday glanced at the guard a few more times that day, but quickly looked the other way when he noticed Le smiling at him.

That night, Tuesday tapped about a time when he took his girlfriend to the 1967 Indy 500. In that heartbreaking race, Parnelli Jones in his whistling turbine racecar lost with a lap to go because of a faulty two-dollar part.

Le did not know if Tuesday's story was accurate. In fact, he did not really understand it. Nevertheless, Tuesday was noticeably excited as he was tapping his story. He said that just before the car broke down, he was excitedly jumping up and down. He felt so confident he was seeing a sure win; he turned to the beautiful brunette on his side, and planted a long kiss on her lips. "I almost married her. In fact, I would have if I had not been drafted."

More silence.

"I wonder whatever happened to her," he added. There was stillness as he thought of what might have been.

After so many years, the prisoners knew when to be quiet, and when to help each other through a difficult time. Survival depended on their support.

In the stillness, Saturday knew it was the perfect time to speak. "Saturday here...I have been thinking of a way to get out of this place. I have devised a plan to get all of us home in just days. What do you think about it?"

Again, nothing.

"What about it? Does anyone want to be free again?"

Finally one prisoner spoke, "Free! Free! Who are you kidding?"

You could almost feel the anger as another soldier expressed his feelings, "Are you being cruel? Why are you saying this? You have to be kidding. Free! Only death will make us free."

Still another, or perhaps the same soldier added, "America has forgotten us. To them we are dead. Probably not even a memory. We will never be free. We are weak and our enemy is strong. Home is too far away. Escape is impossible."

"No, it isn't. We can do it," Saturday protested.

"How? Where would we go?"

Suspicious and apprehensive, another soldier tapped, "I think this conversation needs to end. What if they are listening?"

Saturday tapped, "So, what if they are?"

Exhausted and discouraged, one prisoner offered, "I am sick of the beatings. I just want to die. I'm tired. Please, just let me die."

Even through the tapping, the sadness could be sensed—pure hopelessness, only despondency.

What could Le say? How could he convince them? What more could he do?

Most of them attempted to take their own lives, more than once, only to be brought back from death's sad escape.

Friday tried suicide several times. Once he jumped off a cliff, broke an arm and the same foot General Yo injured years before. He never received medical treatment. The others nursed him back to health, but he walked with a limp. The pain in his arm was a constant reminder—some days worse than others.

Wednesday once slit his wrist with a sharp rock. He lost a lot of blood and teetered on death's doorstep for days, but lived through it.

Both men were still angry at Sunday for saving their lives. General Yo would not have let them die anyway. Their suffering meant too much to him; somehow, he would keep them alive as long as he could.

There was an eerie absence of sound the remainder of the night. Saturday wondered what was going through the minds of these men. Were they fearful it was a trap? Were they so broken and adapted to this horrible life they simply accepted it? Didn't they have any hope left, only despair?

Le recalled reading about how the Nazis captured the Jews in World War II. They forced a man to dig a hole, and then fill it again, repeating the process until his will was broken. At that point, they did anything the Nazis told them to do, including walking to their death.

Le believed this situation was similar. These also were broken men. He had to get their attention another way. If escape would ever be a reality, he needed to discover a method to obtain their trust and cooperation.

Le went home exhausted that night. He collapsed in bed, but could not get the vulnerable prisoners off his mind. As he tossed and turned, he wondered what else he could do to gain the prisoners trust. Time was getting short. The window to freedom would close for all of them soon. Finally, he drifted into a restless sleep.

—⊹— —⊹— —⊹—

Morning came too quickly. Fortunately, Le would be working with Monday again. He had to speak to him on his level. There must be a way to reach him. He had to get him to understand the urgency of his plan.

Le recalled a recent conversation with the American at the orphanage. They were discussing people and their complacency. Le asked Sam, "How do you get through to someone who is contented with his life? How do you explain he is missing something?"

Sam replied, "Share Scripture with him. Tell him how much God loves him. I use John 3:16 often."

Le became familiar with the well-known Scripture and memorized it. It quickly became his favorite verse: *For God so loved the world, that he gave his only begotten Son, that whosoever believeth in him should not perish, but have everlasting life.*

Sam was a wealth of information for the guard. He was knowledgeable in many areas: the Bible, history, geography, military, and even relationships.

Another time Le asked, "What great speech would any American know?"

Sam thought for a moment, and then blurted out, "I know! It's the Gettysburg Address!"

Le was obviously confused, but Sam explained, "It was a speech made by the sixteenth President of the United States after a great battle. The final words are powerful, '…and that Government of the people, by the people, for the people shall not perish from the earth.'"

Le replayed those words in his mind. It was certainly a concept he could not fully understand, but the idea sounded remarkable.

As Le recalled the conversation with Sam, an idea came to him.

As Monday worked tediously, Le approached him and quietly asked, "Can you recite the last line of the Gettysburg Address?"

Monday stared back at Le, not saying a word.

Le took pride of his mastery of the English language. Therefore, he was not sure if his good English or the question astounded the American more. Probably both did.

Le looked straight into his eyes and stated, "…and that Government of the people…"

Monday joined in slowly with his gravelly voice. Together they finished, "…by the people, for the people, shall not perish from the earth."

It was a moment neither of them would ever forget. Two men, who ought to be enemies, reciting an influential speech, written one-hundred and forty-five years earlier by one of America's greatest leaders. The scene was powerful.

With a small tear in his eye, Monday stared back at the guard. What just happened?

Le added, "Those were great words by a great leader. Were they not?"

Monday continued to look at him intently. With reluctance, he nodded his head in agreement.

Le offered him a drink from his water bottle. Monday drank a few sips and handed the flask back.

Shielding his eyes from the sun with his hand, Le looked upward just as a bird flew overhead. Both men watched it glide effortlessly through the air.

The guard took a drink from the bottle and stated, "Oh, to be free like that bird."

Monday stood spellbound, the look of astonishment written all over his face. His eyes firmly fixed on the man who guarded him the past four years.

"Who are you?" Monday quizzed the guard.

The young Vietnamese guard looked around to make sure

nobody was watching. He replied softly, "I'm a friend." He paused, and then added, "A redeemer. John 3:16. Do you remember it?"

The aging POW, touched by the familiar verse, nodded his head. "I remember saying it to myself every night." During the first several years of captivity, he and Sunday recited the verse as often as they could. Unfortunately, somewhere along the way it stopped. When did their faith begin to dwindle?

Le continued to look at the peaceful, blue sky. Suddenly, he glanced at the dense jungle, filled with every shade of green. He hoped to ease Monday's fears, but also kept a lookout for the other guard to return.

Le knew he must act quickly, "I believe what it says in Psalms 33." *Behold, the eye of the LORD is upon them that fear him...'* He looked directly into the eyes of the prisoner and finished the verse. *"...to deliver their soul from death."*

A look of amazement crossed Monday's face, mixed with confusion, and a faint glimmer of hope.

Le spoke softly. "Do you remember Proverbs 3:5?"

Monday shook his head, lowered his eyes, ashamed, "It's been too long. My mind does not even remember yesterday."

Thankful for the opportunity, Le quickly recited it, *"Trust in the LORD with all thine heart; and lean not onto thine own understanding."*

As Le shared the verse, a sparkle appeared in Monday's eyes. "Yes. Yes, I do remember it. But, what does that have to do with me?"

"Trust," Le said confidently. "You need to trust."

The older American looked at the young Vietnamese guard with a blank stare, obviously not fully understanding what he meant.

The other guard returned to resume his duties. The conversation ended.

Nonchalantly, Le walked away uttering the words, "Just think of 'Saturday' when you remember those words tonight." He could not see Monday's expression as his jaw dropped, astonishment on his hardened face.

Another guard took Le's shift for the rest of the day freeing him to go to town to pick up supplies. He looked back at the feeble POW toiling in the rice paddy. The pain in Monday's back was noticeable, agony written all over his face. He managed to turn his head, slowly stood straight up, and glanced at the guard who had given him a spark of hope.

Meanwhile, Le prayed that Monday understood what he meant.

# SIX

# Decisions

---

Le's trip to town took longer than he expected, so he could not hear the conversation that took place on the walls that night. He did not know if anything about the events of the day was shared, but it gave him the perfect opportunity to set the second part of his plan in motion.

He finally had an opportunity to visit Sam at the orphanage. After much thought, he still was not certain how much information he should reveal. He was afraid the authorities were already suspicious of the American.

Earlier in the week, Le heard from one of the other guards that Sam and his team were being forced out of the country because of their Christian teaching. Word spread that the orphanage would close; all the children would be moved to state facilities. Sam was responsible for giving the heartbreaking news to the children. This was the only home most of them had ever known. They loved Sam and the rest of the staff.

As Le and Linh sat eating a bowl of hot noodles, he looked around the humble orphanage. His heart broke for the children. He hoped they would be content in their new home.

Linh, raised in an orphanage herself, felt at home with Sam and his staff. She never knew her parents. Her only family was the other orphans until she married Le. Perhaps that explained her burning desire to volunteer with the children she had grown to love.

Sam joined the couple at the table.

Le looked at him and boldly stated, "Sam, I have a favor to ask."

"Shoot." Sam replied hastily.

"I am a guard at a prison, which is hidden deep in the jungle."

Sam's eyes widened, "Well, that I did not know."

Le thought before he spoke, wanting to tell his friend as little as possible. "Sam, I don't know how to tell you this, but there are six innocent prisoners at that prison. They need to be free. I want to help make it happen. I need to get them out of the country as quickly as possible."

He blew out a deep breath and continued. "At the same time, I need to be sure my family has escaped safely. Do you have any idea how this can be accomplished?"

Trying to gather his thoughts, Sam pondered for a moment, not wanting to appear as shocked as he felt. "I can see that you are serious, my friend. Let me start by saying that my first responsibility is with this orphanage. Does anyone know you visit or that your wife volunteers here?"

"I'm sure they do. We are here often enough."

"Then if the escape fails, or even if it succeeds, wouldn't the authorities know to find you here and punish all of us. What happens to the orphanage and the children?" Sam challenged him.

"I happen to know they have already asked you to leave the country, or should I say ordered you to leave within three days. The children will be put in state facilities tomorrow."

Each man was attempting to learn what the other knew without divulging more information than necessary.

Perplexed, Sam agreed, "That's true. Your sources are right." Taking it a step further, Sam challenged, "Is it because of you, Le? Did you turn us in?" He looked around at his fellow helpers, other young Christians who had given a couple years of their lives to work with helpless children in an underprivileged country.

"No, I'm only a guard, that's all I do." Le looked at Sam for a second and then added, "Until now, that is. Now, I guess I'm sort of a freedom fighter."

Sam looked at Le, and stopped eating. "You are serious, aren't you?"

"Yes, I am."

"It's really important for you to do this, isn't it?

"Yes, it is. I've thought of nothing else the past few months. I have a plan that I think may work. You often told me that Jesus died doing what was right. You said missionaries in other countries died doing what is right, helping others. These prisoners have suffered many years for no reason. I have to help them. I believe it is my duty. It is what is right."

Le's face showed determination. Sam knew his Vietnamese friend well enough to know his mind was made up. No matter what, Le was resolved to follow through with his plan.

Le interrupted his thoughts. "My concern is for my family and for these six men. I am not worried about myself."

Sam stared at Le, and then looked at Linh for a sign that she agreed with her husband.

With a hint of a smile, she gently nodded her head.

Sam remained thoughtful. He sipped a drink and sat up straighter in his chair. "I know some people in Thailand who may be able to help. I will contact them and see if we can set up a rendezvous. When do you want this to happen?"

"In two days."

"Two days? Again, are you certain you want to do this? It sounds awfully risky."

"Yes, I am positive." Le confidently nodded his head.

Sam continued, "That's a pretty short notice. They will be watching us all the time. How will we get away from that?"

Le replied, "We will have to move quickly. I do not want to put your lives in jeopardy. Therefore, you and your team need to leave Vietnam tomorrow. Since the children will be gone by then, they will be safe. The plan is quite simple. I suspect your people in Thailand are the same ones who bring your supplies every couple of months. That helicopter can pick up the prisoners and fly them to freedom."

"You know about that?" Sam said with a look of astonishment.

Le nodded his head.

"If you know about it, does the Vietnamese Government know about my special shipment of supplies for the orphanage?"

"I don't think so. Your secret is safe with me. Be assured my friend, I am on your side. I would have done this last month, but I was not certain I could trust you completely. To be honest, I didn't know who I could trust. Since I heard you were leaving and the orphanage would be closing its doors, I knew it was time to proceed with the plan. This way the children are safe, and if the plan works, we all will be free."

Le cleared his throat and took a drink. "I also believe when the international community finds out what has been going on, the Vietnamese Government will do everything in its power to distance itself from the whole situation. Everything will be denied."

Trying to take it all in, Sam inquired, "Why should we help six of your people escape? Are there not hundreds of innocent Vietnamese people stuck in Communist prisons?"

Le thought hard for a second. He knew Sam served in Desert Storm and believed he could trust him. Everything depended on what happened next.

The young guard looked over at Sam's laptop on the table and asked, "Is your computer on?"

"Yes."

"May I use it?"

Perplexed, he nodded his head, and pushed the computer in front of the guard.

Le typed, "Captain James McCarter."

Immediately, the prisoner's POW web site came up. Le looked at it, and then turned the laptop, so Sam could see it clearly. The former GI stared at it, his eyes grew large, and the expression on his face changed. It was obvious Sam was beginning to understand what Le was telling him.

Sam looked directly into Le's eyes. "You're not saying…." He couldn't finish his sentence.

Le nodded his head enthusiastically.

Sam looked around making sure they had privacy. The three missionaries cleaning the kitchen were busy with their duties, unaware of the conversation.

"I need proof that what you say is true. I can't risk my life, or put my friends in danger. This could be a trap."

Linh finally spoke up, "Sam, this is real."

Le added, "Sam, you talked many times about Jesus dying on the cross between two thieves, right?"

Sam looked at him with an intense look, "Yes."

"One of the criminals asked Jesus to save him. The Savior responded, *Today shalt thou be with me in paradise.*

Sam wondered where Le was going with this. Curiously, he answered, "Yes, I know the story. What does that have to do with me?"

"The thief never questioned Jesus would do what he asked of him. Why was that?"

Sam considered the question. "I'm the one who is supposed to give you Bible lessons. Has the student surpassed the teacher?" He chuckled, and then moved his hand up to his chin as he thought long and hard about the question. "I would have to say because he had faith. He trusted Him."

"You're right. He believed Jesus would do what He said. All I ask is that you believe and trust me. I have no pictures. I have no evidence except what I have witnessed the past four years. You have to take me at my word. I'm asking you to trust me completely."

Sam stood up, pushed his chair under the table, and looked closer at the website. He saw a forty-year-old photo of a young man in uniform, with his wife and two children; a man who may be just miles away, waiting to be freed from four decades of bondage.

Sam looked at Le. "I was getting a shipment in three days, but since I was ordered to leave, I planned to cancel it. Could we do it then?"

"No, I have an eight hour window in two days," Le protested.

"Why?"

"I will be in control of the prisoners for only that amount of time."

Sam weighed the options. He hesitated, "Okay. I'm going to trust you on this. Mainly because we are leaving the country, and won't be permitted to return. Talking about the Word of God has become more restrictive."

Deep in thought, Sam continued, "You do realize the helicopter only has room for ten to twelve people, don't you? In my head, I count fifteen." He paused, "You are going to leave too, aren't you?"

Le's dark eyes showed concern. "My family will leave tonight, headed straight to Laos. I have contacted some friends who will help smuggle them into Thailand."

He paused briefly. "I will lead the men to the rendezvous point. From there, your helicopter will take them to the American Embassy in Bangkok. At that time, I will escape into Laos and catch up with my family. Everyone here must be out of the country within forty-eight hours. It will take the authorities a little time to figure out who was behind this—but they will eventually. Timing is critical."

Sam turned around and scratched the side of his head. "You're telling me…you're saying that there are six American POWs alive and well! They are close to where we're standing?"

Le nodded his head and grinned.

"Six?" Sam reached across the table, grabbed Le's shoulders with both of his large hands, and repeated emphatically, "Six Americans!"

Tears became evident in Sam's eyes and for a split second, Le could tell his mind was in a distant place. "My own father was a POW… for nine months. He was finally freed, but was tortured brutally."

"I know about your father—that's how I felt I could trust you," Le confided.

Sam questioned Le further, "When were these six men captured?"

"1970."

"Forty years ago!" Sam asked excitedly, "Do you know if there are others?"

"I do not know. Maybe. This is an unusual circumstance, unknown even by the Vietnamese Government."

"How can they not be aware of the atrocities?"

"That's a long story. Maybe I can fill you in some day."

"American POWs are alive. I can't believe it." Sam shook his head. "There's not a moment to waste. I will contact my people and move the rendezvous time up."

Le reminded Sam, "Do not tell anybody about this? Not one word to a soul."

"You don't have to worry about that," Sam stated, as he watched the three workers stare at him, curious about the excitement he displayed. A chill ran up his spine. "Forty years, like Moses and the Israelites in the desert."

Le grinned. "I need to head back now. I will be at the pickup site at exactly 10:00 on Saturday."

"Wait a minute." Sam inquired, "Don't you need to know where the rendezvous point is?"

"No, I followed you a couple times. I know exactly where your pickup location is."

The American teased the young guard, "You have been doing your homework, haven't you?"

"Sam my friend, please pray." Le hesitated and looked directly into his eyes. The seriousness of the situation showed on his face. "If anything goes wrong, we are all dead—you, me, and your friends..." Le glanced at Sam's volunteers, "...and my family, as well as the prisoners."

Le walked over to his wife who stood up and smiled at him in a show of support. He embraced her, then whispered, "We are doing what's right, aren't we, Linh?"

"You don't have to ask that question. We are," his wife assured him.

Le spoke straight from his heart. "What if you don't get away? I don't know if I could handle you or the children getting hurt, or worse."

"We will be fine. We are in God's hands. Don't forget that. Since you have to return to work at the prison, I will make sure Sam knows all the details. We will be out of the country within twenty-four hours. Don't worry, just pray."

Le hugged Linh tight. "Take care of yourself and the kids."

The guard reached out his hand to his trusting friend. With a hearty handshake Sam assured him, "I don't know what my part in this is Le, but I do trust you. You have my word; the helicopter will be there when it is supposed to be."

Le began to walk away, and then had another thought. "Sam, make sure you and your staff are out of the country within twenty-four hours. If we are not at the pickup point at the designated time, then something went wrong. Don't look for us. Just get out. Hopefully, my family will be safe."

Le added, "By the way Sam, thank you for telling me about Jesus. If something does go wrong, at least we know where we will spend eternity."

Sam shot him a smile and gave him the "thumbs up" signal.

Le hugged his wife one last time, and gave her a parting smile.

That was the simplest part. Now, Le had less than forty-eight hours to convince six imprisoned men to trust one of their guards. He wondered if it was even possible.

It was early evening when Le arrived back at the prison camp. The prisoners were in their cells receiving their nightly provisions.

Le knew he had to talk every one of them into trusting him, so they would follow his plan. It had to be soon—their window of opportunity was dwindling.

It was Thursday's night to tap. His chat was not about baseball as usual. He told about a time in college when he wanted to cheat on a test. Instead, he took the test honestly and found out later he aced the exam. That was an important lesson for him. He learned if he did the right thing, good would come.

That was Le's opportunity to cut in. "Saturday here. Good could come to you, if you choose."

Instantly someone tapped. "Saturday, where were you last night? Why did you bring this up again?"

"You are going to get us another beating."

There was silence.

Eventually, the conversation started again. "This is Monday. I have an idea where you were last night, why you were not here. Explain yourself."

Le knew he must choose his words wisely. He tapped, "I have discovered a way all of us can be rescued."

"Rescued? Who would bother to rescue us after all these years?" one prisoner asked.

"It's Monday again. Saturday, I want to be free more than anything. I want to go home. Let's be realistic. How can that be possible?"

"You have to trust me. I know it is hard, but you must follow my lead."

"How do we do that?"

"I will let you know the time and place. However, you all must agree to the plan, or it will not work. Every single one of you has to be on board."

"Can't you explain in detail what you are talking about?"
"Not tonight."
"Saturday, I do not like this feeling. I think it could be a trap or another way to torture us." The tapping became more vigorous than before.
"Right. This whole thing is strange. Who are you really?" another added.
"Monday here. Let Saturday speak."
"No! Ask him a question!"
"Yeah, ask him a question that only an American would know. Ask him who the President of the United States is."
"Even we don't know that."
The tapping continued and each prisoner came to life.
"Ask him who won the 1930 World Series," obviously a question from Thursday, the baseball lover.
"I don't even know that. Get real," another prisoner tapped, adding to the lively conversation.
Thursday asked another question, "Saturday, what was the date of our country's independence?"
The question confused Le. He stopped tapping. He had read about it, but did not remember the exact date.
Thursday repeated, "Saturday, did you hear me?"
There was complete silence—the conversation was over—no more tapping.
When Le got off duty that night, he immediately went to a computer on base and typed the words, "America's Independence." He memorized the date.
Now, he was ready for the next step.

---

The next day, Le spent his shift guarding Monday at the rice paddy. Occasionally they glanced at each other, trying not to make the second guard suspicious.

Finally, the other guard walked a short distance away leaving them alone.

Le edged closer to Monday.

Unexpectedly the guard turned around, and came back forcing Le to walk away.

As Le passed Monday, he mumbled softly, "July 4, 1776." The surprising look on Monday's face was one Le had never seen from any prisoner; it was an expression of hope. Le nodded his head, smiled, then whispered loud enough for only Monday to hear, "John 8:36."

The prisoner slowly went back to work in the rice paddy. His mind raced with the details of the recent events. Monday did not know what to think. Eventually, a big smile came to his face as he recalled John 8:36. *If the Son therefore shall make you free, ye shall be free indeed.*

He hoed faster, then smiled at Le and nodded his head acknowledging he understood. Could this guard really be on their side? Was there a chance the end of the nightmare was in sight? He was afraid to believe, yet in another way he felt more alive than he had in years.

As he worked, he began to believe the Vietnamese guard was really going to help them escape. Could it be a trap? He no longer cared. He was ready to end it one way, or another.

---

That night it was Friday's turn to talk.

The tapping began. Le waited for the right time to enter the conversation. This was his last chance to convince the men he was on their side. He hoped Monday would take the lead and provide a good opening for him.

Friday began. "They beat me again, today. I'm worn out, exhausted. I tried to get them to shoot me, but they just laughed. Then they smashed me with their rifles. Won't they ever quit?"

There was silence for a long time, and then the usual tapping continued.

"Monday here. John 8:36."

There was a lengthy pause. Le was about to step in when Sunday responded. *If the Son therefore shall make you free, ye shall be free indeed.*

Monday replied, "That's what I thought it was. It's been such a long time since we talked about the Bible."

"Friday spoke up, "Who are you kidding? We are dead men. Not free. No Bible verse will ever change that."

"Saturday here." Le knew the time was right. *But they that wait upon the LORD shall renew their strength; they shall mount up with wings as eagles; they shall run, and not be weary; and they shall walk, and not faint.*

"Sunday speaking. I think that's Isaiah 40:31."

"This is Monday. What are you getting at, Saturday?"

"Think of me as being an instrument for God."

"Thursday here. That's pretty high and mighty of you."

Le, also known as Saturday, continued, *"Be strong and of good courage, fear not, nor be afraid of them: for the LORD thy God, he it is that doth go with thee; he will not fail thee, nor forsake thee."*

Sunday questioned him, "Deuteronomy 31:6? I never knew you to quote scripture, Saturday. What are you getting at?"

Friday jumped in. "God left us years ago. What is this, some kind of church service?"

"Tuesday here. Saturday, I think you flipped out."

Immediately Monday came to Le's defense. "No, he has not. He is perfectly sane. Let me ask everyone a question. We have all seen each other. We know who everyone is, except Saturday. Has anyone ever seen Saturday?" There was a pause. "Nobody has. Let me rephrase that. Has anyone ever seen the prisoner we know as Saturday?"

Nothing. Absolute quiet.

"Thursday here. What are you getting at?"

"I think it's time for him to come clean. Who are you really, Saturday?" Monday tapped.

Le knew he had to be honest, right here, right now, or they would turn him off and it would be the end.

The young guard tapped, "The real Saturday died forty years ago. Since then, "Saturday" has been twelve Vietnamese guards. I am the twelfth. My real name is Le Huu Trang. I have been "Saturday" for four years. I have seen and felt your terrible plight."

He waited for a reply. There was none. Not one word.

He continued finally, "You have seen me many times. I offered you a drink when you were thirsty. I helped you when you fell. I bandaged your wounds when no one was looking. I was like an angel who came to comfort you. I cannot give back what you have lost, but I can give you hope for the future."

"Friday here. Do you mean you, 'Slant Eyes,' have been listening to our conversations since the beginning? You are crazy. If you really are one of those Commies, I will kill you the first chance I get."

"It's Thursday. Just listen to him, Friday."

Friday responded, "This could be a trap. They aren't going to help us. They want to kill us trying to escape."

"If they wanted to kill us, they don't need for us to try to escape. They would have already done it," Thursday replied.

"Monday here. I know who you are, Saturday. You have helped me many times, while others left me to die. You talk about freedom. How can we be free? We are in the middle of a jungle, miles from civilization. We are weak, almost like dead men walking. We cannot fight. We cannot run. We merely exist."

Le could feel their pain. He tried to encourage them, "For freedom, you can run and fight, if need be. What do you have to lose?"

Friday answered, "Our lives for one."

"Wednesday speaking. Our lives? Is this living?"

"This is Saturday. Wouldn't you love to leave this place and go home and see your wife and family?"

"Friday again. Who cares anymore? Our families have written us off, buried us long ago. All of America has forgotten us." He was his usual cynical self.

"I happen to know that is not true. Although, they have little hope of you returning, your memories still live in the hearts of many Americans," Le implored.

"It's Tuesday. Americans! I have not heard that word for years. Does America still exist? Did it ever exist?"

Le followed through, "I assure you, America does exist. If you trust me, listen to what I say, and follow my instructions, you will see America sooner than you can imagine."

"Monday here. I'm in, Saturday. If it is a trap, then I will go down fighting. I simply cannot go on like this any longer."

"It's Sunday. I agree. When I entered the army, I was a conscientious objector. Now, I will do anything for my…our freedom."

"Monday again. Are all the days of the week in?"

"Let's go for it," Tuesday tapped.

Wednesday quickly cut in, "I'm not sure what month or even year it is, but will we be home by Christmas?"

"You will be on American soil, probably within a week," Le reinforced.

"It's Thursday. How have the New York Yankees been doing, Saturday?"

"Winning, as usual. I have listened to you talk about baseball, so I Googled the Yankees."

Thursday asked, "What is 'Googled?'"

All was quiet. Le forgot that the prisoners had no idea how much the world's technology advanced since 1970. He added, "You will have plenty of time to learn about that when you get home."

"Home! Home is a word I haven't used for years," Thursday replied.

"Monday here. You are the last one to comment, Friday. Are you with us?"

"I'm in, but at the first sign of trouble I will start killing, and Saturday will be my first target."

"Okay. It's settled. Let's go! Saturday, what do we do next?" Monday asked.

"Like I said, follow my lead tomorrow. Right now, get your sleep. You will need to be at your strongest when we travel early in the morning."

Wednesday, too anxious to settle down, pleaded, "What are we going to do when we get out? I suspect our job skills are outdated."

"Friday here. I'm going home to my dairy farm."

"I don't think we have to worry about a job when we get back in the real world. That will be the least of our worries. Besides, in a few years we will be old enough to retire," Monday tapped.

Crowded in their filthy cells, the men replayed the conversation in their minds. Should they dare to hope?

"Goodnight men. Like Saturday said, we need our rest," Monday tapped.

The tapping stopped. They tried to settle down, but sleep would not come. Their minds raced.

In the stillness of his cell, Le reflected. He didn't want to confess to the soldiers that he only made forty-five dollars a month. His thoughts went crazy. Is this worth it? Why couldn't I turn my back on them? It would only be a matter of time until they all died—most likely sooner, than later. He recalled what his friend Sam had taught him about love, freedom, and most importantly, Jesus. What would God want him to do?

Le began thinking about America. It must be an amazing place. Sam talked frequently about his homeland and its freedoms. He explained how people are free to live where they choose. They can even own their home. When they want to travel, they are free to go where they want. A person can walk down the street with his head held high and not be afraid. People can work where they desire, and earn the kind of wage they need to raise their family. He began to realize how different America was from his homeland.

Quickly he snapped back to reality. America would remain a dream to him—something he could never experience personally. At least the prisoners had a chance of returning to that great country.

He must stay focused on the task-at-hand. His responsibility was to get these men on Sam's helicopter tomorrow. Then he would meet his family at their previous agreed rendezvous point. It saddened him that he may never see his parents and sisters again. He determined they would be all right—a long distance separated them from the malicious general.

As Le walked out of his small cell, he looked heavenward. The moon glowed full in the sky, and the stars seen through the jungle foliage seemed to sparkle with hope. He cried to his Heavenly Father. *God, you said you would never forsake us. I believe the promise you made is true. I ask not for my sake only, but for these six innocent lives. I am clinging to your promise. And God, please take care of my family.*

He went to his room on the base to get some needed rest.

Tomorrow promised to be a big day, an important one, not just for the prisoners, but also for their families. If the United States is the country that Le has heard it is, it will be a day when Americans stand united. If all goes according to plan, their children, brothers, fathers, and soldiers who were once dead, were coming home.

SEVEN
# The Escape

---

L e slept soundly for a few hours. He was not certain why he
could rest peacefully. Perhaps it was because his family should
be safe in Laos and soon on their way to Thailand. Maybe it
was because he believed he was finally doing right in God's eyes,
rather than following orders of evil men. Whatever the reason, he
was grateful for the sleep.

~-᚛᚛-~

While still dark, Le dressed, reviewing the plan in his mind.
As he played out each scene, he tried to envision anything that
might go wrong. He knew he had only an eight-hour window,
at best, for the plan to succeed. It should take only two hours
to arrive at the pickup point. He scouted the trail many times
and searched for possible complications. He assured himself that
unless an unexpected problem surfaced, all would be well.

He prayed the helicopter would arrive at the designated time.
He prayed the men would trust him completely. What if any of
the men decided it was too risky and tried to overtake him? That
would be fatal for everyone.

He grabbed his rifle and canteen, tucking them under his
arm. He walked to his bed. Under the mattress was a small, brown
pouch. He picked it up gently, placed the strap around his neck,
and stuffed the small bag inside his shirt. He patted it lightly.

In the pouch were valuables he had collected and stored for
safekeeping. He bought some of them from other guards. A few
items he took from General Yo, over the course of time. They were

the general's trophies from "hunting expeditions." Le intended to return them to their rightful owners when the time was right.

He paused for a moment, and looked around his modest room on the prison grounds. It had been his "home away from home" the last four years.

The stability and security he had known, not to mention his somewhat influential job, would soon be gone. He shivered at the thought. What would he do? He was certain of only one thing; he knew he was doing what God expected of him.

With his heart pounding, he walked the short distance to the small mess hall. His co-workers were already eating. He sat with them, trying to appear calm as he ate his breakfast of sticky rice and a hard biscuit. He wondered if, or when, he would eat again. The thought made him slightly nauseated.

Le knew he had to blend in with the other guards, acting normally. Yet, inside he was anything but calm. His hands trembled; he hoped no one noticed. He glanced over at his fellow guards. He prayed he could pull this off without killing any of them; he wished them no harm. His only concern was saving the six Americans. Realistically, he knew that by the end of the day, there surely would be bloodshed.

Again, he prayed a silent prayer. He asked God to give him the strength emotionally and physically to do what was necessary at the appropriate time.

He had never killed anyone. In fact, he never beat the prisoners. The other guards asked him why he did not join in on the fun. He simply shrugged his shoulders, and explained to them that he was the interpreter, nothing more. They seemed to accept his explanation.

The guards joked and laughed as he drank his milk and finished his breakfast. They discussed some of the "funny" things the prisoners did. At least, they were funny to them. Le couldn't help but think it was a heartbreaking testimony of a sad life.

The hour for freedom was drawing near. They would drop the prisoners off at the labor area, about four miles away. The day's assignment was clearing an old airplane landing strip, now covered with debris. It was a rare occurrence, but for the first time in years, all six men would work together. That aided Le's plan. However, the backbreaking labor would be even more grueling than usual for the men.

In recent weeks, Le noticed that General Yo seemed to be tiring of the prisoners. Perhaps they were getting to be a nuisance. The calloused, elderly tyrant was making life more strenuous for them.

When the guards left the breakfast area, they grabbed a few provisions for the day, including a small amount of food for the prisoners. Le filled a larger bag than normal. The guards teased him about how hungry he must be. Little did they know, he took the extra food for the prisoners' long, grueling day.

The four guards piled into the vehicle, which would deliver them to the landing strip. It was an old U.S. Army ambulance, just right for eight people in the back. Le sat in the back with one guard, while the other two took their places in the front cab.

As they stopped by the cells housing the prisoners, Le noticed the morning's stillness. The tangerine sunrise was spectacular with shades of pink and orange splattered through the clouds. He looked up and felt the refreshing, warm, gentle breeze. It was calm, the start of a beautiful day—peaceful and surreal.

The guards unshackled the prisoners from their cells. They would work free from their usual restraints, but certainly not free from the watchful eyes of the guards. No chains to hold them would be in the POW's favor, and allow them to move around easier.

Le helped the men into the ambulance, nodded, and gave a hint of a smile.

Each prisoner, unsure of Le, glared at him as he passed.

Monday was the last one in. Le looked at him and whispered, "Look at the incredible sunrise. It's going to be a great day."

Monday did not say a word. He paused, and then stepped slowly into the vehicle. Again, he stared at Le. Should he dare hope? Was there any possibility this guard could really be there to help them? On the other hand, could this be another one of Yo's cruel, evil games? Soon they would know.

It was a rough, bumpy ride to the work site; the road rarely, if ever used in the past thirty-five years. Ruts scored deep into the ground.

Dense jungle foliage grabbed the road from both sides causing a dark and eerie path. The sun's rays began to break through the jungle as if they would swallow it. Dew on the leaves danced as the sunlight glistened making thousands of tiny rainbows. The birds sweetly sang their songs of freedom and love.

The prisoners were unaware of the beautiful sounds and sights around them. Any beauty in the world ceased to exist long ago. Life became one endless day, followed by another. To them this was just another day, but soon they would see it as their day to freedom—by either rescue or death. Either way, they would be free from the years of imprisonment, terror, and beatings. Today they were going home—home to their families, or home to their God.

As Le's mind raced, he recalled a time when he read a phrase penned on the side of an American soldier's helmet. "When I die, I'm going to heaven. I've already been to hell." Le often thought about those words. Being Vietnamese, he originally took offense to them. Lately, he studied the Vietnam War and learned what many Americans endured, especially these prisoners. He understood the meaning of those powerful words. They were not a direct insult against his country, but truth about the war itself.

Many times Le wondered what would have happened if South Vietnam had defeated the invaders of the North. Would his country be free now? Le found his mind drifting to what might have been, but quickly snapped out of it coming back to reality. He must stay focused. Did he make any mistakes along the way? Did he forget any important details?

The driver laughed as he crazily sped along the ruts in the road. He knew the bouncing hurt the prisoners. Their tired, aching bones caused them to cringe in pain with every hard jolt. He enjoyed their misery.

One time he hit a bump with such force that those in the back toppled onto each other and landed in a heap. Sunday and Thursday fell onto a guard. The grumbling guard roughly shoved them away. Quickly resuming his position, he hit both prisoners in the head with the butt of his rifle and almost knocked them out. Freeman's head bled profusely.

Le warned the driver to slow down. Then remembered he could not tip his hand and show any compassion to the prisoners. Not yet.

Finally, the ambulance arrived at its destination. It was just before seven in the morning. Le felt confident things were going as planned.

The vehicle slammed to a stop near a rundown, deserted shack. It once served as a tower for a military airfield during the Vietnam Conflict. It was located less than twenty miles from the Laos border.

The two guards in the cab hopped out first. They noticed that nearby an old U.S. Army helicopter lay on its side, abandoned in the middle of the old landing strip, a remnant of what used to be. With piqued curiosity, the two guards walked over to get a closer look. They joked and laughed about how many Americans likely died when the chopper hit the ground.

Le jumped from the back of the ambulance. He looked around and imagined what the airfield was like teeming with American soldiers, helicopters, and small airplanes, four decades ago.

As the fourth guard started to get out, Le sprang into action. Without warning, he raised the butt of his rifle and slammed it into the back of the guard's neck. In an instant, Le replayed the scene still fresh in his mind, when moments before the same guard hit Sunday and Thursday. "How do you like it?" Le sneered sarcastically.

The guard's body fell limp as he collapsed to the ground. The commotion caught the attention of the other two guards who were still gawking at the downed chopper.

Le noticed them watching and yelled in Vietnamese, "He tripped."

They sprinted over and bent down to help their injured co-worker.

Without hesitation, Le struck one of them in the back of his head with the butt of his rifle. The remaining guard, confused, looked up at Le. Then unexpectedly, Le slammed the end of his rifle hard into his face. Blood gushed from his nose as he crumpled to the ground.

The three guards were now unresponsive, sprawled out on the cracked asphalt. Le did not know if any of them were dead, or if they were unconscious for a short time. He only knew he had to act fast.

Le immediately raised his rifle toward the astonished prisoners who were gawking at the scene in front of them.

Their natural response was to raise their hands as if to surrender.

Le noticed his rifle aimed at the prisoners and quickly lowered it. He swung the strap over his shoulder, and urgently ordered the prisoners, "Help me get them into the shack. Now! You'll find some rope under the seat. Quick!"

Sunday drove a similar ambulance when he was a medic in Nam. In fact, he wondered if it might not be the same one. In his normal take-charge way, he pushed the other men back and lifted the seat. The rope was in place, so he grabbed it quickly.

The Americans even in their weakened conditions, and operating on pure adrenaline, piled out of the ambulance and roughly dragged the guards into the nearby hut.

Le shouted, "Who ties the best knots?"

Friday replied eagerly, "I do. I used to calf-rope in the rodeo." He stepped forward and quickly secured the guards. He didn't need a reminder to tie the ropes tight. In fact, he tied them so tight that if the rifle butt to the head didn't kill them, his knots would surely stop the blood circulation. It was obvious he had no pity on them. They had been extremely hard on him personally. It was payback time.

Le double-checked the knots and stretched tape across their mouths. The longer it took for General Yo and his men to locate these guards, the better chance the prisoners had to escape successfully.

As Le stood, he turned and came face-to-face with three of the prisoners. They had grabbed the guards' rifles and aimed them directly at him. They still were not sure they could trust this Vietnamese guard.

Le hesitated, but then reasoned that the prisoners needed him too badly to kill him. Not deterred, he stepped forward and quickly headed toward the truck. "We need to get going. Time's a-wasting." He rushed past the former prisoners who continued directing their rifles at him.

Meanwhile, Monday stared at the words on a corroded, crooked sign, barely hanging from a rusty nail on the old hut. He bent over, grabbed a hat, which had fallen off one of the guards, and tossed it into the small run-down shack. Monday stepped back and shook his head. "I can't believe it. I have been a prisoner all this time, only a few miles away from where I was stationed. This was my army base. Unbelievable."

He turned and was shocked to see his fellow POWs still had their weapons fixed on Le, the man who desperately was trying to help them escape. Taking charge, without batting an eye, Monday instinctively knew it was time to resume his role as Captain McCarter. He quickly sized up the situation and shouted an order, "You heard the man. Let's get going."

He jumped into the back of the ambulance as the three prisoners looked at each other with a blank stare.

"No," Lomack snarled forcefully. "I say shoot him now and take the vehicle." Friday, always known for his quick temper and short fuse reacted in his typical way.

Captain McCarter jumped out of the ambulance, stepping

protectively in front of Le. Glaring at Friday, McCarter's voice grew louder. "Put the weapon down, soldier."

Lomack snapped back. "I see you haven't changed in all these years. You are not in charge anymore. This rifle and these bullets are clearly in charge."

Thursday, otherwise known as Freeman, intervened, "Lomack, put the rifle down. Think. Think of what you are doing." He stepped in front of the captain.

"Oh, I have thought about this. For forty long years, I've thought about this. I don't trust this Commie as far as I can throw him. It's a trap. I know it. I sense it's a VC trick, which will kill us all before the day is over."

"Think of what you are saying. They had forty years to kill us if they wanted to," Freeman bellowed.

"I say take the truck and head west," Lomack gestured toward the road.

Again Freeman taking on his professional role as a counselor with his patient, pled with the distraught soldier, "Lomack, calm down and think. He is our only way out. We may die trying, but at least we tried. If we kill him, we will all certainly die. We have no idea where to go. We don't know what's out there." He pointed toward the dense jungle and continued, "Forty years of growth and industrialization. We have no idea what's going on. They may have flying cars or robots running around on this planet. We need his help. We can't do it alone."

Pfingston, otherwise known as Tuesday, finally agreed, lowering his rifle. "Let's put the weapons down and get going."

Le made a decision to challenge Lomack and end the foolish standoff. "If you're going to shoot me, then shoot me. We are wasting valuable time. We have a helicopter to catch and a psychotic general to escape from." Taking a chance, he hurried to the driver's side of the vehicle.

Lomack glanced around, knowing he was outnumbered, and reluctantly agreed. "Alright, but I'm keeping this weapon on you at all times. One false move and you are history. I still don't trust you."

"Get in the truck now," McCarter ordered. His patience was growing thin.

Lomack glared at Captain McCarter and boldly confronted him. "You may think you are the ranking man here, but that doesn't make any difference to me. Rank died years ago. Now we are equals," he shouted in the captain's face.

McCarter turned to face his comrades, "Rank may be out, but democracy is not. Who wants to shoot this man who is trying to help us?"

There was complete silence. No one budged.

"Who wants to go home?"

Five hands immediately shot skyward, and then a sixth raised slowly—Lomack's.

"Then it's settled. Load up. We're going home." They piled into the old vehicle and quickly were on their way.

# EIGHT

# The Rough Road

---

Le felt the cold, hard steel of the barrel of Lomack's rifle nestled against his neck as they rattled down the abandoned road. Fortunately, he still had his weapons, if he needed them.

So far, everything was going as planned except for the distrusting, paranoid acts of Lomack. They were slightly ahead of schedule, but they still had almost twenty miles to go on the rough road. The mood was tense. Everyone knew the danger involved and was on edge. The uncertainty of the situation made all of them uncomfortable.

McCarter made his way to the front seat. He looked over at Le and began questioning the guard, "Who…are…you?"

Le grinned, "I am Le Huu Trang. Just call me Le."

"Are you Special Forces or something?"

"No, I'm just a guard at your prison camp."

The captain stared at the rough road ahead and replied, "It's not my prison camp." He raised his voice, "None of this makes sense. I mean, how can you speak English so well? You have no accent."

"I don't know for sure. I think it just came natural. General Yo recruited me out of college. He wanted me to listen to the prisoners' conversations. I was unsure what that involved at the time. I really wanted to be an embassy interpreter. But what General Yo wants, he gets."

Captain McCarter paused, trying to take it all in. "Why are you helping us?"

"My heart, I guess. I began to realize that what was taking place in the prison camp was morally and ethically wrong."

The other men moved closer to listen to the conversation.

A question came from the back. Le did not know who asked it since he rarely heard their voices at the prison. The voice sounded hoarse and cracked due to being inactive for years. "How is the war going?"

Le hesitated, struggling to find the right words. "Where do I begin? The war. Well…." He cleared his throat. "Well, the war here in Vietnam has been over for thirty-five years."

Another voice joined in, "Did we win?"

Thoughtfully, Le responded, "Well, yes and no." He gave the out-of-touch soldiers a brief history lesson. "Your nation signed the Paris Peace Treaty with North Vietnam in 1973, and the American GIs went home. All prisoners and bodies of American soldiers supposedly were returned to your homeland."

One of the men shouted angrily from the back, "Not all. What about us?"

Another joined in, "Yeah, why weren't we released? How could they forget about us?"

Le felt compassion for the men. He tried to explain. "You were being held by a vindictive, evil man named General Yo. A bomb from an American plane killed his entire family in North Vietnam in 1968."

Thomas Traber, also known as Wednesday, spoke up, "We weren't here in 1968."

"That didn't matter to Yo. He only wanted to see Americans suffer. Any Americans he captured, he punished. He made them endure horrendous suffering and torture as you all experienced. Even after the Peace Treaty, he refused to release any prisoners keeping them hidden on his personal property. He wouldn't even release the bodies of those that died, totally in opposition to the treaty. He had any dead Americans burned; eliminating all the evidence."

Lomack finally entered the conversation, "How many Americans did that cold-hearted monster kill or capture?"

"Counting you, thirty-two. Thirty-three, counting me."

Lomack continued his line of questioning with his typical sarcasm. "Counting you! You're not American and you're too young to have served in the war."

Le responded patiently, "That's true. You see, I took on the identity of Yo's first prisoner—the one you knew me to be, Corporal Daniel Sparks. You referred to me as 'Saturday.'"

McCarter's head was spinning. Was this really happening? He paused and then finally asked, "Okay. So what happened to Daniel Sparks?"

"I'm not certain. I heard rumors that he died during an interrogation, but I also heard that he was killed trying to escape."

Lomack, finally calmed down, asked, "If the war is over, why are you Commies still in South Vietnam?"

There was no response.

Lomack realized he could not be certain of anything. He continued carefully, "We…we are in South Vietnam, aren't we?"

"Yes, you are. This is all Yo's private property. It borders Laos." Le pointed in all directions with his arm out the window. "The government awarded it to him after the war. For his outstanding service," Le chuckled mockingly. "He's officially retired now, but he still wears the uniform and dishes out orders to his soldiers."

Lomack's voice began to escalate again. He repeated his question, "What are you Communists doing here?"

Le took a deep breath. "In April of 1975, my country, South Vietnam, was taken over by North Vietnam."

Freeman questioned further, "Then we lost the war in Vietnam?"

"That's what the world thinks. However, the fact is my people lost the war. The South Vietnamese people lost the war. America's hands were tied because of the Peace Treaty and the unfavorable position, which many Americans had about the war." Le shook his head in disgust. "Politics, all politics!"

"Unfortunately, thousands of innocent people died when our villages were burned and destroyed by power hungry Communists. It was horrible for people like my parents, and grandparents who only wanted to farm and live peacefully. Now they work hard every day simply to survive. My grandparents and all four of my parent's siblings were killed by the North Vietnamese."

All were silent. No one knew what to say, feel, think, or believe.

Freeman cleared his throat. "What happened in the world in the last forty years?"

The guard pondered the question. There was too much to say. From whose perspective—his own, the prisoners, or the worlds? Le's mind searched for the right answers.

The world seemed smaller due to modern technology. In 1970, it took soldiers weeks to hear from their families. Computers changed that! Instant communication throughout the world is available with a click of the mouse. Immediate news coverage, details shared with the public as they happen, was dramatically different from during the Vietnam War era.

How could anyone explain September 11, 2001, Desert Storm, and the Iraq War? His thoughts were jumbled. The fact that some nations were getting closer to nuclear weapons, or the threat of terrorism was not information he wanted to share at that time. How could the men possibly understand terrorism?

When they went to war, people were listening to record albums and eight-track tapes. Today thousands of songs are stored on a little piece of plastic, the size of a quarter—just one of the wireless wonders, and ingenious innovations available. How could he explain any of that to the returning veterans? They missed nearly a half-century of technology and transformation.

Le pictured them like children in a large toy store with so much to see and learn. Where does he begin? He chose to pay attention to the task-at-hand—finding freedom for the men.

The men patiently waited for a response.

"So much has happened in the last forty years that I don't know where to start. There will be plenty of time to talk later. Right now, let's stay focused. We will be approaching the Laos border shortly."

As he considered the immediate situation, Le asked, "Does anyone know how to drive a clutch vehicle?" Even though it was decades since they had driven, most of the men nodded their heads. Le knew he needed to have the men prepared, in case he was not with them the entire trip. "If anything happens to me, stay on this path for as long as you can. In my left pocket is a GPS unit. The helicopter will find you."

Le noticed the confusion on McCarter's face and realized he had no idea what a GPS unit was. "It stands for Global Positioning System; it's a navigational tool directed by satellites. It traces your exact location."

"Are we expecting company?" McCarter asked.

"Just being realistic; anything can happen. I do mean anything. I think I covered all my tracks, but no one should underestimate General Yo."

"I'd give anything to kill that man. Even my freedom," Lomack yelled.

Everyone pondered his words.

Williams, formerly known as Sunday, spoke up. "Where are we going and who is picking us up?"

"We are driving to the Laos border. There, a helicopter will be waiting for you."

"Who is picking us up?" Freeman persisted.

"A man called Sam. He is a good, Christian man, and the reason I am helping you. He formerly served in the United States Army Special Forces. He operated an orphanage here, but has recently been ordered to close it and get out of the country."

"You mean to tell me you're a Christian?" Williams asked.

Le briefly turned his head and looked Anthony directly in his eyes. "Yes, I am. Thanks to Sam and his missionaries at the orphanage. Actually, everyone in my family is a believer in Jesus."

"No wonder you're helping us." McCarter nodded his head, finally understanding.

Williams continued, "Why was Sam asked to leave when he was helping the orphans?"

"For talking about Jesus," Le replied as he maneuvered around a fallen tree in the road.

"Let me get this straight. He ran an orphanage, and was asked to leave because he was preaching the gospel." Williams could not believe what he heard.

"That's about it. Most Communist and Arab nations are like that these days."

"What about Russia?" Freeman inquired.

"Russia, as a nation, collapsed over twenty years ago."

The men's eyes grew wide. "No more Russia?"

"Well, there is a Russia. All of its satellite countries, Romania, Hungary, and others are free and govern themselves."

Freeman asked, "What about East Germany?"

"Germany is all one country, no longer divided. There is no Berlin Wall. It came down during Ronald Reagan's presidency."

Lomack immediately spoke up. "Ronald Reagan, the actor? Are you saying an actor became President of the United States?"

"Yes, the one and only."

Lomack continued with his line of questioning. "What kind of president was he?"

"History will be good to him. He is considered by many to be the greatest president of modern times."

Lomack grinned, "Wow! Who would have guessed?"

There was a pause in the conversation.

Changing the subject, McCarter asked, "What shall we call you?"

"Excuse me," Le replied.

"I mean, we can't call you Saturday or Sparks. You gave us your name, but I don't remember it. What should we call you?"

"Le would be fine."

"Okay, Mr. Le. Let me ask you this. What are you getting out of this? I mean…a person does not put his life on the line, possibly even kill three fellow soldiers, to help prisoners escape, and not want something in return. I repeat my question, what's in this for you?" Lomack coughed.

Lomack's inquiry prompted Le to question it himself. Why was he doing this? Was it because of his newfound faith? Or, because he saw how wrong it was to imprison these innocent men? Perhaps it was because he wanted freedom for himself. Maybe the reason is part of all of these.

Le reached into his shirt pocket and pulled out six sets of old dog tags on chains. He handed them to Captain McCarter. "If you don't mind sir, please hand these to the soldiers they belong to."

McCarter looked at the tags and realized they were the same ones taken away from them years ago. "Well, I'll be. Our dog tags." McCarter grinned as he handed them to the rightful owners.

"Should we put them on?" Williams asked.

Le responded, "I would. That's the only way the Americans will know who you are when you get to the embassy. When you arrive, they will take your fingerprints and confirm your identity."

"You mean this is real? We are really going home?" Pfingston shook his head in disbelief.

"Unless something goes wrong, you will be landing in the courtyard of the American Embassy in Thailand by sunset. First, they will look at you with skepticism. That will turn to astonishment, joy, and excitement. You can take a hot bath and eat a nourishing meal. You will even have clean sheets and a soft pillow for your head."

Mindful of the time, Le glanced at his watch.

"I hope that within a couple days you will be headed home

to your families. I think the American Government will want to get you to your loved ones as soon as possible."

The men stared at each other, afraid to hope. Too much was at stake.

Suddenly, the silence was shattered when reality hit, McCarter shouted excitedly, "Men, we're going home. We are really going home!"

The men hugged each other and shouted, "We're going home! We're free!" The old ambulance swerved all over the rugged road. The excitement of the newly released prisoners made it difficult for Le to avoid the deep ruts and other debris on the abandoned trail.

Le knew they weren't out of danger yet, but had to smile. He also realized that some of them would face heartbreak when they arrived at home. Their future was uncertain.

For the next hour, the men continuously asked Le questions as the old ambulance traveled just under ten miles per hour. The road was rough and pockmarked, but to the men it was incredible—it was their road to freedom.

They were running on pure adrenaline. Le answered many questions, but as a Vietnamese, he could not answer some of them.

The men finally started to wear down. They were exhausted. Le knew they needed their strength. He finally told them, "Sit back and relax. Drink plenty of water. Go to sleep. Time will pass faster that way."

As much as they tried, it was not possible. They had waited forty years for this moment.

They still needed to get to Laos undetected. As the old vehicle finally quieted, Le took time to pray for continued safety to their destination, uninterrupted by Yo's henchmen.

# NINE
# The Evil Tyrant

Shadowy trees blew in the hot wind and added mystery to the deserted jungle road. The beautiful, deep-green forest went unnoticed.

It took longer than he expected, but they were still ahead of schedule. In less than an hour, the chopper was due to arrive. Everything continued as planned, uneventful.

Le stopped for the men to take a much-needed break as they neared the Laos border. The hazardous road and answering the many questions he fielded was stressful—he needed a break himself.

Everyone stumbled out of the vehicle. Most of the men were barely able to stand, all in pain from aching bones and muscles.

"Hey Le, would you have a smoke? It's been a long time since we've had one," Lomack pleaded.

"Yes, a cigarette would be great," Traber added.

Le looked at them and shook his head in disgust, "No way, men. Cigarette smoking is bad for your health. It causes cancer."

"Are you serious? Who cares?" Lomack chuckled, sarcastically.

"You heard the man," McCarter shouted with confidence. "He doesn't have any. In addition, they are bad for you. End of subject."

The men sipped some water and ate the food Le brought. For the first time in many years, they enjoyed fresh fruit and drank clean water.

The silence of the jungle was creepy. A bird heard faintly

in the distance and the wind rustling the leaves added to the strangeness of the moment.

Suddenly Le sensed something was amiss.

Captain McCarter noticed Le's apprehension. "What is it? You look frightened. What's wrong?"

"I don't know. Something seems weird. I can't put my finger on it."

"It seems pretty quiet to me," Williams confided.

"Too quiet," Le whispered. "Too quiet."

The soldiers stood up and instinctively gathered close in a circle. They scanned the area, immediately raised their rifles, and pointed them towards the thick brush.

Suddenly the jungle came to life, startling the men. The sounds of the birds fluttering as they took flight added to the eeriness. Then there was total silence.

"Get in the truck," Le quietly ordered. "Fast!"

The men scrambled into the vehicle.

"Quick! Ready your weapons. Now!"

Le started the engine and hastily took off. They had driven a short distance and barreled around a blind curve. Blocking the road directly in front of them, a truck with a machine gun mounted over the cab fired over the escaping prisoners' vehicle.

Horrified, Le slammed on the brakes. There was no escape. Something had gone dreadfully wrong.

Two men stepped from the vehicle; weapons aimed at the startled Le.

"Can we fight?" McCarter whispered as his heart pounded.

"Not with that machine gun staring us down. It will tear us to pieces before we fire the first shot." Le sized up the situation. "Everybody, get out the back of the truck. Keep your distance from each other. Captain, you, and I should step out slowly."

"Is this the border patrol?" Williams asked.

"No. It's General Yo's men."

"I knew we couldn't trust this Commie," Lomack shouted. He leveled his rifle at Le.

"No!" Freeman yelled as he shoved the weapon aside. "They'll kill us all if you shoot now."

Lomack glared at Freeman.

The Americans stared with watchful eyes as the backdoor of the intruding truck swung open. The unexpected occurred when General Yo emerged from the vehicle and confronted them. His cocky, arrogant face proudly displayed his victory.

The soldier's nightmare became reality. A sinking sensation overwhelmed Le.

Yo eyed each of the prisoners with his sly grin.

Two of Yo's men stood in front of him with weapons aimed at Le and some of the prisoners. In the bed of the truck, another man pointed a mounted machine gun directly at the rest of the men. The situation appeared hopeless.

At a standoff, the prisoners still had not dropped their weapons.

Yo took out a cigarette, lit it, and blew smoke rings into the air. He strutted closer to Le and stared at him defiantly. "I'm surprised at you, Le. You were one of my brightest students."

"How did you find us?" Le flashed a look of confusion.

The general laughed aloud—his mocking, evil cackle. "Oh, the miracle of technology! We put a bug in your truck. We have been following you all morning, thanks to our GPS. It really was quite simple."

Le knew the escape was well planned and orchestrated precisely. His loud voice echoed through the forest, "How did you know?"

Yo took something out of his pocket and handed it to one of his men nearby. The soldier grabbed it, walked toward Le, handed it to him, and then stepped back.

Le reached for it cautiously, and studied it.

Yo mocked snidely, "It didn't take long to get information out of her. She did not want to see her youngest without a head."

Le's heart sank. He held a photo of his adored wife and children. Bound and gagged; their bloody faces displayed terror.

He couldn't breathe. How could this be happening? What went wrong?

Le's blood boiled. He stomped angrily to confront Yo.

McCarter grabbed his shoulders and stopped him as the enemy's weapons swiveled immediately toward Le.

"How did you find out?" McCarter shouted.

"Well listen to that. He speaks." A sarcastic General Yo smirked and took a puff of his cigarette.

"Le, I heard reports your wife had been working at that orphanage. They stated you were with her. Your house has been under surveillance for months. I knew you were going to do this before you knew it. Such is Christianity. Helping fellow man. So predictable," he mocked. General Yo chuckled, "I was the one that ordered the people at the orphanage to leave. I have also commanded your chopper to be shot down when it arrives."

Then it came again—his sadistic laugh.

"It was obvious when your wife and children left yesterday that something was up. I had them detained and personally got the information out of them. It really didn't take much effort. She was not as strong as the six of you."

He discarded his cigarette butt, crushing it under his boot.

"They will be no problem to anyone again. You will never see them in this life. Maybe your so-called 'Christian' religion will allow you to see them when you are dead," Yo taunted. "I suggest you drop your guns or you will die here. I really don't care."

"Neither do we," Lomack roared as he pointed the rifle toward Yo's head.

Infuriated, Yo hollered, "Your guns do not scare me!"

Lomack stepped forward and fired three shots. The noise of the gunfire was deafening, but General Yo did not fall. Nothing happened.

"Go ahead. Try them all," Yo laughed.

Quickly two other prisoners fired their weapons. Again, nothing happened. Everyone remained standing.

"I was not sure when this would take place, so all I could do was set everything to my advantage. I had blanks put in all the guards' magazines. Even yours, Le."

Le grabbed his pistol from his side and released the magazine. It was true. It was filled with blanks.

"You are mad," Le shouted.

"Not mad, just doing my job as a soldier…for the war…for the cause."

"Job! Job! This is not a job. There is no war. There is no conflict. There is no cause." Le's voice was loud and harsh. "These men should have been released thirty-seven years ago when the peace treaty was signed."

General Yo was infuriated. "Peace Treaty. There is no treaty for those who killed my family. There never will be. That's a joke."

"Your family. Your family!" Lomack yelled. "That was over forty years ago. You are insane."

"Yes, my family. Your people killed my family."

Freeman tried to reason with the lunatic. "No! War killed your family. Innocent people die in war along with the guilty."

"It was not your war," Yo screamed in anger.

"Neither was it yours," McCarter added. "The people of South Vietnam just wanted to live in peace. How many innocent people died when you and your people invaded? How many millions suffered death for your political purposes?"

"How many still suffer today because of your iron-fisted control," Williams shouted.

Yo continued, "They do not know how to take care of themselves. They are subjects of a deeper, more meaningful cause."

"When will it end, Yo? When will it end?" McCarter questioned.

"It will never end as long as there are people like you and Le out there. You are too stupid to realize that Mao is the way. He is the only answer."

"Mao is dead!" Le yelled.

"This conversation is over." Yo was furious, out of control with rage.

Le spoke, "Yes, you have suffered for the loss of your family. But, these men did not do it. A bomb did it."

"A bomb dropped by men, just like them," Yo pointed to the POWs.

"No, the bomb was dropped because of war. Because people can't get along. Because of petty events, miscalculated risks, or misinterpreted thoughts. Do you think what you have done is any better?" Le inquired, his voice more forceful.

"It's justice."

"No, it's not. It borders on insanity. Do you think that once the Vietnamese Government finds out that you have been holding American POWs they will turn and look the other way? Your life will be worthless, Yo. Yes, they will probably kill these six men and destroy any evidence they ever existed, but you will go down, too."

"I did what any professional soldier would do."

"You call keeping a man in a cage for forty years professional. I call it barbaric. You are a terrorist!"

"No, they are the terrorists," Yo screamed and pointed to the prisoners.

"All I see are six shells of what used to be proud men. They are men with families who did what their government told them to do. They have done nothing wrong. They are not the problem. No! You and others like you who refuse to listen to logic, peace, and God are the real problems."

"I am done talking." Yo forcefully ordered his men, "Take them back to the prison. All of them, including Le!"

The Communist soldiers looked at each other, unsure what to do. This was all new information to them. Who was right? What did Le mean?

Le noticed their hesitation and yelled to them in Vietnamese. "Your lives will be worthless, too. Were you ordered to keep your jobs secret? Not to tell anyone about the prison? I know I was.

And why? Because if the Vietnamese Government found out what was going on something would have to be done about it. Your best bet is to end this charade now. Let us go. Turn yourself in. Tell the authorities what happened here. Turn against General Yo, or you will all be dead."

Yo's soldiers looked at each other, uncertain how to react. They were unaware that the Vietnamese Government did not know about the prison and wondered if they made a mistake obeying the general. Should they risk listening to Le and walk away from Yo?

General Yo glared at his men, sensed their hesitation, and feared they were not going to carry out his orders. "Cowards," he bellowed. He pulled his pistol out of his holster and aimed it directly at Le's head. "Die!" he thundered.

Lomack yelled, "No!" He jumped in front of Le as a shot echoed through the forest. McCarter and the other POWs gasped in horror, unable to stop what was happening.

In a split-second, one single shot ended the standoff.

Le stared at Lomack, the man who only hours ago threatened to kill him.

Lomack appeared confused. He turned to face Le and the five other men. He felt no pain. Fear overwhelmed him as he wondered where he had been shot. Perplexed, he looked at his comrades. What happened? Did the bullet miss him?

In unison, all eyes turned to General Yo. He stood with his pistol directed toward the ground. He slumped to his knees, stared at Le with a look of horror, then collapsed in the dirt face first. Motionless!

Without warning three mysterious figures dressed in camouflage clothing emerged from the jungle. A fourth appeared from the trees, and a familiar voice commanded, "Danh tu."

The Vietnamese men did as ordered and dropped their weapons. A tall, black man, dressed in army fatigues, and carrying a military rife showed his face.

"Sam!" Le shouted excitedly.

Sam hurried over and put his hand on Le's shoulder. "Are you okay, my friend?"

Le nodded his head, still in disbelief. "How did you know?"

"I was worried that if you arrived early you might be detected. We landed ahead of schedule just a few hundred yards from here. While we were waiting, we heard gunfire. I suspected something had gone very wrong. We followed your GPS signal and made the decision to fire before things got any worse."

Sam's gaze turned to Captain McCarter and the other prisoners. His hand slid off Le's shoulder and went limp. A tear came to his eye. "Oh, dear God, it is true." He snapped to attention and proudly saluted the six men. "With my highest respect gentlemen, I salute and honor you. God bless you."

Sam walked over to Specialist Anthony Williams. With trembling arms, he gently embraced him.

Then Sam collected his composure and looked at his Vietnamese friend who was helping Lomack stand.

Le extended his hand to Lomack. "You were willing to give your life to save mine. Thank You."

Lomack grabbed his outstretched hand and shook it vigorously.

Freeman smiled as he watched. He knew it was a vital step in his patient's healing process.

The emotional scene had left Sam shaken. Tears ran down his cheeks as he went to each of the men and hugged them, unable to speak. He paused to collect his thoughts. After a deep, steadying breath he flashed a big grin and shouted with authority, "Okay, gentlemen. Let's go home!" With feeling, he repeated, "Let's go home."

"Wait! There is one more thing I must do," Le walked closer to the three Vietnamese soldiers. In their language he begged, "Please tell me where my family is."

They were silent until Sam stomped over to them and looked at them face-to-face. When they noticed him reaching for his pistol, they all started talking at once. "We do not know. Yo captured them near the border and brought them back to the prison."

Le shouted in a loud, desperate voice, "Are they alive?"

One of them hung his head sadly and confided, "I do not think so. Yo took them into the building, but later came out alone. He only had that picture."

Another guard spoke up, "There was a lot of screaming and crying when he was inside. Then it was quiet."

Le looked in the direction of the prison and then at Sam. "I must go back. Even if they are dead, I must go find them."

"I understand," Sam said, putting his hand on his friend's shoulder. "I would do the same thing for my family."

At that moment, the helicopter pilot's voice blared through Sam's headphones. "Sam, we have company. Three choppers are headed our direction."

"How far away are they?"

"About fifteen minutes."

Sam looked at the three despondent Vietnamese soldiers and then at General Yo's lifeless body. "The war is over," he spoke in Vietnamese. "It is done. Go home. Go home."

Sam turned to his men and issued an order, "Disable the vehicles and weapons. Make them walk home. I will take pictures of the evidence. We need to move quickly!"

As if rehearsed, the men sprang into action. They grabbed the weapons, took out the magazines, and smashed the guns across the vehicle. One of the men opened the hood of Yo's truck and the old ambulance, cut the battery cables and plug wires, rendering the vehicles useless.

Sam took a small camera from his pocket and snapped pictures of the POWs, General Yo's body, and the three Vietnamese soldiers.

Another one of Sam's men sent the Vietnamese home on foot, and then turned and signaled "thumbs up."

Sam shouted, "Now we're ready. Let's go home."

Le glanced one last time at the body of General Yo. He walked around it. Some of the prisoners kicked the dead tormenter in the head as they passed him. Lomack kicked him and then spit on the motionless body. "You took forty years of my life. May you rot in your grave!"

The POWs followed Sam through the forest, growing more excited with each step. As they entered a clearing, they could not believe their eyes. Freedom was within their reach—in the form of a large helicopter!

For the first time in forty years, all six men were smiling.

Sam and his men put their arms around the prisoners and repeated the words. "You're going home, men. You're going home."

Sam's aides were formerly in the military. Two were Navy SEALs, and the other was a U.S. Marine. They assisted in many rescues, but this was their ultimate mission. Something they would be proud of forever—a story they would tell their children and grandchildren for years to come. This is what they lived for!

The prisoners were finally on their way home!

Home is where you lay your head. Soon they would lay their heads at home, in America, and experience freedom, real freedom, for the first time in forty long years.

As they reached the helicopter, the soldiers' eyes were moist. Sam's men helped them aboard and strapped them into their seats. They stared straight ahead, never looking out. Their minds were miles away.

Finally, everyone except Sam and Le were in the chopper and the rotors roared.

Sam shouted above the deafening noise, "Le, my friend, you have to come with us now. The men in the approaching choppers will kill you if you stay. Then you will be no help to your family or anybody else."

Le glanced at Sam, then the hostages. He looked back into the jungle. This was his country and life. The only one he had ever known. Somewhere out there were his dear wife and children. Alive or dead—he had to go back for them. "I have to get my family. They are probably dead, but I still must find them. They deserve that much."

"You can't do it by yourself. We will take the POWs to the embassy. We will go through official channels and try to get help for you. I promise we will return to search for your family."

"The embassy—what can they do?"

"Think about it, Le. The Vietnamese Government will soon hear about this. We have taken pictures. It can't remain a secret. I believe they will bend over backwards to help us. Right now, your life is worthless. You have uncovered something big. The world will certainly stand up and take notice. Unless I am sadly mistaken, there will be a public outcry. You are a dead man here. Come. Let me deal with this, the right way, at the right time."

Just then, the pilot yelled out the door. "Sam, we have to leave. Now!"

Le decided Sam was right. He and Linh agreed what they would do in this situation. They both knew what could happen and understood the risks. They had decided together that they would accept the consequences. They would trust God. Yet Le felt the need to protect Linh. Their children were his responsibility. Oh, how he loved his family! He couldn't shake the feeling that he had failed them. However, he trusted Sam. He knew he would keep his word.

The sound of the helicopter blades reminded Le of the urgency of the situation. He threw his rifle down and hopped into the chopper, followed by a much-relieved Sam.

The chopper rose quickly, flying low over the dense jungle. Below, Le saw the abandoned ambulance, and the body of General Yo. He had no pity for him.

Le looked at the rescued men and was confident he did what he had to do. All was quiet as Le watched the trees and the brush beneath him disappear into the distance. The soldiers stared straight ahead in complete silence for a long time.

Le watched Captain McCarter just as the corners of his mouth curved up and a huge smile spread across his face. The captain reached his hand across the aisle and placed it on Le's arm. He realized the tremendous sacrifice this one time "enemy" had made for him. He squeezed the young guard's arm. With misty eyes, and heartfelt words he said, "Thank you! Thank you!"

At that moment, Le believed no matter what happened to him or his family, it was worth it. It was the right thing to do.

## TEN
# The Embassy

---

The Vietnamese helicopters pursuing the Americans were no match for the first-rate flying ability of Sam's pilot. As they crossed into Laos, Yo's helicopters finally retreated. With the general dead, the chase was over.

During the entire flight, the soldiers remained silent; the only sound was the monotonous roar of the chopper.

Sam spent a great deal of time talking on the radio. Occasionally he would look back at the prisoners who sat motionless, staring straight ahead. He could not imagine the thoughts racing through their minds.

Before long, the helicopter entered Thailand's air space. They stopped briefly to refuel at a site previously arranged by Sam.

Just before they reached Bangkok, two United States military helicopters escorted them toward a large compound. They began their descent into the courtyard of the American Embassy.

Le looked at Captain McCarter. The prisoner was staring out a window, his eyes filled with tears. An indescribable look came over his face. The other five men looked up, grabbed each other's hands, and began sobbing.

Le realized why the soldiers were weeping. In a moment of ecstasy, they all caught their first glimpse of a very welcome sight. Flying high in the bright sky over the compound was an enormous American flag. For the first time in forty years, the returning soldiers saw "Old Glory" waving freely in the breeze. Their emotions erupted as the love they felt for their country surfaced with tears of joy.

Le's feelings were also disclosed as tears trickled down his cheeks.

Two military helicopters hovered overhead as they watched Sam's aircraft touchdown.

When the chopper was safe on the ground, the other two landed close by. As the rotating blades came to a stop, the military personnel in the other helicopters jumped out. With weapons in hand, they surrounded Sam's chopper standing at attention. No one moved a muscle.

Sam unbuckled his seat belt. "Wait here," he shouted as he climbed out.

A small group of people streamed out of a nearby building—some dressed in military and others in civilian clothing.

Sam introduced himself and shook the hand of the Ambassador to Thailand, Michael Wagner. He turned his head and pointed in the direction of the prisoners. The stunned look on the ambassador's face showed disbelief. He turned to an aide, "Get some medical personnel out here. Now!"

They walked over and stared at the thin, frail men in Sam's helicopter. The freed captives continued to sit still, noticeably in shock, hands clasped tightly to each other.

Le was concerned their hearts would not be strong enough to handle all that was happening. What were they thinking? Were they paralyzed with fear?

Suddenly the embassy door swung open and an assortment of medical personnel rushed to the helicopter to assist. A soldier with a laptop sprinted to the chopper door and gently spoke to the man closest to him, "Sir, what is your name?"

The prisoner stared straight ahead. Le reached over, patted his knee, and nodded his head in an attempt to coax him into speaking. He wanted to assure him he was safe.

After a lengthy pause, the prisoner's raspy voice slowly responded, "Specialist Robert M. Freeman, United States Army, US 16917813."

The young man with the computer typed in the information.

Within seconds, his face showed disbelief. He turned the computer screen toward the ambassador who looked at it and gasped, "Oh, dear God." Hurriedly, he turned to the medical staff and with urgency in his voice issued an order, "Take care of these men, now! Now, I said!"

Within seconds, the helicopter was bustling with medical aides. After a preliminary check, the two Navy SEALs who helped with the rescue assisted the men out of the chopper and into wheelchairs.

The last ten hours had definitely taken a toll on the soldiers. However, the last four decades left them drained: physically, emotionally, and even spiritually.

The worst of their ordeal was over. Never again would they sleep in rat-infested, filthy, dark, cramped quarters, or forced to work all day in the grueling sun, with little to drink, and garbage to eat. There would be no more physical, verbal, or emotional abuse.

As he stepped out of the helicopter, Le felt a sense of awe he had never experienced before. He could hardly believe he was in the presence of these Americans. Their assistance and kindness defied everything drilled into him by his superiors.

As Le thought about the "Land of the free and the home of the brave," he wondered if his hope of living in America someday could ever become a reality, or merely an empty dream.

Sam stretched his arm around Le's shoulders as they watched the medical personnel care for the now-former POWs. Within minutes, medics wheeled the men toward the building.

Abruptly Captain McCarter motioned the man who was pushing his wheelchair to stop. The captain stood, wobbly on his feet. He turned around and looked at Le. He lifted his hand slowly to his forehead and saluted his former guard. His face beamed.

Le snapped to attention and proudly returned the salute, grinning from ear to ear.

The medical personnel helped McCarter back in the wheelchair. They disappeared quickly into the building.

"You are a hero to them, my friend." Sam barely could speak, his voice cracking with emotion. Never in his life was he more overjoyed to be an American than at that moment.

Le's head was spinning. He was thrilled they pulled off the rescue, but it came at a terrible price. He thought of his family who was probably dead. He hoped their suffering was not prolonged. Le shuddered at the endless possibilities. He and his wife both knew the risks, but still the pain was immense—unbearable. His heart felt like it had been shattered into pieces.

Le looked heavenward and silently prayed, *Dear God, I know you are with them, but I hope they didn't suffer.* In his mind, he replayed the last time they were together. Why did it have to end this way?

Sam respected Le's privacy. He lowered his head and prayed quietly for his friend.

Uncertain what to say, Sam put his hand on Le's shoulder. Then he turned and climbed back into the chopper. The silence was shattered as the helicopter's engines started up and the giant aircraft slowly began to rise. Within minutes, it was out of sight.

Le stood in the courtyard by himself, unsure what to do.

A young woman, who was serving as a United States Marine, hurried to him. She stepped in front of him and looked directly in his eyes. "Sir," she shouted, "Sir!"

Le's mind seemed miles away, but quickly he was jolted back to the real world.

He looked into the marine's deep blue eyes and smiled warmly. She returned the smile. Le estimated she was probably in her early twenties.

"Yes," he finally responded.

"Sir, will you please come with me? We need to debrief you. Don't worry. You will not be harmed in any way." She realized he was frightened, and offered her hand to encourage him.

Glancing at her hand, he imagined Linh's delicate touch.

Heartache encompassed him as he realized he would never feel the warmth of his wife's hand again.

Exhaustion overwhelmed him. In the last week, Le only had a few hours of sleep each night. The marine sensed his fatigue and led him into a comfortable room. Sitting on the small table were bottles of water and soft drinks. A half dozen donuts, arranged neatly on a plate, caught his attention. He wondered what they were.

"Help yourself to a snack. I will be right back." The young woman smiled, then spun around and left the room.

Le realized he was starved. He sat down at the table and quickly guzzled the soda. Within minutes, he devoured five donuts.

As he was eating the last donut, the marine woman returned with two men—an American and a Vietnamese interpreter.

Le stood to greet them.

The American, Lieutenant Jason Rader, introduced himself. He looked at the empty plate and watched Le as he stuffed the last bite of donut in his mouth. "You like those, don't you?"

Le nodded his head as he wiped the corners of his mouth with a napkin.

"I'll get you some fresh ones in the morning. Those were a day old."

Le had no idea what he was talking about, but he was excited to know he could have more of the delicacies the next morning.

"Do you know much English?" Rader asked slowly and precisely

"Yes. I was an English interpreter," Le replied.

Lieutenant Radar turned to the translator and nodded his head to signify that his services would not be needed. The man left.

"Have a seat. We might as well be comfortable while we talk."

The three sat down at the small table. The marine had a recording device and a computer. "This is Corporal Quinn," he said as he pointed to the marine. "She will be documenting your comments. I know you have been through a lot and are tired. However, I need to ask you a few questions. Samuel Jefferson told me about your family. I am truly sorry for your loss. On behalf of the United States Government and the families of the POWs, I want to express our deepest sympathy."

Unexpectedly, he stood up and saluted Le. Then he offered him his hand.

Somewhat baffled, Le stood. He stared at the soldier's extended hand and shook it. Le glanced at the young marine. She was smiling at him.

They sat down. Lieutenant Rader looked at his pad and reviewed the questions he would ask. Before he could begin, a bewildered Le interrupted, "Are you CIA?"

Taken back by the question Radar replied, "No. I am Army Intelligence though. I want to assure you, I'm only here to ask a few questions. No one will harm you."

"What will happen to my friends?"

The lieutenant paused, unsure how to answer the question. "Your friends. That's a nice way to put it. Your friends are fine. They had a much-needed, long, warm shower. I heard they were enjoying it so much they refused to leave the water. Understandably so. I expect it's the first refreshing shower they have had in forty years."

Lieutenant Radar continued, "Soon they will have a complete medical exam. A team is now en route to the embassy. The physicians will examine them carefully and update their vaccinations."

He cleared his throat. "We will have to be careful not to overdo it. They are very weak. They will eat light food for a couple of days, until their bodies…well, their digestive system, can take other food. As I said, doctors and specialists from around the area are flying in to oversee their care. Their physical conditions will be closely monitored. After so many years on a depleted diet their bodies, can and will reject many foods. Nutritionists will see they are fed the right foods at the correct times."

Le continued, "When will they go home? When will their families be notified they are alive?"

The lieutenant, taken aback at this man's heartfelt words replied, "You really care about them, don't you?"

"Absolutely. In a way, I was a prisoner with them for over four years. I know better than anyone does what they went through. I did not endure their suffering physically, but I did mentally. Trust me, I know how much their families mean to them. Shifting his gaze to the marine, Le commented, "I know the names of their wives, parents, brothers and sisters, friends, dogs and cats, and even a couple cows."

They all chuckled lightening the tense mood a bit. Le especially seemed to relax.

Lieutenant Radar leaned on the table with his chin in his hand, still uncertain how much to tell this Vietnamese guard. He knew the plans for the former prisoners were confidential, but somehow he sensed Le could be trusted. After all, he was clearly not the enemy.

"Okay. This is highly confidential. We have not had time to finalize all the details. This is the plan. Keep in mind, it may change somewhat." He leaned closer to Le. "The President of the United States has been informed and will be updated as details develop. Soon he will open a dialog with the Vietnamese Government."

The lieutenant looked at his watch. "The men will spend the night here in the safety of this compound. Late tomorrow morning, they will board a chopper to the Bangkok airport. From there they will be transferred by military jet to Japan. They will go through more medical and psychological tests and get more injections. In their weakened condition even catching a cold could be catastrophic."

He sat straighter in his chair and continued. "Fingerprints on file will verify their identity. It will take time to get that done because we will have to dig into archived files to get their fingerprints. After positive identification, we will notify their families. This must be done delicately. Some of their parents will still be alive. The shock of hearing this news could be more than they can handle emotionally or physically, especially the elderly ones."

The lieutenant sipped his water. "It also goes the other way. Until the time comes to meet their families, the men will not receive any information about their loved ones. We know they are anxious to learn about the families left behind. The truth is it could be traumatizing in their fragile conditions. Some of them will receive bad news. Others may not recognize their loved ones. Forty years must seem like a lifetime to the men. People and situations have changed drastically. There are endless possibilities. We will help as much as we can to assure an easy transition."

"When can they see their families?" Le persisted.

"If all goes well, in three days. That's not absolute. With any luck, within seventy-two hours the men will be rested and strong enough to face the hard-facts of what their years of confinement has done to their bodies, their families, and this crazy world. You know this world is a lot different than it was in 1970. We weren't even born."

Radar continued, "Now on a different note, I need all the information you can give me. Don't leave anything out. Give me every detail. Let's get started please, at the beginning."

The lieutenant took another drink then began, "First, let me ask you an essential question. Did the Vietnamese Government know about these POWs?"

The questioner waited for Le's response. He wondered if the Vietnamese guard would answer these tough questions about his own country truthfully.

Le drew in a deep breath and exhaled slowly. "I do not think the Vietnamese Government, on the whole, knew about them. I do believe some did. Somebody, somewhere, high in the government must have known and gave Yo the help he needed to stay hidden."

"Yo, that would be General Yo? Sam gave me his name. The U.S. military is well aware of his atrocities. Okay, let's start at the beginning. Again, don't leave anything out. Tell me everything you know. When did you have your first contact with this General Yo? What do you know about him and his operation?"

"I met him the first day of my job, if you can call it that."

For the next three hours, Le explained the duties of his job and talked about the treatment of the prisoners. He told them how they used the days of the week for their names. He described how they communicated through tapping. He revealed some of the memories of the prisoners. It was especially difficult when Le tearfully discussed his wife and children.

The marine and lieutenant sat still, entranced by his story. Both of them expressed sorrow for his loss. At times, the marine's eyes were misty. She typed in everything Le said as she listened with compassion. Could this man's incredible story be true?

An aide delivered a meal to their table. As they ate their nourishing meal, they continued the conversation.

Le finally talked about Sam and the rescue, General Yo's death, and the trip to the American Embassy. When the interrogation was complete, Lieutenant Rader stood up and extended his hand to Le.

Le shook his hand warmly.

Rader clasped his hand for a moment, not saying a word. Finally, he nodded his head and slowly blew out a lengthy breath. "Thank you for your bravery and everything you have done for America. I promise, you will not be forgotten."

He turned to the young marine. "Corporal Quinn, please show Mr. Le to his room and make sure he is comfortable."

"Yes, sir." She turned to leave and added, "Mr. Le, please come with me." She motioned to the exhausted man to follow.

He walked behind her. He thought it was strange to see such an attractive woman dressed in military apparel.

"I can't remember your name," he stated as they walked down the hall.

"Corporal Quinn," she replied.

"No, I mean your first name."

"Oh, it's Nancee with two 'e's." She looked back at him.

"Well, Nancee with two 'e's, it's nice to officially meet you." She smiled warmly.

Nancee led him down the connecting hallways and up a flight of stairs to a closed door. She unlocked the door for him and stood back for him to enter.

As the young guard looked at the tastefully decorated room, he felt a warm shudder go down his back. The first thing he noticed was a huge bed with a lightweight green comforter and at least six pillows. The headboard was a large mirror. Next to the bed, were nightstands with lamps lighting the room. Against two of the walls were dressers. A giant, flat-screen television hung on the wall at the foot of the bed. He was stunned as he looked around the room.

"This is your room. It is usually set aside for dignitaries and political leaders from the United States. We have laid some clean clothing out for you. We guessed at your size." She walked over to another door and opened it. "This is your bathroom. There is a shower and a whirlpool. You can take a bath, shower, or both if you want. You can lie in the spa for hours if you choose. We want you to be comfortable."

"What time do I need to get up?"

"I will wake you about seven. Your friends are already asleep. They will be monitored all night long for any health problems."

Still apprehensive, there was a question he needed to ask, one that had been weighing heavily on his mind. "Am I...am I a prisoner?"

Her eyes lit up. "A prisoner? No! Definitely not. Everyone is talking about you and the brave things you did. You're a hero, Mr. Le. I am sorry you thought that."

"I ask because I see everyone staring at me. I am confused

about everything. What will happen to me? I am…I am a stranger here. I'm alone. I have many unanswered questions."

She sensed Le's heartache and desperation. Tenderly she took his hand, cupped her other hand over it, and took a deep breath. How could she answer so he could find peace? What could she say to help him during this difficult time?

After a brief pause, Nancee continued. "They stare at you because of what you did. They wonder why you would sacrifice your life and the lives of your family to save six old men presumed "dead" for forty years. Everyone here has the highest respect for you, Le. You are not a prisoner. You are our honored guest and free to leave wherever and whenever you choose. Whatever you need, I am here to assist you. "

Le listened intently. He was anxious for answers.

She continued, "However, there is something I must warn you about. We are uncertain what will happen if the Vietnamese Government catches you. We are concerned about you. You are safe while in American hands."

She turned to leave, but stopped. "If you need anything, just dial zero on the phone. Somebody will be here to help in a jiffy. Have a good night's sleep, Mr. Le." She closed the door and was gone.

In the stillness of his room, he had a recurring thought, "What am I going to do now?" He kept thinking about Linh. How could he live without her and his children? His heart ached. He felt lost.

A familiar Bible verse replayed in his mind. *Lo, I am with you always, even unto the ends of the earth.* He looked heavenward and asked for divine intervention.

After a few moments, a thought hit him. Maybe, just maybe, my family is alive. He assumed Yo killed them. Is there a possibility they could be prisoners somewhere? What could he do? How could he find them? Could they still be at the same prison camp where he worked? Should he return to Vietnam? These questions burned in his mind.

He took the pouch from around his neck and gently laid it on the covers, between the pillows, on the bed.

He heeded Nancee's advice and took a long hot shower. Following that, he sat in the hot tub for nearly an hour as he mentally replayed the events of the very long day. How could he have protected his family? What went wrong?

As he slipped between the fresh-smelling sheets, he thought about his friends. Tonight they too were sleeping in a bed like this. How strange it must be to them. Many people crawl in their comfortable beds night-after-night, and never realize how blessed they are. Meanwhile, millions wonder where they will lay their head or get their next meal.

Exhausted, he grabbed the pouch and held it tightly as he fell into a deep sleep.

# ELEVEN

# First Day of Freedom

---

Children were laughing and playing. An angelic-looking woman dressed in white, opened the door, and glided gracefully into the room. She turned and smiled at the children. That was when he saw her beautiful face—his Linh, with their dear children. He called to them, but they didn't hear him. He summoned her repeatedly, but still no response. He started to walk to her.

Suddenly he heard pounding. What was it? Was there someone at the door who could help him get his wife's attention? Finally, he heard his wife's sweet voice. "Mr. Le, are you awake?"

He did not want to wake up. The pounding continued. Startled and groggy, he sat up. He realized the voice at the door was not his wife. The marine he met the day before was calling him.

"Yes?" he muttered, trying to sound alert.

"Are you awake?" the voice queried.

"Just a minute. I will be right there." Le stumbled out of bed and opened the door a crack.

Nancee's pleasant smile greeted him. After the time they spent together yesterday, he felt she was a friendly face in the middle of chaos. She helped him when everything was new and frightening. Her presence was refreshing.

"Good Morning. It is nearly 7:00 and we have a busy day ahead of us. Would you like to eat breakfast in your room, or come down to the cafeteria with me?"

He replied eagerly, "Give me a few minutes and I will be ready to go."

"I'll be back in ten minutes." Le closed the door and hurried to get ready.

This was a new day for him and his friends. It was their first full day of freedom and he was anxious to see them. At least he hoped to have the opportunity to visit with the men. He was not sure what the embassy officials planned for him on this day.

Le washed quickly and dressed in the clothes provided for him. He slipped on a new pair of jeans and a light blue shirt, which had the United States Marine emblem on it. Le had never worn jeans before. The first thing he noticed was how comfortable they were, unlike the military khakis he wore.

He smiled as he admired the marine emblem on the front of his shirt. He often read about the marines on the Internet—The Few...The Proud...The Marines. He knew the Marine Corps was the smallest branch of the U.S. military, but a choice fighting force.

He combed his hair and before long was ready to face the uncertain day. Le opened the door to the hall where the marine was waiting patiently. "My, don't you look dapper," she said cheerfully.

He smiled and started to close the door. Suddenly he remembered something and stopped abruptly. "Just a minute." He hurried back into the room, grabbed the small pouch, put the strap around his neck, and stuffed it inside his shirt.

Nancee observed with interest, but said nothing.

Le had an uneasy feeling. He noticed her blue eyes focused on the string around his neck. Obviously, she was curious about the pouch. He feared someone would take it from him. He hoped not. It was his most valuable possession. Trying to get her focus off the pouch Le announced, "Okay, I'm ready. I'm really hungry."

He walked beside her down the hall. They took an elevator to the cafeteria. The noise of the busy dining hall took Le by surprise. People were talking and laughing as they stood in the food line waiting their turn, holding their trays. Others were sitting at tables, deep in discussions, while they ate breakfast. Several dozen people had gathered already; a few were dressed in civilian clothing, but most in military uniforms.

Le noticed people stared at him as he entered the room. They stopped what they were doing and the room suddenly hushed. Then it happened—it began with one person clapping. Then two, then four people. Suddenly, everyone in the cafeteria broke into applause and stood to their feet. A group from the kitchen joined in the ovation.

Nancee smiled, and said softly, "I told you, you're a hero. Nobody here is going to let you forget it."

As the young Vietnamese soldier walked through the cafeteria to get his tray, the applause continued. Some patted him on the back. Others shook his hand. Le was overwhelmed!

The applause finally died down.

One of the cooks handed him a tray with silverware, then ushered him and the marine to the front of the line. Another man dressed in white stepped next to him. "Sir," he said to Le, "What can I get you for breakfast? You name it."

Le thought for a second. "Can I get one of those round things with a hole in the center?"

The man put his hands on the former guard's shoulders and looked him straight in the eyes. "Hole in the center?" he asked. The confused cook glanced at Nancee for help.

"I believe he wants a donut," she said matter-of-factly.

He looked at Le. "A donut! You want a donut," he laughed, now understanding what the Vietnamese hero meant.

Nancee politely nodded her head.

Le repeated, "Yes, a donut. I think they are very good. I never had one before yesterday."

"Sir, for you I am going to get the freshest donut I can find." He turned and walked briskly to the kitchen as everything went back to normal.

Le went through the food line with Nancee and helped himself to some bacon and eggs, and a cup of coffee. The variety and amount of food amazed Le. They took a seat at a table near the back of the room.

Le bowed to give thanks to God for the food. He prayed also for the six men and their families as well as his own family.

Nancee noticed him bow his head. She looked around to see if anyone was looking, and then slowly bowed her head.

Suddenly the man in white came bursting through the door with a dozen fresh donuts and set them in front of Le. His eyes lit up as he looked at the platter and then back at the man who brought them. With a wide grin, Le gratefully responded, "Thank you."

"Anything you ever want, just ask for Sal. I will personally get it for you." He walked back to the kitchen.

"He's nice," Le commented.

"Most people would disagree with you. He runs this mess hall with an iron fist, but his food is always topnotch. He has taken a special liking to you. His grandfather was a POW during the Korean War."

Le picked up one of the donuts. He thought it was the best food he had ever eaten. In just minutes, he had downed three donuts and started on his fourth.

Nancee chuckled. "Those things will make you sick, if you eat too many."

Le raised one eyebrow and grinned. "Yes? But they sure taste good." He gobbled the remnant of donut in his hand.

All of a sudden, there was a commotion. Le looked up to see Captain McCarter entering the cafeteria, followed by the rest of the men. Everyone in the room jumped to their feet and a thunderous applause erupted.

Nancee also stood and a huge smile spread across her face as she joined in the celebration.

Le stood up slowly. He froze, as he stared at his new friends. They looked so different from yesterday. Over-sized clean clothes replaced the smelly, drab rags they wore for years. They had on tennis shoes. The men were all clean-shaven, even their heads, probably the best way to do away with mange.

All the soldiers enjoyed the first full night of sleep they had in forty years. Apparently, it did them good. They were bright and cheerful.

They walked past Le and totally ignored him. Disappointed and hurt, he did not know how to react. Surely, they could have said hello after what they had been through together. Maybe they didn't recognize him in civilian clothes. Did they care?

About a dozen men, some high-ranking officers, followed the soldiers. Medical personnel were present to oversee health concerns.

Military escorts showed McCarter and his men to a large table. Food had been prepared specifically to meet their needs. The nutritionist planned a bland breakfast, since their weakened systems demanded caution. They would have to adapt gradually to normal eating again. Their breakfast consisted of a scrambled egg, oatmeal, a slice of dry toast, and weak, green tea.

The applause continued. The men were uncertain how to react to the situation. Some of them had a slight smile, while others kept their heads down and looked toward the floor. The medical personnel motioned for them to sit.

The applause subsided as the men took their seats. Everyone in the dining room sat and conversations and eating resumed.

Captain McCarter looked up and noticed Le still standing and staring in his direction. The captain rose and the room instantly hushed. McCarter strode slowly toward the former guard. When he reached Le, they stood face-to-face.

All eyes in the cafeteria fixed upon the scene as it unfolded.

Tears flowed from the captain's eyes. He placed his arms around Le's neck, pulled the young man close, and held him tightly. He finally regained his composure enough to speak. "Thank you. Thank you."

Stirred by the action and words, Le faced his new friend, Nancee, who watched through teary eyes.

Le's eyes weld over with tears. The other men formed a line behind McCarter and waited to acknowledge their former guard. The men he knew as Sunday, Tuesday, Wednesday, Thursday, and Friday took this opportunity to express their feelings. Some said nothing. Words were inadequate to convey their wide range of emotions.

Sunday uttered a simple, "God bless you."

Le was unsure what to expect when Friday neared him. He remembered that just twenty-four hours ago Lomack wanted to kill him. Wearing new glasses, he approached Le. For the first time in what seemed to be a lifetime, Ronald saw clearly—he saw the world in a different light. Through tearful eyes, he looked up at Le. He raised his right hand and softly placed it on Le's shoulder, but couldn't speak. He nodded his head. Then without warning, he grabbed the former guard's neck and cried, "Forgive me for the way I treated you."

Le drew a slow, deep breath. "It's all forgiven. I understand where you were coming from."

A smile lit up the soldier's face, something Le never expected to see. Lomack turned, walked to his table, and sat down. The entire room erupted in another hearty applause. Things died down when the men began to eat their first breakfast as free men.

Captain McCarter asked, "How's the food?"

Impulsively Le shot back, "I love the donuts."

James laughed, along with a group of people nearby.

Le stared at his friends and then turned to his newest friend, Nancee.

"What are you thinking about?" she asked as they sat down.

"I wonder what they are thinking. What are they feeling? Is it excitement, joy, relief, or apprehension?" He toyed with the food on his plate, and then glanced around the room searching for some way to express his feelings. "I would like to know if any of the people in here know what real sacrifice is. Sure, they are away from friends and loved ones for a while, but they are in a clean room with good food, watching flat screen TVs. It's a far cry from where those six men were yesterday."

With a glimmer of a smile, he added. "It's hard to believe that in a couple hours they will be on their way to Japan, and then home to America. Me? Where will I be? What will I do?"

Nancee looked at him bewildered. "Nobody told you, did they?"

"Told me what?"

"You'll be with them. Last night your six friends decided they were not going anywhere without you. You are one of them. They know you can't return to Vietnam. Where would you go? What would you do? You're going with them to live free in America."

Le appeared confused. Was it a dream? Surely, it had to be a mistake. It would be a privilege even to visit America. Yet, she did not say he was going to visit. She said he was going to live in the greatest country on earth. Live in America! His heart pounded so hard with excitement he thought everyone could hear it. At the same time, he felt empty because he would not be sharing the experience with his family. The moment was bittersweet. Things were happening quickly, and he had not even had a chance to mourn his tragic loss.

## Twelve
# Headed Home

---

In spite of Le's broken heart, somehow at times he felt a sense of inner peace. Even though he had many unanswered questions, he felt God's presence in an unexplainable way. Other times, the darkness engulfed him as if he was drowning in a sea of despair, unable to swim. One thing he was certain, God had a plan for his life and it would be revealed in His time. He had to trust God, similar to the way the prisoners needed to trust him.

Following breakfast Nancee escorted Le back to his room. She briefed him on the latest details of his upcoming trip. "The chopper will be leaving at precisely 10:00. You and the former prisoners will be chauffeured to the nearby airport. From there, you will fly together to Japan aboard a military transport plane."

She paused. "The rest of the world does not know about you and your friends yet. Nothing will be released to the media until fingerprints confirm the identity of the former POWs. Then their families will be notified." A smile tipped her lips. "However, from everything we can gather, they are really who they say they are."

She looked into Le's sad, confused eyes. Her heart broke for her Vietnamese friend. His love for his family was evident every time he spoke about them. She touched his hand gently, "I will come back to get you in an hour. Please be ready."

Le nodded his head, signifying he understood.

With that, the marine was gone.

In the stillness of his room, loneliness engulfed him. He collapsed onto his bed and wept. How he missed his family! How could he go on without them? He felt as if his whole world had come crashing down and there was no one to help him pick up the pieces. Without his family, what kind of future could he have? Fear rippled through Le. His life seemed uncertain. He had never felt so alone!

Trying to reassure himself, he cried aloud repeatedly, "I did the right thing. I did the right thing." The warm expression of appreciation and thanks in the cafeteria proved it. Why did he feel miserable? Why did he feel like his heart could quit beating at any moment?

He sat upright and looked at his watch. It was almost 9:00. He collected his few personal items. He eyed a Bible on the desk; his was back home, hidden from the Communists. Fortunately, many Scriptures he had memorized, and they were permanently etched in his mind.

Sam once told him, "When your heart is broken and you need an answer, read God's Word. A verse will always come to your rescue and calm your hurting heart, just when you need it most."

He had a few extra minutes; Le picked up the Gideon Bible and began to read. A verse jumped out at him. He read the words of Jesus. *Lo, I am with you always.* He has been with me always, he thought. Always means now, as well as past, and future. This assurance gave him the inner peace he needed. He continued reading the Scripture as he waited.

Nancee arrived precisely at the moment she said she would. He noticed she was always prompt and he appreciated that.

He picked up the pouch, carefully put it around his neck, and gently placed it under his shirt.

His carry-on bag contained a change of clothing, a shaver, toothbrush, toothpaste, deodorant, and a comb. He grabbed his few possessions, and hurried to the door.

Nancee greeted him with her usual smile. They made their way down the hall to the elevator. As they walked, they chatted about their lives.

"Nancee, may I ask where you are from? How did you end up in the United States Marine Corps?"

"I'm from a city in Arizona called Flagstaff."

"Oh yes, I've heard of that. You have skiing there?"

"Yes, we do. Have you ever skied before?"

"Me? Oh no, there aren't very many places to ski in Vietnam," he said with a little laugh.

"What did you do there for fun, Mr. Le?"

"Fun—what do you mean by fun?"

"You know, like play baseball, bowl, swim, horseback riding—things like that."

"All my life, I simply tried to survive. I spent most of the time learning to do something beneficial. My parents wanted me to amount to something, to live a worthwhile life. They forced me to study all the time. I guess you could say I had the gift of learning." He chuckled. "That's what I did for fun. I read everything I could find. I spent days at a time reading and learning on the Internet."

"Learning what?" she asked.

They stopped walking for a moment. He looked at her. "Mostly, your language. English is a very difficult language."

"So I've been told," she agreed.

Le, determined to probe her past continued, "You didn't answer my question."

"And your question was—what is a nice girl like me doing in the marines, right?"

He nodded and they both laughed.

She cleared her throat. "Well, to make a long story short, my father is a marine. He always wanted a son." She stopped and faced Le. She spread out her arms and laughed, "So here I am, my father's son."

"Wow!" he said, sounding sincerely surprised. "We never had soldiers like you in the Vietnamese Army."

"Do you disapprove?" she asked.

"Disapprove of you, or the fact that you are a marine?"

"Both," she said, looking at him.

"Well, I certainly do not disapprove of you. You have been

very helpful to me. I appreciate you. As for you being a soldier, I can't really say. We were taught in our army that men are powerful; women are weak and need to be kept in their place."

"What do you think?"

"What do I think?" he repeated, unsure how to respond. "First off, it's really none of my business. Second, well… second is, that I personally would find it hard to fight with a woman beside me because I would tend to…to protect her." As soon as he said the words, he stopped dead in his tracks.

Nancee kept walking and finally noticed that Le had stopped. She turned to look at him. "You are thinking about your wife and family, aren't you?"

"Yes, I wonder what I could have done to change the way it all turned out. Could I have protected them somehow?"

Nancee's eyes clouded. Her look became solemn. "Le, I'm sure when the time comes and the announcement is made about the former prisoners, the U.S. Government will question the Vietnamese Government and demand answers about your family."

Le spoke up. "You can demand any information you want. You don't understand. They will deny everything. They will even refute my family or I ever existed. It will not bring them back. Maybe I should have stayed there to fight for Linh and the children, as well as myself." He looked around. "I feel helpless. I can't do anything here. So much is confusing."

"Do you pray about it?" she asked boldly. "I noticed that you pray before you eat, and I saw a Bible on your bed."

"Are you a Christian?" Le asked.

"Me?" She paused. "Define Christian."

Before Le could respond, she started down a somewhat unfamiliar path. "I was raised in a military family. Power was everything." She looked around. Her mind was searching for the right answer. Finally, she looked directly in Le's eyes and said, "I was taught you pray in foxholes, but that's as far as it goes. I'm not sure what I believe."

Le walked silently, listening, trying to understand the marine at his side.

Nancee persisted. "You never answered my question."

"You mean about praying?" Le asked.

She nodded her head.

"Yes, of course I pray. That does not alter the fact that my family is dead. They were savagely murdered by a madman."

Scraping up courage, she added, "You don't know that for sure."

"True, but I do know how Yo operates. I have seen it firsthand."

"Listen to me, Le. America will get to the bottom of this. The Vietnamese Government will admit to these horrific war crimes. They will have to."

No further words were spoken. They walked in silence, each in deep thought.

Just as they reached for the outside door, it flew open, startling them. There stood Lieutenant Rader. "There you two are. Let's go. Do you have everything?"

Business-like, Corporal Quinn answered quickly, "Yes, sir. My gear is already on the chopper. Le has his belongings with him."

"Let's go. You will be on the second chopper with two of the POWs and their escorts."

"You are coming with me?" Le asked Nancee with surprise in his voice.

"Yes. I have been designated to escort you all the way to America."

He was relieved. She had been a good friend to him. He felt comfortable with her at his side.

"May I ask you one more thing?" Nancee probed as they reached the door of the helicopter.

"Sure."

"What is in that bag that you keep close to you? Why do you guard it so carefully?"

Le felt the pouch, held it tight to his chest, and patted it tenderly, but did not reply.

She smiled at him and added, "Family mementos?"

"I guess you could say that. In fact, that is probably an understatement."

They climbed into the chopper. Freeman and Lomack were already aboard. Le took a seat directly across from Nancee. He smiled and greeted the soldiers with a cheerful, "Good Morning."

Freeman returned the smile. "That would be putting it mildly."

"What do you mean?" Le asked.

"Good!" Lomack spoke out loudly as the helicopter's blades began to whirl. "Good Morning. No, it's not just a good morning; this is probably the best morning of our lives."

Nancee commented, "From here on, gentlemen, hopefully each morning will only get better."

Le leaned slightly toward Nancee and spoke softly. "May I ask a favor of you?"

"Sure," she replied.

"This." He motioned to the pouch under his shirt. "This is what I live for now. This little bag means everything to me." He bent over further and she leaned toward him, making sure no one else could hear. She sensed the importance of what he wanted to tell her.

"I planned originally to give this to Monday, I mean Captain McCarter. Now since I am going to America, I believe it is my responsibility. Although, I'm worried it might be taken away from me when I get there."

Startled, she sat up straight. She realized that whatever was in that pouch must be extremely significant to him. "It won't be," she reassured him. "I'll see to that. We are in this together from now on, my friend."

Le smiled broadly and thanked her. The relief he felt was evident.

They watched the ground disappear beneath them as the helicopter rose. The crowded, little homes below grew smaller. Le realized this would probably be the last time he would see this part of the world; the only life he ever knew. He would never be able to return to his native country. His face reflected a change in his demeanor; a look of hopelessness and despair replaced his smile.

Unexpectedly, a hand touched his knee. Surprised, he looked up and saw Specialist Robert Freeman. The action was a simple reminder that he was not alone. No words were needed between the two.

All of a sudden, a smile crept across Le's face when he realized how many people cared about him. It gave him a renewed sense of peace and comfort. A new life awaited him, and he would not face it alone. He closed his eyes, and thanked God for his new friends, and new life.

Shortly after, they landed at the airport near a military transport plane, which awaited them. As they disembarked the helicopter, Le grabbed his small bag of belongings. Nancy reached for her duffel bag, and Le immediately took it from her.

"I can do that," she said, quite forcefully as she tried to get the bag back.

"Lead the way, Miss. Lead the way."

She decided not to persist when she realized it might be a cultural tradition in his country to help women. Reluctantly she thanked him, and they headed to the waiting airplane.

After they had gone a few steps, a Military Policeman (MP) halted them, and demanded to search Le.

"He's with me," Nancee spoke protectively.

"Sorry, Corporal. Our orders are to search anyone who is not in military uniform. It's the policy. No exceptions."

"Do you know who this is, soldier?"

"No, but actually I don't care if he's the President of Thailand. He's not in military uniform; therefore, I have orders to search him."

"Is there a problem, soldier?" a voice boomed from behind them.

The MP snapped to attention.

Captain McCarter stepped forward. Dressed in his army fatigues, and his captain's hat and bars, he stared at the young soldier, brow tight, without a hint of a smile.

"No, sir. I just need to search this man."

McCarter looked sternly at the MP, then at Le. He immediately stepped between them. "No, you don't. You see, he's with me, and I don't want to see him harassed. Do you understand?"

"I have my orders, sir."

"Now you have new orders, understand soldier?"

The MP continued standing at attention and shouted, "Yes, sir!"

McCarter continued as if nothing happened. "Mr. Le, would you and the young lady kindly accompany me onto the plane?"

"We would love to," Le replied, following McCarter. He avoided making eye contact with the young MP. Although the event unnerved him, he felt reassured. Le thanked the captain for his assistance.

"Le, I will go to my grave defending you."

McCarter peered at the strap around Le's neck, which was obviously hiding a treasure, something of great significance. "Maybe one day you can tell me the importance of what is being held so close to your heart."

Le looked back at him, clutched the pouch, and nodded his head. "One day. One day."

As the former prisoners took their seats on the plane, the other passengers who were there to assist the soldiers watched curiously. They wondered what hardships the men endured during their long, grueling captivity.

However, many eyes focused on the young Vietnamese guard. Who was he really? Why would this man risk so much for six forgotten American POWs?

Many questions remained unanswered.

## Thirteen
# America

On the flight to Japan, the former prisoners were overwhelmed as they discovered the latest technology. A few of them inquired about the laptops some individuals were using. Some were curious about the tiny earpieces many wore.

One passenger, whose dress and demeanor indicated he might be important, was talking on a cell phone. Traber noticed it. "Look, that phone is not attached to anything. It looks like that thing Captain Kurtz used on that sci-fi show."

One of the aides nearby wisely corrected him. "I believe that would be Captain Kirk."

"Beam me up, Scotty," Freeman remarked, quite loudly for all to hear.

Everyone on board laughed. The mood on the plane lightened. Laughter had been unfamiliar to these men the past forty years. There was not anything to evoke laughter. The joyous sound encouraged the other passengers.

When the men left America's shores in 1970, the world was a different place. Now returning to their former lives, what surprises are in store for them? How will they adjust to the many changes they will face?

As they descended to the Tokyo airport, the men's eyes were wide with wonder. They looked down and noticed massive skyscrapers and a huge, bustling city.

The army would protect the men from the outside world for a brief period. Family members would be notified before the news of their escape was released to the public. The plan was for the soldiers to be en route to the United States at that time. The world's media would demand access to the former prisoners as soon as they learned about them. To prevent a leak before the designated time, security measures were in place. It could prove disastrous for the families, who for years believed their soldiers were dead.

The plane came to a stop on the runway, and six black limousines drove alongside. They landed at a secluded area of the airport, away from a crowd of anxious reporters who were trying to sniff out leads for a big story.

The men boarded the limos, which whisked them away to a specially prepared facility in a high-tech military hospital. Skilled physicians awaited their arrival. The medical team's sole purpose would be to care for the needs of these very special returning soldiers.

For eight hours, the men underwent a multitude of tests, shots, MRI scans, X-rays, and eye and ear exams. Psychological evaluations were also scheduled. After a few hours, the men grew weary of all the probing and injections. Yet they knew they were about to enter society and needed to be ready physically and emotionally.

Each of the soldiers spent individual time with psychiatrists and counselors evaluating their mental health. The physicians were doing everything possible to make a smooth transition for their return to society. The professionals realized they could only partially prepare them for their homecoming. No one could predict what the men would experience when reunited with their families.

The day was grueling and exhausting. However, the medical team pushed on. Their goal was to return the men to their families as quickly as possible; they wasted no time performing the necessary exams.

Le received many of the same treatments, especially the shots. By the end of the day, he commented that he felt like a human pincushion. He was tired of the probing, injections, and especially the endless questions.

Le was drilled with certain questions repeatedly. Why did you risk your life for these men? How will you react when they find the bodies of your family? Will you be willing to denounce your country to become an American citizen? To ensure clarity, the questions were asked in Vietnamese and English.

Much was at stake for Le, for America, and ultimately for the world.

The whirlwind of events confused Le. His quiet room away from the fanfare sounded better to him as the day wore on.

Finally, they boarded the limos and headed to the hotel designated for them. Le sat next to Nancee. Though bewildered by the strange surroundings, he felt strengthened by her presence.

As Nancee escorted Le to his room, she reminded him she would be next door. "Just bang on the wall if you need my help. Next stop is America!" In a parting remark, she whispered, "Take care of those mementos." Without another word, she slipped away.

Le closed the door. He took the pouch from his neck and placed it carefully in the drawer of the nightstand next to his bed. He removed the Gideon Bible and laid it on top of the stand.

Worn out and fully dressed, he collapsed on the bed, thinking about all the events of the day. He wondered what tomorrow would bring. In minutes, perhaps seconds, he was in a deep sleep.

---

Fingerprints authenticated the identities of the men. Any lingering doubts were gone. Six men—presumed dead—were going home. Alive!

Word spread fast that the men would jet to the United States on a new 747, which was on its way to Tokyo. They would head to America the following afternoon and spend their first night on American soil in Los Angeles. The next morning, the heroes would fly to Washington, D.C. The plan was for their families to meet them there.

Visits to their closest relatives by their congressional representatives, along with military and medical personnel, were already taking place across the United States. Many family members were now elderly with multiple health issues. Those breaking the news to them would be delicate and use utmost caution.

━━━━━━

The persistent ringing of the phone awakened Le. A pleasant female voice greeted him, "Good Morning, Mr. Le. This is Nancee. It is 0500 hours. We are due to eat in fifteen minutes. I haven't heard your shower, so I figured you were still sleeping."

Le jumped out of bed and shouted into the receiver, "I will be ready. I'm sorry. I will hurry." It was the fastest shower and shave of his life. He dressed quickly in clean traveling clothes and ran over to the nightstand to grab the pouch. As he picked it up, he noticed the Bible. He softly uttered, "Thank you Lord, for your guidance today."

Nancee met him with her usual warm smile as he opened the door.

Due to high security, the hotel restaurant was open only to their group. After the soldiers ate their breakfast, they were hustled to a secure location in the hotel. For the next six hours, some of the men were fitted with glasses and hearing aids. Medics shared their test results with them. Physically the men were still weak, but in overall good health.

At 1400 hours, the men hurried into the elevator, which would take them to the underground parking garage. Security was everywhere. There seemed to be a strange, unexplainable feeling in the air, which most of the men sensed. Something was not quite right as they piled into the limousine.

Dozens of police on motorcycles quickly surrounded them. The men's personal escorts ordered them to sit back and relax. The dark windows of the limo allowed privacy. When the police were satisfied it was safe, they escorted them out of the garage and into the hustle and bustle of afternoon traffic.

Within minutes, reality hit them when they saw thousands of people screaming and cheering in a cordoned-off area. Dozens of police officers were trying to maintain order and keep the crowd under control. The news was out! Hundreds of cameras were flashing. The United States military had gone to extremes to protect the identity of the POWs, yet somehow word leaked out.

The massive crowd indicated that their homecoming was something bigger than any of the POWs could have imagined. Lining the streets, many American soldiers dressed in military uniforms saluted the returning soldiers as they passed. Children waved enthusiastically. Parents held small ones on their shoulders so they could see the caravan of heroes. People everywhere held "Welcome Home" signs.

Le watched the shocked expressions on his new friends. The looks on their faces displayed happiness, astonishment, and confusion created by the fanfare.

Forty years ago, there were protesters, violence, bloodshed, and death in the streets of the United States due to opposition to the war these soldiers fought. What a difference! With this greeting in Japan, what would it be like in America?

At the Tokyo Airport, the limos pulled up next to an impressive new 747. Emblazoned on the aircraft were the words, "United States of America." The American flag stood out brightly on the tail. On the side of the plane was "The Presidential Seal." It was the newly commissioned presidential plane, "Air Force One!"

Thanks to an order from the president, they would have the honor of flying home on the most distinguished airplane in the world. They were true-life heroes who endured the unthinkable, the reprehensible, and they were finally coming home, in style.

Once aboard the splendid aircraft, the soldiers looked around in awe. There were three levels, and over four thousand square feet of floor space. The medical suite could function as an operating room. There were two large food galleys, which could easily serve everyone on the flight simultaneously. Dozens of people were on board for only one reason—to make the soldiers' trip home pleasant and comfortable.

Each soldier sat in a soft, high-back seat. As they buckled their seatbelts, a personal television dropped down in front of them. The screen lit up and a well-dressed man appeared. With a broad smile, the man introduced himself. "Good morning, gentlemen. My name is Nathan Alexander and I am the President of the United States. I would like to take this opportunity to welcome you home."

The men stared at the screen as the president read each of their names, slowly and precisely. "Captain James McCarter... Specialist Thomas Traber...Specialist Anthony Williams... Specialist Robert Freeman...Specialist Ronald Lomack...Sergeant Brent Pfingston. Welcome home, men. America excitedly awaits your return."

He continued, "I trust you are being treated well. We cannot give you back the forty years you have lost. All we can do now is to make the rest of your life the finest we can. We, the American people, owe you an immeasurable debt of gratitude. I look forward to meeting you personally. You are six of the bravest men the world will ever know. If there is anything you need, feel free to request it. The staff on board is available to assist you."

The president cleared his throat and with fervor explained, "We have planned a welcome home celebration to honor you in Washington, D.C. You will be amazed at the outpouring of love shown by the American people. Right now, thousands are on their way to our nation's capitol to give you the reception you richly deserve. Your families and friends are among them."

The men stared at the screen, each deep in thought. They were still trying to grasp the significance of their return.

President Alexander continued, "Forty years of alienation from your loved ones is incomprehensible. You realize that more than anyone does. I must warn you that some of your family members are no longer with us. For your loss, you have my condolences. I regret that an earlier rescue simply was not possible."

With added emphasis he continued, "Those who are responsible for your imprisonment and brutal treatment will be held accountable. Trust me on that. I assure you, we will do everything in our power to prevent this from happening to anyone in the future. As a fellow Vietnam veteran and president of this great country, you have my word."

The men's hearts were racing, their heads spinning. They tried to comprehend what they were hearing. Each wondered how it would affect him personally.

President Alexander added, "Gentlemen, there is one more very important matter. I understand we have a special guest among us. Mr. Le, thank you for making this possible. Your sacrifice is one of honor. I thank you sincerely, and the American people thank you. You are also a hero."

Lomack turned toward Le, nodding his head in agreement.

"Sit back gentlemen and enjoy the ride. It is a privilege to provide special transportation for your trip home. Consider this your 'Freedom Bird.' It is the least we can do. Again, thank you. God bless you." The screen displayed an American flag waving in the breeze.

The men looked at each other. No one knew what to say, so they remained silent, each absorbed in his own thoughts. Could this really be happening after all these years?

As Le studied the men and their reactions, he especially noticed their faces. Le dreamed of this moment and it was here. The men's faces expressed real joy and why not? They were finally going home.

After a short time of silence, there was an unexpected

eruption of excitement among the returning soldiers. It was as if reality finally hit them. They unfastened their seat belts and began to dance in the aisles, chanting, "We're going home. We're going home!" It was similar to a sports team after winning a championship game.

Williams grabbed Le to join the celebration. Before long, everyone on the plane participated in the clapping, cheering, and dancing. Many had wet eyes. All of them had hearts filled with gratitude. The rejoicing continued for the next several minutes.

The men finally settled down and returned to their seats. The thrill of it all filled their hearts. The air was electric with excitement!

When the plane took off, the soldiers watched out the windows as Tokyo faded into the distance. Ahead, was the place the former prisoners thought they would never see again—the United States of America.

The trip back to the States seemed to take forever. The men's anticipation was beyond comprehension. A multitude of thoughts flooded their minds as they wondered what the future held.

An aide gave each man an MP3 player with music to help pass the time during the lengthy flight. At first, they just looked at the gadget, unsure what to do with it. A few of the aides demonstrated them, but they were still confused. How could such a small device, which could fit in the palm of their hand, hold thousands of songs?

The ocean below was expansive and inspiring. Their memories of such beauty had faded through the long years.

With delight, the flight attendants served anything the soldiers requested. A couple of the men had sensitive teeth and needed to be careful. Their stomachs were still fragile and getting used to regular foods and beverages–alcoholic or carbonated beverages were out of the question. Ice was a special treat. Cold water was the most popular drink—they thought it strange that it came from a bottle.

The men were fascinated with the attractive features of the

female flight attendants, especially their long hair. Thomas Traber reached out and gently stroked the hair of one of the women. She looked at him and smiled. He pulled back immediately, like a frightened child. "I'm sorry," he stammered. "It's been so long since I've seen such beauty, and your hair is so soft."

"You don't have to say you're sorry. I'm the one who should apologize." She bent down and gave him a heartfelt hug.

A dam of emotions broke and his tears flowed freely as she knelt and nestled his head close to her. She began to cry, too. She could not imagine how much he and his comrades suffered. "In just a few hours you will be reunited with your family, she reassured him."

His voice sounded shaky. "They won't tell us who is dead, or who is alive. We don't know what to expect when we land. We're scared to death."

"I know, I know." After a short time, the caring flight attendant released the soldier and stood. Her face radiated empathy as she tried to comprehend the dilemma of these brave men.

"Thank you. I needed that," Thomas responded.

Education about the past and present could help ease the men's entry into society. During the long flight, they viewed film clips of America's history during their years in captivity. The videos, shown on the personal screens, contained valuable information: the eight presidents of the lost years, the advancements in the space program, the latest information in the entertainment and sports world, and the progression of technology.

The lack of clothing on the girls surprised the men. The foul language used, and the tattoos and earrings in both men and women astonished them. Whenever they noticed a man with an earring, they laughed. Why were so many people wearing their baseball caps backwards?

In addition, clips of new movies were popular with the returning soldiers. The special effects amazed them, and they asked for certain scenes to be played repeatedly. Some of the soldiers asked, "How did they do that?" They were unaware of modern computer-generated graphics.

Each soldier saw forty years of historical highlights pertaining to his hometown, and state. Authorities knew they would be wondering about events at home.

Sports updates on baseball, football, basketball, tennis, and car racing were of special interest to the returnees. The most excitement came when they heard about a baseball game in St. Louis on September 8, 1998. A man named, Mark McGuire, smashed a homerun which broke the record Roger Maris set in 1961—the same homerun that Robert Freeman witnessed as a young boy. A shocked Freeman watched in silence, not believing that anyone could ever top Maris' record. Disappointed, he hung his head.

In racing, Pfingston noticed that Indy was no longer king; stock car racing replaced it. He could not believe his ears.

On the screens, movie celebrities welcomed them home, as did well-known singers and songwriters. Sports personalities also wished them well. The men laughed and cried when updated on the last four decades.

When the announcement they were waiting for came, the men moved rapidly to look out a window. America was in view! In the distance was a small, dark silhouette of something not quite discernible.

As the plane neared the coastline, they could make out the lights of Los Angeles in the distance. They stood in awe and watched the huge city come into clear view. America! Home! They were almost home! The plane began to circle the "City of Angels."

Below, thousands of lights flashed repeatedly. "Why are all the lights flashing on and off?" Lomack asked.

One of the flight attendants stood beside him and looked out the window. "That's for you. That's all for you. Los Angeles is welcoming you men home."

They buckled their seat belts in preparation for landing and stared out the windows the entire time. Their heads reeled with an array of emotions. Finally, the plane began to descend. The excitement in the men's eyes was evident; the anticipation was almost more than they could bear. The plane landed and slowly drew to a stop.

Expectation was high as the men waited patiently to disembark. Finally, the doors opened. Each one thanked the crew for the flight home. The attendants gave each man a long, cordial hug.

Nervously, the former POWs stepped out the door into the warm, California air. They were home. They were in America where a new life awaited them.

Everyone on the ground stood at attention as Captain James McCarter descended the stairs of the plane, and stepped on American soil for the first time in four decades.

Cameras snapped everywhere. Official photos, taken by a select group of military photographers, would not be released until after the returnees reconnected with their families.

A hand reached out to McCarter, but he hesitated as the rest of the men stepped behind him. "I'm sorry," Captain McCarter apologized to those gathered around them. "The greeting will have to wait."

He turned to his fellow former POWs and said solemnly, "Gentlemen, there is something we must do."

The six soldiers formed a circle, clasped each other's hands, and lowered to their knees. Together they kissed the hard, black asphalt, the ground of their homeland, the United States of America.

On bended knee, Williams led them in prayer. *Lord, we thank you for your love. Thank you for remaining with us during the years of captivity. We recall your promise in Isaiah 40:31. "They that wait upon the Lord shall renew their strength; they shall mount up with wings as eagles; they shall run, and not be weary; and they shall walk, and not faint."* Choked up, he continued, *Renew our strength. May we live our remaining days of our lives like eagles. Free.*

*Free, as you created us to be. Thank you, Lord.* The men responded with a hearty, *Amen.*

Then, they stood up and greeted those awaiting their arrival. The Vice President of the United States, the Governor of California, and the Mayor of Los Angeles were first to welcome them. Famous entertainers, who they did not recognize, thanked them for their gallant service. The celebrities were all anxious to welcome back the six unsung heroes of yesterday.

While the soldiers appreciated the pleasantries, they only had one thing on their mind—their families! They could not wait until tomorrow.

The only secret now was Le. Nobody knew about his role yet. He stood in the background watching the events unfold, trying to stay out of the limelight. He remained with the soldiers wherever they went. At the right time, his significance would be revealed.

The men were escorted to limos and whisked to a local hotel where penthouse suites were reserved. For the next ten hours, security precautions demanded the men remain in their rooms. Secrecy was still vital.

Tomorrow they would travel to Washington D.C. for an early-afternoon welcome home event.

They were still under close medical supervision. The physicians were pleased how well the men were adapting to the new environment. None of the men had adverse reactions to the medical treatment, diet, or stress. The doctors could not explain it. One of them termed it, "miraculous."

At times, they looked out the windows of the hotel where thousands of people gathered below chanting, "Welcome home. Welcome home." The city was bustling with honking horns. Helicopters flew overhead. Cameras and video recorders were everywhere. Many were desperately trying to get the first photo of the freed POWs.

The humble men catapulted to celebrity status, without warning. They only wanted to go home.

Most family members were on their way to the nation's capitol. Out of respect to the men and their families, the returning prisoners' names had not been released to the public. However, excited friends and family leaked a couple identities. Persistent investigative procedures by the media narrowed the search. The news reports showed high school pictures of Pfingston and Traber. The other four POWs remained unidentified, but the names of their hometowns were announced. It would only be a matter of time until the press unraveled the personal details, and released all the privileged information. It was a race against the clock.

Celebrations at school and sporting events were planned in many cities around America. Churches were having special praise services. Specials about the Vietnam conflict aired on television. The names of thousands still-missing POWs and MIAs scrolled across the bottom of television screens. America's news programs brought reminders of those still missing to the forefront of daily reports. The entire world watched the events as they unraveled.

In his hotel room, Le clutched the pouch, still protected under his shirt. He contemplated the contents. The idea was never far from his mind. He knew what he had to do with it. Would he be permitted to carry out his plan? Would he be able to cope emotionally? It would take a lot of strength on his part, and he may face rejection. Le opened the pouch, retrieved a small item, and held it in his hand. He closed his eyes and quietly uttered a prayer, *God, please prepare me for this endeavor.*

## Fourteen
# Meeting the President

Stars twinkled in the still-dark, early morning Los Angeles sky. The guests were escorted secretly to the hotel roof, where helicopters waited to deliver Le and the six men to the airport. The chaos from the excited citizens and extremely heavy commuter traffic made a limousine drive to the airport impossible. They boarded the chopper for the short flight to the airport.

Reporters in news helicopters hoped to catch the breaking story. Therefore, a number of newshounds were trying to get the first pictures, even to the point of breaking the law. They knew the invaluable photos could make them a fortune. Military helicopters quickly escorted the news choppers away from the airport. The delay irritated a couple of the soldiers. They complained because it slowed the process of getting home. At last, the area cleared and the helicopters landed safely.

The majestic "Air Force One" stood ready, waiting for its honored passengers.

They quickly boarded the plane for their trip to Washington. Euphoria mounted.

The anticipation of the men was at a peak. Each man had mixed emotions. There was fear and dread of the unknown. They were all astonished by the hype over their return. Most of all, there was thankfulness to God and Le for their freedom.

Air Force One, lifted into the clouds, headed east to the nation's capitol. Time seemed to stand still during the flight. The freed men stared out the windows. A cloud of uncertainty plagued them. Although briefed on the upcoming details, much did not sink in. The entire idea was more than their minds could comprehend, too overwhelming after the many years of captivity.

The men enjoyed a healthy breakfast and spent quiet moments looking at places of interest below. At times, the plane would alter its route to show the men sights they had not seen in years, if ever. The plane flew lower over the Grand Canyon to allow the men to see its majestic beauty.

The snow-capped Rocky Mountains were another spectacular sight; such beauty was put on hold during their imprisonment. McCarter especially was enthralled with the mountains. He recalled the experiences with his family, as a pilot, flying over the towering peaks. Memories of special times flooded his mind. He smiled as he thought of Wendy. He took a deep calming breath.

The plane was due to arrive about noon. They were served an early lunch as they neared their destination, although most were too nervous to eat more than a few bites of the delicious food.

Nearing the East Coast, one of the flight attendants stood near the men. Choked up she spoke, "Gentlemen, if you look out your windows you will see the great city of New York. We were ahead of schedule, so we gained special permission to fly over the 'Big Apple.' The entire city below is honking their horns and flashing their lights welcoming you home. The pilot thought it appropriate for you to view 'The Statue of Liberty.'"

The men were stunned as they looked out the windows. There she was as big and beautiful as ever. The "Lady of the Harbor" welcomed home the brave and now-free soldiers.

Williams looked at New York's picturesque skyline and stated, "It hasn't changed a bit."

Freeman concentrating on the sight below added thoughtfully, "Yes, it has. Something is different. I remember two extremely tall skyscrapers under construction. I don't see them. Where are they? What happened to them?"

The flight attendants looked at each other, and wondered

how to explain what happened to the Twin Towers on September 11, 2001.

Reluctantly one answered, "That's a story in itself." She paused a moment as the men stared at her waiting for a response. "I guess you'll find out soon anyway. Terrorists hijacked two passenger jets and crashed them into the Twin Towers. The buildings collapsed."

"Terrorists? What do you mean?" Williams questioned.

"Collapsed? The whole buildings are gone?" Freeman inquired.

"How could that happen? How does a huge building like that collapse?" Captain McCarter asked.

"It just did," she recounted. She was struggling how much to say. "It was a terrible time in American history. The worst imaginable."

Williams asked the inevitable question, "Was anyone killed?"

"About three thousand people perished on that awful day."

"Three thousand people!" Williams repeated. "That's impossible!"

The soldiers looked at each other, bewildered, unsure what to say next. Then it hit them—the only news disclosed to them so far was "good" news. They wondered what else happened on America soil while they were captives.

"Did we catch the ones that did it?" Williams persisted.

"They all died in the planes." One flight attendant decided to continue, "That's not all. One plane crashed into the Pentagon, too."

"The Pentagon? The military headquarters? Are you serious?" McCarter questioned.

The attendant nodded. "The men who did it were Islamic terrorists."

The news of 9-11 was taking its toll on the men, leaving them visibly agitated. The medical team tried to protect them from bad news, unsure whether their weakened bodies and strained minds could take the pressure. This incident happened before the medics could intervene.

Williams would not let it go. "What kind of planes did they use?"

One of the nearby physicians suggested they drop the subject. "You will hear all the details later. Right now, let's focus on your homecoming."

"One last question," Captain McCarter persisted. "I would assume these terrorists were not Americans. Did we make their countries pay for these horrific deeds, or did we just turn our backs like we did in Vietnam?" He asked an important question, one that needed addressing.

Le knew the answer, but he watched and waited to see what the response would be.

One of the nearby aides spoke up. "Yes, we waged a war on terrorism." He opted not to tell the soldiers the war was ongoing.

The plane became strangely silent, each person in deep thought.

They continued their flight and soon began their descent to Washington D.C.

Finally, the pilot's voice boomed over the speakers and broke the silence. "Gentlemen, I want to thank you for flying with us. It has been an honor to bring you home. I have been a pilot for many years, for many dignitaries. However, this flight with you heroes has been my highest privilege. My father fought in Vietnam. He is a proud marine and will join the crowd to welcome you home."

He paused for a moment and then continued. "I have been asked to inform you of the day's events. It is going to be a busy one. Thousands of Americans came here today, for you. Do not be alarmed. Be honored. They are here to welcome six brave heroes home."

"Seven," Lomack blurted, as he looked straight at Le.

The pilot did not hear him and continued, "First, we will

land at Andrews Air Force Base, where the President of the United States will greet you. Your relatives will watch you land, but you will not meet them at that time. Upon landing, you will go through the usual welcome by the president and other dignitaries. Next, a limo will take you to an airplane hangar where your families will be anxiously awaiting your arrival. You will have approximately one hour to visit with them.

"After that, you'll be chauffeured to the foot of the Capital building for the ceremony. That's where you will be introduced to the world. At that time, you may make a speech, if you wish. Following the celebration, an aide will take you to the Vietnam Veterans Memorial, built in honor of those who fought and died in that war. You will undoubtedly find that a memorable experience. I assure you, this will be a day you will remember forever."

The pilot hesitated, "When you are finished there, you will truly be free men. You can live the life you dreamed of for the last forty years. I am sorry that you lost that time. Again, I want to say on behalf of myself and my crew, as well as all Americans, thank you and welcome home."

The men looked out the windows in silence while the plane landed. As it taxied down the runway, they could only imagine their families watching with anticipation. There could be no comparison as to who was most excited. Yes, the men had endured hardship beyond comprehension, but their loved ones—parents, siblings, wives, and children had gone through tremendous heartache as well.

None of the men knew who would be there to greet them. The doctors thought it best for them to find out in person, rather than tell them bad news of a loved one who passed away, or remarried, believing the soldier to be dead.

Unexpectedly Le stood up, walked over to James, and sat in the empty seat next to him. A subtle smile appeared as he reached into his shirt pocket and pulled something out. Clutching it in his hand, he reached over to the weary soldier who watched him curiously.

Instinctively, McCarter opened his hand as Le laid the item in it. James stared at the object in the palm of his hand. It was a gold ring. James picked it up and read the engraving on the inside. "Love forever. Wendy."

Le returned to his seat.

Tears filled McCarter's eyes as he stared at the ring—his wedding ring, which Wendy gave him over forty-five years earlier.

James made eye contact with Le. A huge smile expressed his gratitude. James had a look of peace on his face.

Nothing was said. Nothing needed to be.

When the plane came to a standstill, there was an eerie silence. The men acted composed, but their hearts were pounding. They walked calmly to the door of the plane. As they deplaned, the flight attendants gave each returning soldier a heartfelt hug and a quick kiss on the cheek.

"Oh, great! I'm going to be meeting my wife after forty years away and I'm going to have lipstick on my collar." Captain McCarter chuckled as a couple of the men broke out singing an old Connie Francis' song, "Lipstick on your collar, going to tell on you."

Everyone laughed and the door flew open.

Standing near the plane was a group of about fifty people in front of a long line of stretch limos. A red carpet stretched to the foot of the plane's stairs.

Captain McCarter was the first to exit. Immediately he noticed the cool temperature, something he had not experienced in Vietnam. Forecasters predicted snow this evening in Washington.

The returning men would shake hundreds of hands and meet many important people on this special day. However, their focus was on the airplane hangar where their families waited. They knew the eyes of their loved ones were gazing at them from a distance and wondered what they were thinking.

The soldiers were directed to the tarmac. From the earlier videos, they recognized the man in front of the gathering as the President of the United States. Standing next to the president was a man neatly dressed in full military uniform.

The six frail soldiers stood at attention and saluted the leader of the free world.

President Alexander returned the salute, and then warmly shook their hands. Choked up, he spoke, "Gentlemen, welcome home. On behalf of all American citizens and free people in the world, I say again, welcome home." The president was uncharacteristically at a loss for words.

He took a deep breath and continued, "In moments, you will be reunited with the loved ones you left behind forty years ago. I can't imagine the depths of your emotions. You must be bursting with excitement, yet fearful of the unknown. You do not know what the next few hours will hold, let alone the next few days or years. I assure you, America will be there to aid in your transition to civilian life."

President Alexander gestured to the man standing beside him. "Now, I would like to introduce you to the Chaplain of the Army, Brigadier General Norman Kingman."

The cross on the officer's lapel was the first thing Captain McCarter noticed.

It was unclear how much the soldiers were absorbing. Their demeanor was difficult to read as their eyes kept searching for a sign of a loved one, anyone they recognized.

General Kingman stepped up and saluted the soldiers. He spoke in his usual straightforward manner. "This is indeed a privilege. Gentlemen, President Alexander and I, think it appropriate to pray with you before you visit your family members."

Captain McCarter took a step forward and replied with certainty, "Sir, it would be deeply appreciated."

The frazzled soldiers bowed their heads, along with the President of the United States, as the chaplain prayed. *Lord, we want to thank you for bringing these men home safely. They have been gone a long time and suffered much. Enable them to adjust to the changes they will encounter. Please calm their nerves and give them physical stamina to endure what they are about to face. We ask you to grant calmness and peace as they meet their families. Give them and their loved ones patience and understanding. Thank you for the young Vietnamese guard who made this possible. We thank you for your abiding love and care. We ask this in the name of Jesus. Amen.* Slowly, they all raised their heads.

Captain McCarter noticed Le standing a short distance away. He signaled for him to join them. "Mr. President, this is the man who engineered the rescue, Le Huu Trang."

President Alexander's face lit up with a bright smile as he greeted Le with a firm handshake. "It is my privilege to meet you."

Le responded, "The honor is mine, sir."

The president turned to the soldiers. "I know you men are excited and I shall not delay you any longer. I will not join you in your reunions. This is your special moment and should be private."

The president and chaplain stood tall, raised their right hand to their brows, and once again saluted the brave heroes. The men knew normal protocol called for the lower rank to salute first. Humbled by this extraordinary act the soldiers snapped to attention, and saluted the President of the United States, and the Army Chaplain.

Photographers were taking pictures and videos. However, the pictures were for these men and their families, not for the public. The journalists would have their chance soon enough.

Le followed the men to a single limo. As he approached the vehicle, he suddenly remembered Nancee. He looked toward the crowd and noticed her standing in the front, her face beaming. Le walked over to her, "Are you coming with us?"

"No," she said shaking her head. "This is your time. My job is completed."

"Will I ever see you again?"

"Maybe I will see you tonight at the White House. Following the banquet, I head back to Thailand."

Le looked in her compassionate eyes. He recalled the kindness and support she gave him the last few days. "Thank You."

"For what?" she asked.

"For being so helpful to me. You were my friend when I needed one. I don't know if I could have done this without you. Thank You."

"It was my pleasure," she replied.

He realized he was delaying the men from seeing their loved ones, so he rushed off. He waved, stepped inside the limo, and watched her as the vehicle drove off. When she was out of sight, he turned his attention back to the men.

He watched as each man stared straight ahead, motionless. There was soft music playing in the background. No one recognized the song, but it was a peaceful melody.

Within minutes, their hopes and dreams of the last forty years were about to become real. What would they find? Who would be there to greet them?

# FIFTEEN

# The Reunions

T he authorities, still concerned with protecting the men's privacy, arranged a location for the reunion that would be away from the swelling crowd. The limo drove into the hangar that usually housed Air Force One, at the end of the runway.

Cheerful teenagers, in formal dress, greeted each man as he stepped out of the vehicle. The youth—a boy and a girl, welcomed their assigned veteran by name and stood beside him. They each took a soldier's arm and escorted him to a large room, which had been partitioned into six private visiting areas with comfortable chairs and tables.

A crowd of people stood nearby holding signs and banners welcoming home the heroes. American flags of every size waved briskly. The on-lookers were strangers to the returning soldiers. Some small children sat on the shoulders of adults, seeking a closer look at the historical event unfolding before them. As the men neared the group, they noticed many of the unfamiliar faces had tears in their eyes. Unrecognized, but not for long. These were their loved ones—memories, which had dimmed through the years.

Many years ago, the soldiers had funerals. Since their bodies were never recovered, they were listed as MIA. Consequently, there was never full closure for the heartbroken families. Although some parents, spouses, and siblings kept a faint glimmer of hope their soldier would return someday.

Le stayed inconspicuous, a short distance away, as the men met with their loved ones. He knew this would be an emotional time for all. He did not want to intrude on these private moments. Yet, his heart was racing also. He almost felt out-of-place.

⟶⟶⟶

Le watched Specialist Anthony Williams approach a cluster of cheering people. Signs read, "Welcome home, Tony. We love you."

As "Sunday" neared the group, he suddenly stopped in his tracks. The noisy distractions surrounding him went unheard for the moment. His eyes fixed on the man who stood unsteadily in front of him—his eighty-year-old father. His white haired dad was thin and frail, but a huge smile radiated across his face.

Anthony stood just a few feet away, unable to hold back a river of tears. His hands trembled. He almost collapsed, but the teenagers steadied him. Finally, he fell into his father's arms. They held each other in a tight embrace as they both wept.

"Dad," he cried.

"My son, is it really you? Welcome home. I can't believe this moment has come. You're really here."

They embraced with such force they could feel the pain from old age and years of abuse, but at that moment neither man cared about the pain from the past—only the joy of the present and the hope of the future.

Anthony learned that his mother died from cancer eleven years earlier. Two of his siblings also passed away. Greeting him were his remaining sisters with their husbands and several nieces and nephews.

The homecoming was incredible. Since he had been "dead" himself for those long torturous years, there were no tears to cry for those who had died during his absence. On this momentous occasion, Anthony would only have tears of joy.

Williams looked around the group of well-wishers, past his father and sisters. He spotted a woman with a small family standing quietly to the side. Her beauty immediately told him who she was—his wife, Abigail. He approached her cautiously as she bowed her head slightly. The look on her face hinted how much things had changed. He was uncertain what to do.

She made the first move and walked closer to him. She threw her arms around him and exclaimed, "Welcome home, Tony." It was a long embrace, but not filled with passion.

His dad joined him and spoke softly. "Son, she waited five years for your return. The army said you were likely dead. Her life had to continue. Your son needed a man to guide him, a father. Finally, she remarried."

Abigail released his neck and looked at him through tears. "Tony, may I introduce you to your son and his family?"

He looked at his son, the spitting image of himself years ago. The muscular young man stood next to Abigail with his wife. Next to them were three children, ten, sixteen, and twenty-years-old.

"I was going to name him after you, but I knew you liked the name Logan. I named him after the character in that silly book you used to read so often. Logan, may I introduce you to your father?"

Anthony looked at his son. "Logan. Yes, I remember *Logan's Run*."

"It was made into a movie," Abigail said nervously, trying to make light of a difficult situation.

Anthony stared at his adult son whom he had never seen or held. Not sure what to do, he reached out his hand. The young man shook his hand and said, "Welcome home, sir. It is an honor to meet you." Tears blurred the soldier's eyes as he struggled to keep his conflicted feelings under control. Anthony wanted desperately to hear his son call him "Dad," but realized that was asking too much. Someone else had raised his boy, and apparently did a good job. He was his father by blood, but another man was his dad.

"Son, meet your grandchildren," Anthony's father said pointing to three handsome young men. The awkwardness of the situation was obvious. No one could have prepared for it. Each person reacted differently, dealing with the situation in his or her own way. His oldest grandson stepped forward to shake his hand. The other grandchildren greeted him with a nod.

After meeting his family, he was introduced to some good friends from his past. Sadly, he felt more comfortable with them than his own family.

He glanced one more time at his relatives; they were a reminder of how much life he missed. He knew it would take time for everyone to get to know him. Fortunately, he had plenty of time.

------

Sergeant Brent Pfingston, formerly known as "Tuesday," was amazed how different the world looked to him. Fancy cars, electronic gizmos—like those on Star Trek many years ago were now reality.

His young escorts took him to the area where his family awaited. Brent saw his name on dozens of signs held high.

The long years had taken a harsh toll on him. Fortunately, he had not seen himself in a mirror during his captivity, or he would have been dismayed. Even with his new glasses, none of his family looked familiar. He could only imagine how different he looked to them.

Each of the visitors wore a nametag for identification. He discovered his five sisters first. Each of them hugged him sincerely, and joyfully welcomed him back to America.

After a bit of light talk, he found the courage to ask about his Mom and Dad. Since they were not there, he expected the worst. His sister reported that both of his parents had perished in a house fire twenty years earlier.

Another sister added, "Until the day they died, they never gave up on you being alive. They were very active in the POW/

MIA movement. They started a chapter in Minneapolis, which they personally financed until the day they passed away."

His siblings gave him time to come to grips with the sad news, and then he met his many nieces and nephews. He knew he would not remember all their names. It was evident many of them did not know who he was. He sensed apathy in some of today's youth. They seemed more interested in the press coverage than the real reason they were in Washington D.C.

The scanty clothing the girls wore seemed outlandish to him. The foul language many people used shocked him. He would have had his mouth washed out with soap if he spoke to anyone that way. It did not seem necessary. The lack of respect some youth showed disappointed him.

He realized a new chapter in his life would begin today. It would not be a continuation of the old, but a new start, in a new life. A huge challenge was ahead of him. Was he ready? Were any of these brave men?

The teens escorted Specialist Thomas Traber to his designated area where a large banner read, "Welcome Home, Thomas."

Wednesday spotted two women standing with an elderly lady in a wheelchair. He recognized his two sisters immediately. They ran excitedly toward the returning veteran, threw their arms around his neck, and gave him a loving, welcome home hug.

His eyes then focused on the woman sitting hunched over in the wheelchair. Instinctively, he knew the gray-haired, aged woman was his dear mother.

The mood changed with the sight of her. A cloud of sorrow replaced joy. He knelt down and took his mother's hand looking deeply into her shallow, empty eyes.

"She had her hip replaced just a couple of weeks ago after she fell and broke it," one of the sisters explained in a sorrowful tone.

"We thought about not bringing her, but the doctors felt it might be good for her, and for you."

The other sister sighed, and then spoke sadly. "Thomas, she's had Alzheimer's for about eight years. She does not remember anything or recognize anyone. Dad took care of her until he died four years ago."

He stood up and looked directly into his sister's distressed eyes. Choked up he asked, "Dad's dead?"

His sister, with tear-filled eyes nodded. She barely could get out the words, "I'm sorry."

Thomas stared at his sister, and then back at his mother and asked softly, "What is Alzheimer's?"

He listened carefully as one of his sisters explained the debilitating disease. The term Alzheimer's became familiar while Thomas was away. What used to be senility or dementia now had a specific name. They told him how their mother suffered memory lapses, confusion, and a decline of mental ability. She no longer recognized anyone, and was unable to communicate verbally.

The heartbroken GI looked down at his mother, compassion written all over his face. Holding back tears, he knelt beside her wheelchair, and whispered gently in her ear, "Hello, Mom." He cupped her thin, frail hands with his. "I'm finally home, Mom. I am sorry I was not here when Dad died. I wish I could have been. I love you." He did not know what more to say. He stayed on his knees next to his mother, his eyes focused on hers.

"She can't understand you, Thomas," his oldest sister whispered. "Mom has been incoherent for over two years now."

The medical team accompanying the soldiers throughout the trip monitored them closely during each event. They also kept an eye on each of the family members. A heart attack could occur in either the returning soldiers, or older family members. They were there for any medical emergency. An ambulance and a medical helicopter waited outside the airport hangar.

The physician with Thomas had been watching the reunion

carefully. The doctor noticed something unusual happening with his mother, and leaned over the wheelchair to observe her more closely. The doctor said to Thomas, still on his knees next to his mother, "Look carefully at her eyes."

His mother's eyes were noticeably red. Slowly, they filled with tears. Then one word came out of her mouth, crisp and clear— the first word she had spoken in nearly two years. "Thomas."

Astonished, the doctor stepped back. He stared at the elderly woman and then back at Thomas. "Some things happen, which doctors cannot explain. I can't explain this, except that it is a miracle. Thomas, your mother recognizes you. She knows who you are."

The soldier could hold back the tears no longer. He embraced his fragile mother with tenderness. Tears flooded his eyes. His sisters knelt next to him, and held him tearfully. No one observing this scene would ever forget the sight. It was the love of a family, still held together after forty long years of separation.

Finally, his sisters introduced him to their husbands, nieces, nephews, and his many good friends he left behind.

He asked about the little Kansas town he once lived in. He was surprised that it was no longer a small town, but a growing city.

He realized how much times had changed.

---

Specialist Robert Freeman's parents were there to greet him. Both had remarried while he was gone. In fact, his father married three more times. At least for now, they were together for this special occasion.

Thursday was grateful to find his parents in good health. What more could he ask? He hugged his mother and shook hands with his father.

Compared to some of his friends, his was a small reunion. Robert was an only child; neither parent had any additional children. A few childhood friends from Cooperstown came to welcome him home.

His father strode over and handed him a small box. Robert opened it and grinned. He reached in and gently took out a glass case. Inside, was the baseball Roger Maris had signed and given to him so long ago. Speechless, he looked at his father and smiled with approval.

Robert looked over at his fellow comrades and saw the commotion and excitement in the large crowds at their reunions. His gathering was almost non-existent when compared to his fellow soldiers. There were no signs or banners. Yet, he was not disappointed—nothing could sadden him. He was free!

He pulled the baseball close to his chest and then did something completely out of character. He looked upward and uttered the words, "Thank You, God."

He realized this was the first day of the rest of his life and he would make the most of it!

Ronald Lomack's reunion was of special interest to Robert Freeman. For the entire confinement, Robert tried to help his patient, Friday, who was traumatized when a landmine exploded killing his comrades. Freeman wondered if he succeeded in helping him. It warmed Robert's heart to see Ronald's parents hugging their son enthusiastically and welcoming him home. What would the rest of his life be like?

Two of Ronald's brothers were also there for him. David now operated the family farm. Gary moved to California to get away from small town life and have more excitement. Friday was introduced to many nieces and nephews.

After a few moments of chatter, the brothers shared heartbreaking news with the returning soldier. Thirty years ago, on graduation night, a car crash killed Ronald's youngest brother. The school curse continued. The driver was intoxicated.

Five young men in his brother's class of fourteen died needlessly, including his brother.

The parents were devastated over their son's death. Times on the farm were tough. They were on the verge of bankruptcy. During that time in America, many family farms failed. When their parents needed help with the farm, Ronald's brother, David, responded to the challenge.

David married his high school sweetheart, and built a comfortable house on the farm property. Their five grown children also left for big city life. "I need your help operating the farm. There is a job waiting for you at home," David pled.

Ronald smiled. "I'd like that. More than anything, I looked forward to returning to the farm."

All eight classmates from his graduating class of 1969 showed up to welcome Ron home. It was almost a class reunion.

———

In a nearby area, the young people with Captain McCarter showed him to his visitors.

One face in the crowd grabbed his attention. His eyes met hers. Wendy was as gorgeous as he remembered. His wife had taken the time to have her hair fixed exactly as it was when she said goodbye to him in 1970. She even had on a dress similar to the one she wore that day. He instantly recognized the scent of the same brand of perfume she wore many years before. It was as if time stood still. He stood motionless, unsure how to react. Should he hug her or shake her hand? Thoughts raced through his head. Surely, she had remarried and had other children. Who could blame her? Of course, she assumed him dead. He tried to prepare himself mentally for whatever news she would tell him.

James noticed a man and a woman standing beside her. They gently held her arms, supporting her trembling body. James whispered softly, "Could those be my children, Kaylie and Braden?"

The woman made the first move. She let loose of the two people holding her arms and ran to James. She threw her arms around him, squeezed his neck hard, and repeated tearfully, "James. James. James." Then without warning, she planted a long kiss on his lips. She stepped back just a few inches, not wanting to let go of him. She held up her left hand, and showed him the ring he put on her finger that night in the park when he proposed to her. She had waited for him—she never remarried, or even removed her wedding ring.

He raised his left hand and showed her his wedding ring. It was on his middle finger because of his huge weight loss.

She smiled and clung tightly to his neck.

He always knew Wendy was amazing. She raised their two children with the help of their parents. Wendy's parents were now deceased. James' mother died just three years ago. Wendy took over his insurance company and ran it successfully. Now, their son Braden operated the business.

James could not believe his eyes! He glanced over to see a frail, elderly man sobbing uncontrollably. His father! He hurried to his dad and hugged him. They held each other tight, neither one willing to let go.

"Son, Son," he repeated. "It's really you. After all these years!"

"Dad, I thought you were dead." His mind flashed back to the letter he received from Wendy on the day of his capture telling about his father's critical illness.

Wendy stepped in, "The doctors couldn't explain his recovery. Once given the news that you were missing in action, he suddenly began to improve. It was as though something or someone was keeping him going. That is how I knew you would return, and why I never married again. God assured me you were still alive."

James' heart was racing and tears coursed down his cheeks. He stepped back, looked at his father, and turned again to face his sweet Wendy. He stared at the man and woman on each side of her.

"James, these are our children, Kaylie and Braden."

They rushed over and embraced their long-lost father. Time did not erase the tender memories they had of their daddy. Their warm welcome was evidence of the love James showered on them as children.

A thrilled James met his six grandchildren as Kaylie and Braden introduced them one-by-one.

The heartwarming scene, when he met his three-day-old great-grandson, touched all who watched. The baby was born the same day they received the news that James was alive—the news that altered all their lives forever. Plans changed that day for the new parents. They were going to name the newborn, Nathan, after the President of the United States. Braden handed the infant to the tearful great-grandfather and through sobs said, "We are honored to introduce you to "James," named after you, Dad."

Le stood in the background, noticing the tears streaming from his friend's eyes.

Others stood nearby waiting to greet this returning hero, but had to wait their turn.

However, James focused his attention on a well-dressed man in the crowd who stood slightly lopsided. He did not have an inkling who the man was, or why he was there.

Kaylie noticed where her father's attention was, so she walked over to the man, took his hand, and led him to James. "Daddy, this is Bobby. You may not remember him. When I was a little girl, I gave a man in a wheelchair a dollar. You got him a job at a cabinet shop. Do you remember?"

James was stunned. So much had already happened and now this!

James grabbed his hand. "I remember. A fellow vet. Oh, how well I remember!"

"Sir," Bobby said boldly, "Welcome home. I want you to know how...what you did in my life. I mean...." Bobby's emotions made it difficult for him and he struggled to maintain his composure.

He felt a soft hand take his. Supportively, Kaylie smiled at him, and then looked back at James.

"That act of kindness..." Streams of tears ran down Bobby's cheeks as he related his story to James. "That act of kindness you and your daughter showed me years ago changed my life. After given that job, thanks to you, I pulled my life together. I worked hard, returned to school, and earned a business degree. I opened a hamburger franchise. Now, I own ten others throughout the state."

James grinned. He asked a question, which surprised the old veteran. "Did you ever get to see your daughter again?"

A huge smile lit up Bobby's face. "You do remember! I can't believe it. Yes, a few years after you found me that job I got a call from her. We had a wonderful visit. Her mother remarried, but I had visitation rights. In fact, I did something I never thought I would be able to do. With a lot of rehabilitation and hard work, I walked her down the aisle on her wedding day."

His voice cracked, "My grandchildren visit me frequently. I even married a beautiful young woman. We had three more children. I owe it all to you. You believed in me when no one else did, James. Thank you."

Bobby looked at Kaylie and smiled. "Welcome home. Thank you for serving our country." The sight was indescribable as these two veterans embraced.

James' homecoming was perfect. He could not have asked for anything more.

Suddenly through the tears, James' eyes widened. He slowly backed away from Bobby. James continued to stare into the crowd. Standing behind Bobby was a tall man with golden-colored hair. He was dressed in a suit, and held a book in his hand.

"Goldie?" James said. "Is that you?"

"In the flesh," the man shot back.

The quickness of James was surprising as he rushed to give his old army friend a hug. Again, tears flowed as the two embraced.

In fact, there was not a dry eye anywhere. Finally, James stepped back and looked at his friend, Goldie.

James spoke first. "I thought many times about you when… when…" It was difficult for him to talk about his painful ordeal when he was Monday. After a lengthy pause, all he could manage was, "What have you done with your life, buddy?"

Goldie responded. "James my friend, you saved my life not once, but twice.

James tilted his head, looking confused, puzzled.

"The first time you saved my life was when you gave me your seat in your helicopter. The second time came a couple years later when I met your wife and family. You were presumed dead. I stopped by to meet them. James, I saw the same thing in them that I saw in you. I knew I wanted that for my life. I started going to church." Goldie held up the book in his hand. It was a Bible. "This book changed my life. I gave my heart to God and before I knew it, I became a preacher. I have been preaching ever since. I am pastor of a church in Dallas where I have served God for thirty-three years."

James put his hand on Goldie's shoulder as they continued to chat.

Goldie spoke fast, knowing time was short. "I want you to know I have prayed for you every day since you were captured. I mean every day, James. On my desk in my office is a picture of the two of us in front of your helicopter, taken the day before you disappeared. Every morning when I came into my office, I looked at the photo and prayed for you. You are an answer to prayer, my friend."

"It's great to see you, Goldie. I prayed for you many times, too. In fact, my fellow prison-mate Sunday, I mean Anthony, prayed for you also. Without him and his faith, I don't think I would have made it. I guess you could say we helped each other through it all."

The hour sped by. The two friends said goodbye and promised to keep in touch.

James reached for Wendy's hand and held it tight. She rewarded him with a smile.

There were a number of other friends and relatives at James' remarkable homecoming. He wished his mother could have been there. However, later he mentioned to Le that he missed his mother, but at least she knew he was alive. When Le questioned what he meant, all he said was "I'm not with her," and then added, "yet!" By that, Le knew what he meant. James' mother was in Heaven and since her son was not there, he must still be alive.

—————

The gatherings lasted almost an hour when an official announced it was time to move on to the next event. Some of the men still clutched the hands of loved ones. Further memories and stories would have to wait.

Now it was time for the world to meet and thank these six brave heroes—finally!

The men made their way to the limos, while continuing to look back at their families. They just became reacquainted. Now, they had to part for a brief time. Soon, after the big event, they would be together again—to go home.

However, there were still medical concerns.

As they climbed into the limo, Le felt uneasy. He wondered what he was doing here. This was the returning prisoners' day. He would continue to maintain a low profile.

The cars moved away from the huge hangar toward the Capitol Building. For the first time the world would view the six men making history. A sea of people lined both sides of the streets waving American flags. Cameras were everywhere. The returnee's tears dried up during captivity, but now there seemed to be no end to them.

The limos traveled down streets roped off for the occasion. The caravan moved slowly, so the men could view all the sights, especially the throngs of people cheering and waving. Soon they arrived at their destination—the Capitol Building.

Never in their life had they seen such a sight! It was an extraordinary outpouring of support and appreciation. Every direction they looked, they saw excitement. Flags waved. Signs and banners with messages such as, "Welcome Home Heroes," or "America Thanks You" were in abundance. The men were awestruck. Words cannot adequately describe the scene. Yet, nothing would compare to what they were about to face.

SIXTEEN
# Welcoming the Heroes

---

As the heroes stepped out of the vehicles at the capitol building, they hardly noticed the dropping temperature. Music heard in the distance only added to the soldiers' exhilaration. The overwhelmed men followed a parade of people the short distance to a stage. The U.S. Army Band was playing lively patriotic music.

As they neared the side entrance to the platform, men and women rushed to them. All of them, hoping to be among the first to meet them and be a part of this important historical event.

An energetic young woman welcomed each of them with a hearty hug. She spoke rapidly, in a take-charge way. "Gentlemen, let me thank you right now before we get started. My name is Ellen Burns. I am sort of the stage director. My job is to ensure that everything runs smoothly."

She paused briefly to take a quick breath. "I cannot imagine what you must be feeling right now. However, I can relate to the emotions your families are experiencing. My father was a POW in Vietnam. Fortunately, he was one of the lucky ones, released when the war was over. He told me to thank you. I certainly do the same. Thank You." She clutched each of their hands warmly.

Ellen, jittery, and bubbly, continued, "Now before you go out there, let me explain a few things so you know what's going on. U.S. Army, Chief of Chaplains, General Norman Kingman, has a short presentation and prayer before the president speaks. The president will introduce you to the nation, actually to the world. Let me warn you of something, which will astound you.

Hundreds of thousands of people have gathered here today. That's right men. It has been just a little more than forty-eight hours since the details of your release hit the news. Americans have traveled from all over the country just to welcome you home. People have come from other countries, too."

Ellen pulled her hood up on her coat, noticing the drop in temperature. "This event has created worldwide excitement. It is unbelievable, I know. Reporters from almost every major newspaper and television network in the world are here. People are viewing on live television around the world. The six of you are bigger than any movie star or sports figure. You are the biggest celebrities in the world right now. Isn't that exciting?" By now, Ellen was so on edge she could hardly stand still.

The men looked at each other in disbelief. Each had thoughts racing through his mind as he tried to comprehend the enormity of the occasion. Apparently, not everyone had forgotten them after all! Could this really be happening after all those miserable years of confinement and torture?

Pfingston, confused, asked, "Why would so many people want to come and see us?"

"You are heroes, sir. All of you."

"We are not heroes, ma'am. We are… we are POWs. Captured prisoners," Freeman stated with conviction.

As the music grew louder, so did Ellen's voice. She spoke passionately, "Sir, let me try to explain something. Since your capture, America has changed more than you can imagine. We have experienced wars. We have seen this country go from 'Leave it to Beaver' to reality TV. We went from genuine sport heroes to athletes using steroids in order to set world records. Many of our heroes today are people who at one time in America would have been thought of as…how should I say it. Well, sort of unsavory characters. Our children used to play baseball in the street, but now they sit in front of a computer playing video games for hours every day. Our nation needs this special time. We need valiant men like you. America needs real-life heroes. You may not consider yourselves heroes, but everyone else does. That is why they are here. Gentlemen, please accept the honor. If not for yourself, then do it for the country you love."

The men knew it was futile to argue the point, so they just listened and tried to retain as much as they could.

Ellen glanced at her watch and then continued. "Gentlemen, your name will be called individually. If you do not want to say anything, do not feel obligated. Oh yes, one more thing. There are hundreds of chairs in the front where your friends and families will sit. You will be able to see them. I trust you may draw strength from them."

She turned to walk away and then added an afterthought, "I hope we can get through this before the storm hits us. We are expecting about four inches of snow tonight. Welcome home soldiers, welcome home."

The men sat in a row of chairs offstage to catch their breath. Physicians stood nearby, occasionally asking an ex-prisoner how he felt. They were also concerned about the effect of the cold and damp weather in their weakened condition. The prisoners did not know how they felt. They were numb. Every emotion imaginable flooded their minds.

The music came to a stop.

General Kingman, U.S. Army Chief of Chaplains, a decorated soldier from the Gulf War, stepped up to the microphone. He could read clearly from the Teleprompters on each side of the podium.

The excited crowd settled down and listened attentively. Giant screens throughout the mall projected the exciting event.

"We gather today to honor six brave men. Those of us who have had the privilege to serve in the military understand the personal sacrifice many of our brothers and sisters have made to defend this country. At this time, I would like to ask everyone to stand as we sing our *National Anthem*."

At the back of the stage, a giant American flag lowered slowly. The audience gasped at the breathtaking sight. The talking stopped as hundreds of thousands of Americans stood and proudly placed their hand over their heart. Appropriately, the U.S. Army Band played, *The Star Spangled Banner.*

The freed men stood tall, with gleaming faces as they earnestly sang the well-known melody. Tears were streaming down the faces of multitudes, as well as the former prisoners.

General Kingman stepped to the microphone and issued an invitation for all to join him in the *Pledge of Allegiance.* The scene was indescribable as people all over the National Mall recited the oath of loyalty to the flag and to the Republic of the United States of America.

When it was finished, a thunderous applause engulfed Washington, D.C.

Finally, General Kingman raised his hand to quiet the enormous crowd and the men took their seats.

"We honor six returning POWs today. However, we must never forget the thousands of soldiers who still have not returned. This is for them, too."

"During the past forty years, while these men cowered in filthy cells, we enjoyed freedom to work, play, eat, worship, and love. These six men, as well as countless others, have not experienced those freedoms. In captivity, their meals consisted of a couple handfuls of rice a day. If they received meat...well, I'll let your imagination guess what it was."

In the audience, many shook their heads or murmured comments of disgust.

The chaplain pointed to a small round table with a chair. "In front of me is a table—not just any table. It occupies a place of dignity and honor at the front of this platform. Notice that it is set for one, symbolizing the fact that some members of our armed forces are missing from our ranks. A family member is absent. Maybe your soldier never returned. People refer to them as POWs, 'Prisoners of War' and MIAs, 'Missing in Action.' We call them 'comrades.'"

He stepped closer to the table and somberly continued. "They are unable to be with their loved ones tonight, so we join together to pay our humble tribute to them and bear witness of their continued absence. This table set for one is small, symbolizing the frailty of one prisoner alone against his or her oppressors." The chaplain pointed to the table. "The tablecloth is white, symbolic of the purity of their intentions when they responded to their country's call to arms."

He pointed toward the flag. "On the front of the table is an American flag. It represents this great nation and the principles on which it was founded."

He held up a small vase. "The single red rose in the vase signifies the blood, which many have sacrificed to ensure the freedom of our beloved United States of America. This rose also reminds us of the family and friends of our missing comrades who keep the faith while awaiting their return."

The audience was spellbound. Many had tears in their eyes.

"The yellow ribbon on the vase represents the ribbons worn on the lapels of the thousands who demand with unyielding determination a proper accounting of our comrades who are not among us tonight."

The chaplain lifted a small plate. "The slice of lemon on this plate reminds us of their bitter fate." He sprinkled some salt from a shaker on the same plate. "The salt reminds us of the countless fallen tears of families as they wait."

The chaplain picked up a small, black book. "This Bible represents strength gained through faith to sustain those lost from our country, founded as one nation under God."

Chaplain Kingman held an upside-down glass. "The glass is inverted—they cannot toast with us tonight."

He directed the crowd's attention to the single candle on the table. "The candle is reminiscent of the light of hope, which lives in our hearts to illuminate their way home, away from their captors, to the open arms of a grateful nation."

All eyes turn to a chair as the chaplain motioned toward it. "The chair is empty—they are not here."

Chaplain Kingman raised his arm heavenward. "Let us pray to the Supreme Commander that all of our comrades will soon return. Let us never forget their sacrifices. May God forever watch over them and protect them and their families."

The chaplain stepped back as a lone bugler walked to the microphone to play the moving, haunting, musical piece, *Taps*.

The audience was deeply moved as they listened to the famous melody.

After a moment of silence, the chaplain spoke again. "People of this great nation and people of the world, let us pray." He bowed his head reverently.

Everyone stood. Throughout the massive crowd, men removed their hats. People of all races, ages, and religions lowered their heads; many closed their eyes, and came together in unity as one nation before God Almighty.

*Heavenly Father, we come to you today thanking you for bringing these courageous men home. We can only imagine what they have gone through during their captivity. However, you know because you were with them every step of the way. You helped them through each dark night when they could only dream of being free. You enabled them to endure the pain and healed their broken bodies after frequent beatings. You were with them in recent days as they made their daring escape to freedom. Lord, they were always in your hands. I look out across this vast sea of people who came to celebrate the return home of these six brave souls and realize there may be more POWs who have not yet escaped the clutches of tyranny. For them we pray. We ask that you protect them as you did the men we honor today. Lord, bring them home. Bring them home to their families and loved ones. Bring them home to this great nation, the home of the brave and the free. Amen.*

Silence reigned over the attentive crowd. Tears trickled down the cheeks of many. Others stood quietly contemplating the events that brought them together. Some family members of POWs began to have a glimmer of hope for their missing soldiers.

General Kingman said solemnly, "Mr. President." The chaplain stepped aside as the president appeared on the platform and neared the podium. President Nathan Alexander glanced at the six heroes sitting quietly off stage.

Everyone stood; thunderous applause billowed from the crowd.

Ellen looked at the stage and then back at the honored guests. "Okay. Get ready. This is your moment, gentlemen."

Finally, the crowd quieted. The people in the front, mostly family and honored guests, sat anxiously in their chairs. Anticipation was high awaiting their leader's words.

President Nathan Alexander began his address. "My fellow Americans and honored guests. We gather this afternoon to welcome home and honor six men who for the last forty years were prisoners of war. Forty long years! That is two generations. We cannot imagine what these six men have endured during their captivity. I have had the privilege to meet them. They are thin and frail, but ready to begin their new lives."

The men watched and listened, completely still, thoughts racing through their minds. They still could not comprehend all the publicity and fanfare associated with their arrival home.

"The past seventy-nine hours have been a whirlwind experience for them. To achieve freedom was not easy. They began their trek in a Vietnam prison camp, and traversed through Laos and Thailand. They traveled over rough, almost impassible roads, and through dangerous jungles. They were in a perilous gun battle. The obstacles were many. Finally, they flew thousands of miles to get to America's shore. Why, you may ask? Why?" His voice grew louder. "For freedom!"

The crowd went wild.

The president glanced briefly at the men, and then continued his passionate words. "In the last few days these returning soldiers have received dozens of injections and undergone innumerable examinations and tests. Some were fitted with glasses, and now see clearly for the first time in many years.

"As Americans, there is one thing each of us should cherish." The president's voice grew louder and more forceful. "Freedom is a blessing we should treasure, but often take for granted.

"I was informed when these brave men first saw the American flag at the United States Embassy in Thailand they began to weep. Even after four long decades in a prison camp, they remained patriotic. They still loved our great country. Why? Why after all those years when they saw the American flag did they weep?"

The president's voice cracked. He paused briefly and pointed to the American flag. "Because of what it represents. It stands for the one thing, which millions of people for two-hundred and thirty-four years have been seeking in this nation. Men, women, and children have been coming to this wonderful country to find what these men yearned for. Throughout the world, it has been denied to millions of people. It is what my own grandfather sought when he emigrated from Germany in 1917. In one word—freedom. Freedom!"

The audience broke out in a deafening applause that lasted for several minutes.

The president finally spoke again. "I look at this tremendous reception for these six Vietnam War veterans, and recall a huge difference in my homecoming in July, 1971. The greeting many of my fellow Vietnam veterans and I received was far different from today. I believe this homecoming is not just for them, but also for us. Each veteran who came home to protests, violence, hate, and ridicule after serving their country did not deserve that treatment. In a sense, this homecoming is for every Vietnam War veteran—from the one who is a successful business owner, to the one who lives on the street with no place to call home. I hope and pray it will be for all of us a time of healing, so that we can finally put behind all the bitter memories. After all, we did our duty as Americans when our country called us."

The audience went wild, waving flags and signs, whistling, shouting, and cheering.

The men sat silent, awed by the president's words and the crowd's reaction.

Finally, the Mall quieted enough that President Alexander could continue. "On a more somber note, I have information that the remains of twenty-seven other brave soldiers are also returning home. Unfortunately, their return is not a joyous one. In the next few weeks, twenty-seven families will be notified in person that their loved ones made the supreme sacrifice in the Vietnam War. For the families of these fallen comrades, I pray you will finally have closure. As your president, I offer my sympathy and that of a grateful nation."

He continued, "I am reminded of what a great president said to a family in another unpopular war—The Civil War. The mother had lost five sons. Five sons…I cannot even imagine a loss of such magnitude. Abraham Lincoln wrote to the grieving mother the following words: 'I feel how weak and fruitless must be any words of mine, which should attempt to beguile you from the grief of a loss so overwhelming. But I cannot refrain from tendering to you the consolation that may be found in the thanks of the Republic they died to save. I pray that our Heavenly Father may assuage the anguish of your bereavement, and leave you only the cherished memory of the loved and lost, and the solemn pride that must be yours, to have laid so costly a sacrifice upon the altar of Freedom.'"

Sniffling and quiet sobs rippled through the audience.

"Freedom. There is that significant word again. In all wars, there are casualties. Freedom is not free. It never has been, nor ever will be. It is purchased with the blood, sweat, and tears of many brave men and women."

With resolve in his tone, the president continued with his historic speech. "I am reminded of the Germanic tribal leader, Arminius, who in 9 AD stood against thousands of Romans to free his countrymen. The warrior, Queen Boudicca of England, formed an uprising against the occupying forces of the Roman Empire to gain freedom for her country in the first century. We cannot forget William Wallace, the Scottish patriot, who fought for freedom against the English invaders."

The president scanned the immense gathering, and then focused directly on the honored guests sitting in the front rows. "America has also fought for freedom. The forefathers of this great country sacrificed much. Our Constitution and our Declaration of Independence go to great lengths to protect it. The Civil Rights movement came into existence for that cause. Today, that privilege is restricted in many countries throughout the world where there is no freedom to worship, choose their own leader, or protest things that they believe are wrong. Freedom is costly! Arminius, Boudicca, Wallace, Martin Luther King, our forefathers, and countless others can testify to that." He held up an envelope. "These twenty-seven names can be included; brave men who gave their lives for liberty."

He paused briefly. The crowd was listening intently. "Why would anyone fight and die for this cause? A few days after the famous Battle of Gettysburg, where eight thousand Americans died, President Lincoln uttered these immortal words, engraved on monuments throughout America. 'That we here highly resolve that these dead shall not have died in vain—that this nation, under God, shall have a new birth of freedom—and that government of the people, by the people, for the people, shall not perish from the earth.' Citizens of America and people of the world, these twenty-seven soldiers, and others who died in prison camps did not die in vain."

The ovation started slowly as people contemplated what their leader said. When the truth of his remarks settled, the applause swelled to a deafening roar.

After several moments, the president added, "As an American and the leader of the free world, I have the great honor of introducing six of America's bravest men. They came from all walks of life. Each one had hopes and dreams that were shattered the day of his capture. I am certain that every day for the last forty years this band of brothers dreamed of freedom. I would expect that near the end of their captivity they never planned to see it. America, here they are. Welcome them home, please."

The crowd roared with delight.

President Alexander waited patiently for the crowd to hush.

Several minutes later, he read the names of the brave heroes honored: "Captain James McCarter, Specialist Anthony Williams, Sergeant Brett Pfingston, Specialist Robert Freeman, Specialist Ronald Lomack, and Specialist Thomas Traber."

A thunderous ovation echoed throughout the National Mall as the President of the United States recognized the six free men. He motioned them to join him on stage.

# SEVENTEEN

# The Award Ceremony

---

The men stood in awe. The years of quiet isolation in captivity affected them in various ways. They were apprehensive of the gigantic crowd, their nerves jittery; their social skills lay dormant for all those years. No one was sure how the former POWs would react to the stress of the day. They remained in place, afraid to move. People nearby gently coaxed them toward the president.

Reluctantly, Captain McCarter led his men gradually to the front of the platform. All were dressed smartly in new military uniforms.

Le watched in the background enjoying the poignant scene. As they moved toward their president, he attentively observed the men who he had grown to respect and admire. He was proud to be their friend.

"Sir," Ellen whispered, "you need to be with them."

"No," Le replied. "This is about them, not me."

"That's where you are wrong. It is about freedom, as the president said. Without you this moment would not have occurred. You made it all possible."

Le barely heard Ellen's words, not wanting to miss a moment of the festivities.

James turned and looked back at Le. Unexpectedly, the captain walked over and reached his hand toward his former guard. Le grabbed his hand and James shook it heartily. An insistent Captain McCarter put his arm around his friend's neck and whispered, "Come, Le Huu Trang. I want America to meet you."

Without hesitation, Le and James walked side-by-side to join the waiting president.

The six worn American soldiers and the young Vietnamese guard stood beside the President of the United States. History was made as a hurting nation came together in unity, with one purpose. It was an unforgettable day. As far as the eye could see, people of all ages, ethnic groups, and religions waved American flags and cheered.

The men did not believe they were heroic. They believed the true heroes were the men and women who came back to the protests and ugliness of a split nation. The real heroes were the soldiers who did not make it back alive, or were still missing.

At last, the crowd settled and the men sat down in a row of chairs behind the president. Soon each man would have his deserved moment in the spotlight.

"Specialist Thomas Traber, please step forward," President Alexander ordered.

Thomas stepped to the front. Raised in a small town and out of touch with the world for years, he was noticeably nervous. Yet he marched forward, stood at attention, and smartly saluted the President of the United States.

The president returned the salute.

Two soldiers moved a small table close to the president. Wooden boxes and framed certificates were on the table.

President Alexander shook the trembling soldier's hand firmly and held it for several seconds. Camera shutters clicked in every direction as news photographers and spectators alike captured the historic event.

"Specialist Traber, I am deeply honored to pin these stripes on you. Thank you for your years of service. As President of the United States, I officially present you the rank of Sergeant First Class. With these stripes, you will have all the benefits that accompany it."

President Alexander reached toward the table and picked up a plaque. "Now, I present you an honorable discharge from the

United States Army. You will receive a pension and back pay for the time you were held a prisoner of war as the rank of Sergeant First Class."

A smile replaced Traber's serious look when he began to understand the significance of the leader's words.

An aide handed the president a box from the table. He took the contents and spoke with authority. "I also am proud to present to you the 'Prisoner of War Medal.'" President Alexander held the medal high for the spectators to see. "This medal may be presented to any person who was a prisoner of war after April 5, 1917—the start of World War I. President Ronald Reagan signed the proclamation into law in 1985. It is awarded to any person who was taken prisoner or held captive, while engaged in action against an enemy force of the United States. The prisoner's conduct during captivity must have been honorable."

He turned to face the men seated near the back of the stage. "Gentlemen, I have it on good authority that your captivity was honorable."

The president pinned the medal on Sergeant Traber.

He selected an official document and read the inscription to the hushed crowd. "Specialist Thomas M. Traber, United States Army. On September 21, 1970, while on a mission in Vietnam to pick up injured comrades, his helicopter that he served on as a gunner was shot down. Subsequently, he was captured and spent forty years in a prisoner of war camp, where he did not break under harsh treatment and continued torture. His gallantry and indomitable spirit, while a POW, are in keeping with the highest traditions of military service and reflect great credit upon himself, his unit, and the United States Army."

President Alexander handed the certificate to the humbled soldier. "Sergeant Traber, I am honored to present you another significant medal. By a special order of the United States Congress and as Commander in Chief of the Armed Forces, I proudly present you 'The Medal of Honor.'"

Sergeant Traber stood stunned when he heard the

announcement. He looked over at his fellow prisoners and noticed the shocked looks on their faces.

President Alexander held up the nation's highest military decoration. "This is the only military medal that can be worn around the neck. 'The Medal of Honor' can only be awarded to a member of the United States Armed Forces who has distinguished himself conspicuously by risking his life above and beyond the call of duty, while engaged in military action against an enemy of the United States. The deed performed must be one of personal bravery and self sacrifice." He placed the medal over the neck of a very proud and emotional Sergeant Traber.

The president watched the other five soldiers' faces, which registered surprise and humility as each heard the awards. The men looked into the crowd, noticing their family members proudly smiling and cheering for them.

President Alexander stepped back, "Sergeant Traber, as President of the United States and a retired Colonel of the United States Marine Corps, I salute you as a 'Medal of Honor' recipient." The president proudly saluted the humbled sergeant.

Sergeant Traber returned the salute as people all over the world watched.

"Is there anything you would like to say to the American people?"

He shook his head. "No, sir. Captain McCarter will be our spokesman." Traber again saluted the president and returned to his chair.

Thomas showed his fellow prisoners the medals he received. They all shook his hand and gave him a cordial hug.

Sergeant Brett Pfingston, Specialist Robert Freeman, and Specialist Ronald Lomack were honored next. Each had his own moment of glory as he received the same medals as Sergeant Traber, and promotion to Sergeant First Class.

The president continued the award presentations.

Specialist Williams stepped forward when the president called his name.

President Alexander read the inscription on a document. "Specialist Anthony C. Williams, United States Army Medic, August 3, 1970, while on a campaign to 'search and destroy' enemy combatants in the villages of South Vietnam, pulled three wounded men to safety while receiving enemy fire. In the process, Specialist Williams received a wound to the head that knocked him unconscious. He regained consciousness, and with the help of a fellow soldier fled into the jungle. After three days on the run, North Vietnamese troops captured them. Subsequently, he spent forty years in a prisoner of war camp where he was brutally beaten and tortured. Williams never succumbed to the numerous beatings he received, and remained faithful to his fellow POWs and his country."

The President of the United States pinned "The Purple Heart" on Williams. Like the other men, he received "The Prisoner of War Medal" and "The Medal of Honor."

They saluted each other. Williams returned to his seat by his comrades.

President Alexander asked Captain James McCarter to come to the podium. Captain McCarter, in his confident style marched forward, proudly saluting the President of the United States. The president returned the salute.

"As Commander in Chief, I am honored to promote you to Colonel." The rank was pinned on him, and the massive crowd cheered. Some whistled. Others yelled, "You deserve it" or "God bless you."

Colonel McCarter saluted the president and then looked down into the massive crowd. On the front row was his wife, Wendy. He smiled at her and pointed to his new rank. He could see tears streaming down her proud face.

"Colonel James McCarter, as President of the United States, and on behalf of Congress and the American people, I want to thank you for your service to the United States of America. I present you the 'Prisoner of War Medal.'" The president pinned it on McCarter's uniform.

President Alexander picked up another medal. "For your gallantry in action against an enemy force, and for your bravery in saving the lives of Captain Richard Jenson, and Specialist Anthony Williams, I am honored to present you the 'Silver Star' for gallantry in action."

James stood at attention as the president pinned the medal on his uniform.

When the noise of the energetic crowd died down, the president continued. "Captain James McCarter, Helicopter Pilot for the United States Army. While on a 'Search and destroy' mission in Vietnam on August 3, 1970, bravely and heroically, without regard to his life, forced his helicopter down among enemy fire to pick up survivors of three disabled units. Captain McCarter's helicopter was loaded to full capacity. Captain McCarter noticed a fellow pilot, Captain Richard Jenson, seriously wounded. He sacrificially gave up his pilot's seat to his injured comrade. While running through the smoke-filled battlefield, Captain McCarter encountered resistance. Firing his pistol, he downed an enemy patrol, which was attacking the fleeing helicopter piloted by Captain Jenson.

The President continued. "He found Specialist Anthony Williams, unconscious from a bullet wound to the head. Discovering the soldier was alive, Captain McCarter took time to aid Specialist Williams. The two ran into the jungle to escape enemy forces. He bandaged Specialist Williams wounds, saving him from probable death. Captain McCarter assisted Williams the next two days as they trekked through the jungle. Enemy forces captured them on August 6, 1970. Captain McCarter and Specialist Anthony Williams were taken to a prisoner of war camp, where they were tortured repeatedly over the course of forty years. Due to the help of a Vietnamese Guard and Captain McCarter's strong leadership, the six remaining prisoners finally escaped the clutches of their captors. Captain McCarter's leadership, while a POW, inspired his fellow captives and was instrumental in their eventual escape. His extraordinary heroism, at the risk of his own life, is one of gallantry and to be commended."

President Alexander reached for the medal. "Colonel McCarter, with honor I award you this medal, the highest decoration any soldier can receive, "The Medal of Honor." James leaned forward, so the president could put the distinguished medal around his neck.

President Alexander saluted Colonel McCarter, and he returned the salute.

Again, the crowd roared its approval.

James looked at Wendy, her glowing smile and sparkling eyes just as he remembered. He found comfort in her presence. She was as beautiful as the day he married her many years ago.

Perhaps it was divine intervention, but a strange sight briefly interrupted the ceremony. Over all the noise, a faint honking echoed in the distance. It was unnoticed by most people. First, Colonel McCarter looked upward. Then the other five men lifted their eyes to view a flock of geese flying overhead. They stared at the formation, mesmerized by a sight they had not witnessed for years. No one uttered a word.

A simple scene—birds flying free, captured their attention. Most people would not understand how meaningful that display was to the men who had lived in terror, filth, loneliness, and hunger for forty years. The crowd quieted, undoubtedly wondering what the men were thinking. What could be so meaningful that it stopped the ceremony?

An aide walked up to the president, whispered something in his ear, and handed him a paper. The president read it, stood thoughtfully for a moment, and then glanced over at Le. The nation's leader stepped to the microphone, "It is often little things of beauty which we take for granted." He gestured to the winged visitors. "Perhaps each of us should do as these soldiers are doing and take a moment to observe our feathered friends. Let us remember this impressive sight, and allow it to serve as a reminder to appreciate the unexpected occurrences in life, which happen every day."

Everyone was gazing skyward. Parents pointed out the fascinating formation to their children. For a brief time, the focus of the gathered spectators was on the wedge of geese, which soon disappeared in the distance as the skies again quieted.

Drawing the significant interruption to a close, the president returned to the planned activities. "Colonel, would you like to say something now, or should I present the next award?"

President Alexander handed Colonel James McCarter the paper he received from his aide. James silently read the note and a huge smile spread across his face. He returned the paper to the president and stepped close to the microphone, still grinning. "Mr. President, would you please present the next award? After that, I would like to address the people of the United States and the world."

The commander in chief readily agreed. "Then so be it."

The president glanced at the Vietnamese guest, and surprisingly announced his name. "Le Huu Trang!"

A startled Le looked at the president. His heart raced. What was wrong?

The president continued. "Will you please come forward?"

Le strode forward hesitantly, uncertain if he should salute or shake hands. As he neared the leader of the free world, he was stunned as he saw the crowd standing, cheering, and applauding him enthusiastically. He looked at the former prisoners of war, now his friends. They were clapping wildly, broad smiles on their faces.

He tried to comprehend what was happening. Life had become a sudden and complete whirlwind overnight. Just a few days ago, he was a prison guard for the Vietnamese Government. Now he's standing in front of the President of the United States with a countless mass of spectators.

He did what was natural for a military man. He saluted the president, who returned the salute.

"Le Huu Trang, as President of the United States of America, I present a unique award to you. I understand that your name means 'decorated' or 'honored.' How fitting." An aide handed him a medal. "This is the highest award a civilian can receive in America. You certainly deserve it. It is 'The Medal of Freedom.'" He placed it carefully around Le's neck.

The president shook Le's hand as thousands of cameras captured the presentation.

When the crowd quieted, President Alexander reached for a document. He smiled at a nervous Le and read, "'October, 4, 2010, Le Huu Trang is hereby granted American citizenship.' I have signed it on behalf of the American people. It bears the great seal of the United States of America. Mr. Le Huu Trang, this recognizes you as an American citizen, a special privilege you richly deserve."

He handed the certificate to Le. He was overwhelmed and uncertain what to say or do. For years, he dreamed of being an American citizen, now his dream was coming true.

"Mr. Le, responsibilities come with citizenship. You have the responsibility to vote, honor the flag, and defend it. You will be privileged to pay taxes."

A faint chuckle rose from the audience at the mention of taxes.

Le smiled. The incredible moment was bittersweet. He felt joy and heartbreak at the same time. How he wished his family could share in this momentous occasion. It comforted Le to know his family was in Heaven, smiling down on him. At least he knew, someday they would be reunited for eternity.

President Alexander turned to Colonel James McCarter and said, "Would you like to present the next award to Mr. Le?"

The colonel snapped to attention and saluted the president. "I would be honored, sir."

James stepped in front of Le and took his hand. Looking directly into the younger man's eyes he spoke sincerely. To the onlookers, it was one good friend talking to another.

"Le my friend, what you did for us went far beyond bravery. It was selfless. At great personal risk, you saw a wrong, and believed you could and should make it right. You engineered a *righteous rescue*. We thank you sincerely for being courageous enough to do the right thing. We thank you for bringing us home."

The colonel smiled at the president.

"Le, this took a lot of doing, but it was worth it." Colonel McCarter's voice cracked and his eyes moistened. Unable to speak further, he looked behind the former guard, nodded his head, and motioned Le to turn around.

From the back of the stage, Le's mother, father, wife and three children sprinted toward him. Unable to move, he stood in total disbelief. Could this really be happening? As he held them tight, he knew it was real. As they embraced one another, tears generously flowed. In fact, there were probably not many dry eyes watching the reunion in person or on TV.

The family was unaware of everyone and everything around them as they clung to each other, rejoicing in the unbelievable moment.

At last, Le composed himself enough to look at the president, and then back at his friend, Colonel McCarter, the man he had known in prison as "Monday." With tears streaming down his cheeks, Le asked the colonel, "How? When?" He could not find the words to frame his thoughts. He paused to decide what to say, how to say it.

Colonel McCarter, sensing what Le wanted to express, finally managed to get out the words, "You can thank your friend Sam for this."

Right on cue, Sam bounded from the back of the stage. His face beamed with his well-known smile.

Le released his grip on his family and hugged his good friend Sam; the one who helped make this reunion possible.

President Alexander stepped to the microphone for a surprise announcement. It was time to disclose the contents of the paper he received earlier. "The Vietnamese Government sent a statement saying it will abide by all the treaties we have signed. They have issued a proclamation to assure there are no other POWs. There will be an immediate investigation of this entire affair. The United Nations is welcome to oversee the investigation. In addition, there will be an extensive search of Vietnam for any other POWs, or the remains of any. They will be returned immediately. As a goodwill gesture and an apology, the Vietnamese Government released the family of Le Huu Trang."

The president looked directly at Le, who held his family close. "Mr. Le, not only have you saved six American lives, but you have opened an essential, stronger dialog with the Vietnamese Government, which I trust we can take to heart. I believe thanks to you our relations with them will improve."

The crowd roared with excitement.

When the crowd finally silenced he added, "I also express appreciation to Mr. Samuel Jefferson. Without him, this day would not have been possible. As an American, he operated an orphanage in Vietnam. He established friendships with Le and his wife, Linh. Just a week ago, the escape plan was put into effect. There was no military backing, nor United States assistance. These two men, Le and Sam, developed and executed the entire plan by themselves."

President Alexander cleared his throat. "Sam shared Le's vision, the urgent desire to do the right thing. Because of their perseverance, the six men we are honoring today are going to live their lives in freedom. Mr. Samuel Jefferson will be an honored guest at our banquet tonight. Now, I have the privilege of awarding Sam the 'Medal of Freedom' to express our nation's appreciation."

A shocked Sam stood before the crowd unable to believe what was happening. Unexpected tears pooled in his eyes and he tried to blink them away.

The tribute became real when President Alexander placed the award around his neck.

As the celebration continued, Le introduced his family to the six men he had grown to love and respect, and to the President of the United States.

The audience finally settled down and watched as Colonel McCarter stepped to the microphone. "Mr. President and fellow Americans, it is hard to believe that only four days ago my comrades and I had given up all hope. An evil General Yo held us prisoners. We were living in a small, dingy cell, no bigger than a refrigerator box. Every day we received dirty rice, drank polluted water, and worked twelve or more hours a day. We had no shoes for our sore, calloused feet, or hats to shield us from the scorching sun. There was no protection from the mosquitoes, flies, cockroaches, and rats."

Colonel McCarter glanced at his wife. She sniffled, but gave him a slight smile for moral support.

"Through our years of confinement, we seldom conversed with each other. Vocal communication was strictly forbidden. If we disobeyed and the guards caught us, the consequences were horrific. Many of our comrades died from the punishment." Colonel McCarter drew a deep breath. "We started out with about thirty or thirty-five men, I do not recall exactly. We were moved to different locations several times, but the conditions were always brutal."

He shook his head as he recalled the bitter memories. "We never knew what day of the week it was, let alone what month, or year for that matter. We lost track of time. Each tedious day was the same as the previous one." The colonel's face registered sorrow. "I believe it was about twelve years ago…although I am not certain, we planned an escape. We knew we might never make it to freedom, but we had to try. I think there were thirteen of us at the time. We planned the escape through a unique system we developed similar to Morse code. We tapped on the wall with our feet or hands, whatever we could use to communicate."

He turned to his comrades for support and took another deep breath. "The escape plan turned out to be a trap. We never understood why the attempt failed. The guards beat us for days afterward. They took great joy in our suffering. Some of my fellow inmates were beat to death."

Colonel McCarter's rough voice ceased. He could not continue. The emotional toll was too much. He stepped away from the microphone.

Suddenly, a voice behind him boomed, "We are with you, brother."

Colonel McCarter turned to look directly at his spiritual partner, Sergeant Anthony Williams.

The encouraging words from his friend were all it took for the colonel to regain the strength to continue. "There were only seven of us left. For safety reasons, we code-named each of us a different day of the week. We had an idea who each of us was, but were quite confident General Yo did not. Never did we suspect that the seventh day was actually a Vietnamese prison guard. We called him, 'Saturday.'"

Colonel McCarter paused and cleared his throat. The speech was straining his already weak voice. "A few years ago, a new prison guard was hired. He was not brutal, like the rest of them. He did not hit or kick us. Occasionally, he even smiled at us. You must understand we trusted no one, especially after the failed escape attempt."

"It was not until a few months ago, I began to notice a difference in this guard. You see, we had forty years of hatred and bitterness pent up in us. Therefore, for a while we did not even notice his kindness. We did not hear the gentle words he spoke when the other guards were not around. Now as I look back, I remember times when he smiled at me, or extended a helping hand when I fell."

Colonel McCarter glanced at Le as he still held his family close. "Once, when I was really down and hurting, I walked by that guard and heard him say, 'I'm sorry, GI.' I could not believe it! Those three words stuck with me. Soon after, he shared his bottle of water with me. I will never forget the taste of that cool, fresh water. Oh, it was good! What shocked me most was when I realized I had almost finished the entire bottle. I knew a beating would follow. I handed the bottle back, watched the guard raise it to his mouth and sip the last few drops. He did not whip me! No punishment! Instead, he said…he said," choked up, Colonel McCarter hesitated, and then looked directly into Le's teary eyes. "You know what that guard said, he said, 'It's a great day to be alive.'" He paused. "I remember thinking, who is this man? What does he want? Could this be a trick?"

"Over the next few days, the guard showed me something about myself. He shared scripture from the Bible. I began to see that Le was a soldier for righteousness. His kindness reminded me that I was missing something in my life. Something I had at one time, but let slip away. That was God. I am ashamed to admit that I…we, all of us, had given up hope in America, in ourselves, and even in God." He looked down and remorsefully shook his head.

"Since returning to America, I realize although some had forgotten us, many had not. The outpouring of love and support you have shown today has overwhelmed us. We never expected a welcome like this."

As he looked into the vast crowd, he continued, "I see those black flags out there." He pointed to a number of POW/MIA flags in the audience; veterans dressed in camouflage clothing, some in wheelchairs, carried most of them. "You sir, what is your name?" He directed his question to a rough-bearded man carrying a large black flag. He wore a shirt that read, "POWs never have a nice day."

The veteran snapped to attention. "Sergeant Dennis Shelby, United States Marines. I served in Vietnam 1967 to 1969, sir."

"Sergeant Dennis Shelby, I thank you…we thank you." He gestured to the other men. "We thank you for never giving up, Sergeant Shelby."

Colonel McCarter's passionate speech kept the onlookers spellbound. "Last night before I went to bed, Le helped me run a search on a computer. I wanted more information about what

Americans refer to as 9-11. I was horrified as I watched the planes hitting the buildings, and Americans jumping out of the flaming inferno to certain death. Then the horrible collapse of the towers! I can only imagine what you felt that fateful day. In my research, I discovered many Americans have become complacent since then. I will never forget those terrifying scenes. So many lives were lost needlessly that September morning in New York. I pray nothing like that ever happens again in America, or even in the world! I also hope and pray another American soldier never becomes a prisoner of war."

The crowd responded with enthusiastic applause of affirmation.

"You may wonder if we ever gave up. Yes, we did. Each of us did. We gave up on America, and sometimes even on God. But, you know what? We now realize some of you continued to be steadfast. People like Sergeant Shelby never gave up. Neither did God. He never forgot us, nor did He forsake us. No, quite the contrary. He brought us an angel in a Vietnamese guard uniform to help us. Who would have guessed?"

The colonel smiled at Le. Admiration was evident by his remarks.

"Many times in recent hours, I asked Le why he helped us. Why would he sacrifice his life and the lives of his family for six forgotten American prisoners? His reply was always the same, 'It was the right thing to do.'" Colonel McCarter's voice slowly intensified. With resolve and confidence, he continued, "Today America, I challenge you. Do the right thing, everyday. Do the right thing."

He beckoned his comrades to join him. They still needed to do something. Together, the former POWs locked their arms, and in front of the vast gathering, tapped the floor rhythmically with their feet.

McCarter stepped to the microphone. "That was the code we used for communicating with each other during those years of confinement. I am sure you wonder what we tapped." His voice cracked. "We said what every American should affirm daily. 'God bless America.'"

The crowd began to chant, "God bless America."

When the refrain died down, the Colonel concluded, "We thank you for your warm reception. God bless you."

Colonel James McCarter and his band of liberated POWs waved to the audience as they walked off the stage while the ovation continued.

Spontaneously the crowd broke out singing, *God Bless America.* Those present or those viewing on TV will never forget the sights and sounds of this incredible event.

Le stood with his arm around Linh. He could hardly believe he was in America and for the first time in his life was free. Really free! The best part was sharing the experience with his family. Le noticed each of his loved ones had a look of fear, uncertainty. Beyond the joy of the moment were understandable concerns about their future. Monumental concerns!

All Le could do was assure them with a confident, loving smile. Somehow, he knew things would be all right. God reunited his family. He guided them through perilous times and protected them. He must have a plan for them.

As the reality of their situation began to sink in, unpredictably Le started to laugh and a peace enveloped him. As he remembered God's promise of His presence, he was thrilled beyond words.

Colonel McCarter and his comrades returned to the stage and greeted Le's family.

President Alexander joined in the reception.

All the men were exuberant, except Lomack who was noticeably disturbed.

Freeman and Colonel McCarter noticed his demeanor and approached him. Lomack was staring at the medal he received only minutes before.

When his friends neared him, Lomack noticed their concern and remarked, "I keep thinking how I got here. Each of you deserves these medals, but me…me, I flipped out forty years ago.

I might have been court-martialed, given a medical or perhaps even a dishonorable discharge for my actions. I don't deserve this honor." He looked down, dejected, and ashamed.

"Ron," Freeman pleaded. "You can't look at it that way. None of us knows what we would have done in your place. You spent forty years in a POW camp where you were tortured excessively. You never cracked. In fact, you challenged your captors. You did not break."

Lomack hesitantly nodded his head in agreement. Yet deep in his heart, he still felt unworthy.

It started to snow gently as the event began to wind down. Le looked up and smiled, allowing some snowflakes to melt on his face. Snow was something he had never experienced before. He thought it was another amazing thing about an already incredible day!

Le noticed Sam standing alone offstage, watching the events. He knew Sam was instrumental in the reunion of his family. He rushed over to him. "How can I ever thank you for bringing my family back?"

"No thanks are needed. I gave you my word. I did what I had to do. You said so yourself, it was the right thing to do."

"Yes. I did say that, didn't I? How did you find them?"

"I contacted a friend in the Vietnamese Government. The U.S. authorities had already notified them, and they were working on the situation. I was permitted to participate in the storming of the prison compound. We found your wife, children, and parents locked in cells with about twenty-five other missing people. They released your family immediately, no questions asked."

Sam continued, "My chopper flew to the site. We left with the Vietnamese Government's blessing. A few of the other prisoners were missing dignitaries held by Yo. They were in captivity because they found out about him and were going to turn him in. Yo is despised in Vietnam. If he were not already dead, he would be now. There is more good news—that horrible prison is no more."

Le shook his head, sadness clouding his face. "I'm glad it's over. What a relief."

The former guard, observing all the excitement around them, turned to face Sam, "What do I do now, my friend?"

"Le, the sky is the limit. Tell your story. Write a book. Make a movie. Go on a lecture tour of universities, anywhere in the free world."

Le considered the ideas. "Write a book. Yes, I could do that."

EIGHTEEN
# The Wall

---

The honored guests arrived at the White House at the prescribed hour. The staff ushered them into the State Dining Room.

The soldiers, who only days ago were imprisoned in filthy, repulsive conditions, gazed around the banquet room. It was luxury at its finest. The décor and furnishings were magnificent. Priceless art decorated the walls. Tables were set with fine china, crystal, and linens, as they would be at a dinner for a visiting head of state. A tuxedo-clad live orchestra played softly in the background.

The guests, including the soldiers and their immediate families, were dressed in formal attire. The returnees tried to focus on the occasion, but the beauty surrounding them captured their attention, distracting them.

Before dinner, the men mingled with one another as they delved into the delicious hors d'oeuvres. Their appetites were improving, and they were permitted to eat more foods to help regain strength and stamina.

The soldiers proudly showed each other and their loved ones their new ranks and coveted medals while they visited.

Le and his family received special attention from his friends and the attendants. Le's parents appeared to be adapting to the cultural changes easily. They were laughing, and having a great time speaking Vietnamese with some of the American men and women.

Le tried to absorb the scene around him. He still couldn't

believe this was happening. He was dining in the White House with dignitaries, including the President of the United States and the beautiful First Lady. Could it be any more unbelievable?

His blessings were abundant. His family was alive and celebrating with him. He was with new friends who genuinely cared about him. The tables were filled with more food and drink than he had seen in his entire life! What more could he desire? Yet, he sensed something was missing.

Suddenly, a strange sensation swept over him as if someone was watching. Glancing across the room, he was amazed to see a beautiful "angel" standing in the doorway, dressed in a stunning, sparkly, red dress.

A wide smile crossed his face as he noticed his friend, Nancee. He walked over to greet her.

"Hi," she said softly. Her big blue eyes and her captivating smile made him feel comfortable.

"Hi. I'm delighted you could make it."

"I would not have missed this for the world."

They both looked around the room at the guests, most of them strangers to Le.

"Some party," she commented.

"Yes, but they sure have a lot of strange food in America. Some of it is delicious though. Fortunately, there are some familiar dishes from my country. I guess I should say the country I was born in; America is now my home." He proudly boasted.

Le reached for her hand. "Come, Nancee. I'm anxious for you to meet my family." Together they walked over to his family who was laughing and visiting with some other guests.

"This is my wife, Linh. Honey, this is Nancee. She accompanied me all the way to America and was a remarkable help to me. Nancee motivated me and helped me get through the confusing transition. I don't know if I could have done it without her. She has become a good friend."

The women greeted each other with a hug.

"Thank you for taking care of him," Linh remarked genuinely.

"I was so worried about him, and I know he was concerned about us. I prayed that someone would be there to help him. You were the answer to my prayer. Thank you, Nancee."

"It was my pleasure. He often talked about you and the children. He prayed for your safety. Le is a kind and gentle man. You are fortunate to have him."

Le reached for Linh's hand as he summoned their children and introduced them to his American friend. They individually thanked her for helping their daddy.

"You have beautiful children," Nancee offered. "You are blessed."

"I sure am," Le readily agreed. "Would you like some punch?"

"I'd love some."

Le turned to Linh, "I'll be back in a moment."

Le walked over to the serving table with Nancee. He poured her a glass of sparkling red punch, handed it to her, and took one for himself. They stood away from the crowd chatting comfortably like old friends.

"You have a lovely family, Le. Are they doing okay?" she asked, sipping her punch.

"Yes, they are doing well. Linh has a few burn marks inflicted by Yo. My youngest has a badly cut finger. They will heal. They'll be fine."

With concern, Nancee inquired, "Le, what are your plans for the future?"

"I am unsure what the future holds, but excited about some possibilities. I am not certain how I will support my family. Sam suggested I write a book, or go on a lecture tour, but I don't know how to do that."

"Hmmm… lecture tour. Yes, that is a great idea and could be quite lucrative."

"How does that work?"

"Perhaps you could speak at schools, universities, and public events. Often an agent is retained to set up a speaking itinerary for a client."

"Are there many opportunities?"

Nancee smiled, "Thousands of them."

"How much do they pay? I made forty-five dollars a month. Can I make more than that?"

Nancee laughed a cute chuckle. "Oh my, yes. I have heard of people making fifty-thousand dollars or more to speak at various events. You may be surprised at the opportunities that come your way. Speaking engagements at churches might be a possibility, too. They do not usually pay like that, though! There is no limit to where you can go, what you can do, or how much money you can make."

Le was shocked to hear this, but thrilled and hopeful. He realized he and his family would be all right. This was the beginning of an adventurous new life.

As he sipped his punch, he glanced at his family and then back at Nancee. How could he thank her for the kindness she showed during his time of heartache? He concluded it was not necessary—after all, Nancee was also doing the right thing.

Le would see Nancee again a few times in his life. She invited Le and his family to her wedding two years later. It was a spectacular military ceremony, just like her father wanted. She married a Christian; he was also a Marine.

⟶⟶⟶

The banquet was exquisite. The chefs prepared a superb six-course dinner, which the men and their families enjoyed. As they dined, they caught up on each other's lives and plans for the future.

After the banquet, chauffeurs drove the men to the Vietnam Veterans Memorial. Le and his family accompanied them in a separate limo.

When they arrived at their destination, it was snowing

heavily. The freshly fallen snow had been cleared from the area around the Wall.

Visitors, reporters, and photographers were kept at a distance. It was vital for the six men to visit the site in private, and pay tribute to the men whose names were listed on the Wall. This was not a time for media, or even family members. No one could understand how sacred and special this time was for the men.

Le knew his friends needed this special time together, free from the watching world and activity of the past few hours.

As the men walked down the path to the memorial, emotions ran high.

The two black granite walls were striking with light gray lettering. It was larger than they imagined, spanning two hundred and forty-six feet long, and standing ten feet at the highest point.

The men stared solemnly at the 58,261 names listed on the Wall. Grief overwhelmed them. It was amazing they had any tears left after their eventful day. Somehow, more tears coursed down their faces as six brave soldiers wept for those who paid the supreme sacrifice.

They paid particular attention to twelve hundred names listed as MIAs and POWs. Among them were many familiar names, twenty-seven names were men they knew very well.

Colonel McCarter pointed to Corporal Daniel Sparks' name. Too emotionally drained to speak, they stared at his name. For forty years, Sparks was one of them, in name only. Yet seeing his name was a reminder of how real Corporal Sparks was.

It was especially poignant when they saw their own names listed on the spectacular memorial.

After a lengthy time of reflection and memories, now exhausted, they were ready to leave. It had been a draining day. The worn-out soldiers and their families would soon head in different directions. That would be strange for them. Something they dreamed of through their long imprisonment would soon become real. There would be many obstacles to overcome in their lives, but they would do it. After all, this was a new life of freedom!

They walked back to the limousines quietly, thoughtfully.

It was time to say goodbye to each other and to Le. The handshaking, hugging, and the farewells were difficult and the tears would not stop. They were anxious to go home with their families, yet they had been through so much together. They were the only ones who understood what happened in the course of those long years. During that time, they depended on each other, even if only through the tapping in a dark cell. No one expected the goodbyes to be this difficult. Could they survive without each other?

Finally, the inevitable moment came when they parted and went their separate ways. Le watched as the last limo disappeared into the darkness, tires kicking up the new fallen snow. Consumed with loneliness, he felt totally lost. Maybe fatigue dulled his senses.

He stood still for a second, then turned and noticed his family standing in the falling snow, waiting patiently by the limo. He fought the impulse to break down and weep. He drew a slow, deep breath. He would miss his friends greatly. Even though he had been with them for only four years, it felt like forty. He had been one of them, both physically and emotionally.

⟶⋆⟶⋆⟶

Le's family stayed in Washington, D.C. for three weeks while being processed for American citizenship. The luxurious five-star hotel provided comfort they never knew existed. They toured the city and enjoyed the sights Le had learned about on the Internet. It was a helpful time of transition for them.

A major university in Colorado offered Le a position teaching his native language. He readily accepted the offer. He would live near the mountains and be close to his special friend, James. This job would give him summers off and enable him to go on lecture tours.

Just as Sam and Nancee said, speaking engagements were abundant—churches, schools, universities, and public rallies. Because of his role in freeing the prisoners, he was in high demand. His flexible schedule was beneficial.

First, there was something unfinished—something he still needed to do.

# Nineteen

# Honor Due

---

Le's picture and story were in almost every major newspaper in the world and on the cover of many news magazines. His face appeared often on the Internet and even on some billboards. All of America seemed to recognize the Vietnamese VIP.

Although he was still a little uncertain what the hubbub was about, Le kept his focus on one thing and one thing only—the pouch. He set in motion the project he had to finish. He took the carefully guarded pouch from around his neck and studied its contents for a long time. He had already received permission from military leadership and President Nathan Alexander to implement his plan. The authorities made the necessary arrangements for him to carry it out.

His first mission was to meet the family of Corporal Daniel Sparks, the soldier whose identity he assumed for four years. He was relieved to discover that Daniel's parents were still alive. He boarded a military jet to Butte, Montana.

At the airport in Butte, an official vehicle awaited to drive him to the Sparks' home.

Le was uncertain how the family would respond to him. Would they see him as an enemy or friend? The army informed the Sparks family ahead of time about Le's coming, but didn't tell them the reason for his visit.

As the car stopped in front of the simple, ranch style home, Le whispered a short prayer. He climbed out of the car and took a deep breath in the cool, brisk air. *Please God, help me as I meet this family. I want to help them, not hurt them.*

He walked to the door slowly and noticed the curtains move to one side. He saw the face of an older woman peeking out. Seeing her sent a shiver down Le's back. How will they react when they meet him? After all, his country was responsible for the death of their only son.

He rang the doorbell and looked around at the freshly fallen snow. Three birds sat on a feeder nearby, singing a delightful melody.

The door squeaked as it opened. An elderly couple stood in the doorway holding hands, seeming to draw strength from each other. Le knew they were in their eighties. Although they moved slowly, they appeared to be well. The Montana climate has been good to them, he thought.

Le smiled at them and broke the ice saying, "Hello. I am Le Huu Trang."

"Good Morning," they replied pleasantly in unison.

"Come in, please," Daniel's mother said as she moved aside, gesturing for him to enter.

As he stepped into the cozy room, Le noticed the aroma of bacon lingering from breakfast. The home gave the feeling of warmth and love.

"Would you like to sit?" the man said pointing to an old, flowered sofa.

As Le sat down the woman offered him a cup of coffee.

"That would be nice."

"Sugar and cream?"

"No, thank you. Black will be fine."

She disappeared into the kitchen.

For a moment, it was a little awkward sitting and waiting in the quaint surroundings. It appeared the couple lived a comfortable life, but certainly nothing elaborate.

Le noticed a lone picture in the center of the fireplace mantle. It was a photograph of a young man in military uniform. An MIA ribbon draped over the photo. He immediately knew the identity of the soldier.

Le walked over and stared at the picture. "May I?" he asked, pointing to the photo.

"Sure, go ahead."

Knowing how much it meant to them, Le picked it up respectfully.

The elderly man spoke in short sentences, never wasting any words. "That is our son, Daniel. Our only child. Doctors said if Mary had another baby, it would kill her. Danny was a good son. Great athlete in high school. Best high jumper in the state, two years in a row."

Le touched the ribbon as he stared at the photo, listening to the proud, but grieving father.

"Joined the army fresh out of high school. Said it would pay for his college. He felt he had to do his part for America. My, he looked fine in that uniform. He was in the army, like me. Went missing in Nam. They tell us he's dead. It's been forty years. They are probably right. We had a funeral. Tombstone and everything. Just no …no Daniel."

Tears began to well up in Le's eyes as he listened to the father speak so admirably about his son. He studied the picture. It was almost as though he was looking at himself. How would he explain the situation to the hurting parents?

Daniel was a good-looking young man, lean and tall in stature. In the photo he was only nineteen years old—certainly too young to be fighting a war so far away.

Le carefully returned the picture to its original place, trying not to disturb anything else on the mantle. He sat down waiting for the right time to tell the Sparks the reason for his visit.

The conversation changed to small talk when the host asked Le about his trip.

Finally, the woman returned with a steaming cup of coffee. Le immediately stood as she handed it to him. He thanked her and brought it slowly to his lips.

As he sat down, his eyes were drawn to the photo again. He

realized the hopes and dreams of these parents were shattered with the notice of their son's missing in action status.

Le closed his eyes and uttered another silent prayer. *God, give me strength. Please help me.*

"Is it too hot?" the woman asked.

"No, I like it hot. It is delicious. Thank you."

There was an uneasy silence as he sipped his coffee.

Finally, Le broke the stillness by explaining the reason for his visit.

Mr. and Mrs. Sparks already knew who he was and what he had done for the six prisoners. How could they not know? The entire world heard about Le and his friends. When the news first broke, they desperately longed for one of the rescued men to be their Danny. However, their hopes faded when the names were announced. On the other hand, they were excited for the families of the soldiers who were alive. It gave them at least a flicker of hope for their son.

Le found it painful to share his experience. With all his strength and with God's help he began. He told them what relationship he had to the men in the prison camp. He watched their reactions carefully as he told them each intricate detail. He explained how he and the guards before him assumed their son's name, Corporal Daniel Sparks. He confessed to being recruited by General Yo to listen to the conversations of the prisoners. He told how the prisoners knew him as "Saturday." He related to the eager parents everything he knew about their son.

Le only knew the information the other guards passed down to him through the years. He believed some details should not be revealed. They did not need to know how badly the guards treated the young soldier after his capture, only how brave he was. That's all that mattered at this point.

The dreaded question came from Mr. Sparks, "How did he die?"

"I am not certain, but I do know where his remains are. President Alexander assured me that his remains and those of the other twenty-six missing soldiers would be returned to America."

Le took the pouch from around his neck. He opened the small bag carefully, removed something, and clutched it in his hand. He walked over to the proud father. "Sir, with great honor and sorrow I present this to you."

The bereaved father carefully took the item from Le's hand. He knew immediately what it was. He had received a similar set while serving in World War II. He held Daniel's dog tags, still attached to the chain. They were worn, but shiny and readable— the army's means of identifying a soldier.

"When I received them they were rusty. I tried hard to keep them in good condition in case this moment ever came."

The heartbroken father read the inscription aloud. *Sparks, Daniel M. RA 16917813 AB+ Protestant.* "My son's dog tags," the father lamented. He looked at Le, then over at his wife as tears began to fill his eyes. He handed the treasure to her.

She took them and held them delicately. Of course, they weren't breakable, but they represented something precious to them. They were representative of their son's life, a tangible remembrance, possibly the last thing he touched before he died.

Mr. Sparks stood up slowly and faced Le. Neither man knew what to say or do.

Le spoke from his heart, but was uncertain how the sorrowful parents would react. "Mr. and Mrs. Sparks, on behalf of myself and my people, I am truly sorry for your loss. Your son died trying to give freedom to my country, the Vietnamese people. Your great leader Abraham Lincoln, in the Gettysburg Address referred to a life not given in vain. Your son's life certainly was not given in vain."

The man and his wife looked at Le, carefully concentrating on his words. The elderly couple began to sob quietly as they embraced Le, "Thank You."

Le was uncertain if their tears were out of gratitude for the dog tags, or because they finally had some information about Daniel's death. It didn't matter.

Finally, they released their grip on Le. He turned and walked slowly to the door. This caring couple needed time alone. They could finally grieve their beloved son. Healing could come because now they knew with certainty what they always wondered.

As Le departed, he glanced back to see them still embracing each other tearfully. How he wished he could have brought them good news! He closed the door quietly and headed to the car.

Le looked at the young military driver waiting for him. Sadness and compassion showed on Le's face. The driver noticed how shaken he was.

Le's mind was reeling from the impact of what had just transpired. Reflecting, he stood at the limo, laid his arms on the door, and rested his head on his arms.

The birds on the feeder, suddenly startled by a nearby noise, flew by chirping loudly. The house door sprang open and the father yelled, "Young man, please stop!"

He turned to face Mr. Sparks wondering what he would say. Le was afraid he would condemn him and leave him shattered by his remarks. He knew how words could crush a man; he saw it repeatedly with General Yo.

In a shaky voice, the elderly man said with sincerity, "Thank you Mr. Le. God bless you."

Le smiled and replied, "He already has sir. He already has."

The driver, deeply touched, looked through red eyes as he opened the car door for Le. He nodded his head and smiled at the former guard, both of them feeling the deep emotion of the incident.

As he sat back in the seat, Le removed the small bag from around his neck and stared at the contents. Inside were twenty-six more sets of dog tags, each representing a man, a life who died at the hands of General Yo.

For the last couple of years Le searched for, traded, and bought the tags, usually from other guards. Some he took from Yo. He intended to send them to the men's families. The last thing he ever expected was to hand them to their relatives face-to-face.

The next three weeks would be busy and very stressful for him. He planned to visit each family of the twenty-six soldiers, apologize to them, and give them back a remembrance of their lost loved one—his dog tags.

✈ ✈ ✈

After thousands of miles and endless hours, Le visited the last family. He reached his goal, and visited with representatives of each soldier's loved ones. Most were gracious, some were bitter, but all were grateful they could close this part of their lives.

When he was finally finished, Le was exhausted. The ordeal had taken a huge emotional toll on him. He felt drained physically, emotionally, and spiritually.

As he was leaving the last small town in northern New Hampshire, they drove by a picturesque white church. It resembled a Christmas card scene.

Le asked the driver to stop. The military vehicle pulled up to the church and Le stepped out carefully. He looked around, and breathed in the fresh, crisp air. He closed his eyes briefly and quietly said, "I wish Sam was with me. He could lift my spirits. He knew when I needed encouragement and always helped."

He strode toward the serene church. It surprised him to find the front door was unlocked. Curiously, Le opened the wide, wooden, red door and entered the foyer.

He looked around for a few moments. It was a homey church with a striking sanctuary. The old fashioned, wooden pews could probably seat a couple hundred people. He paced up front to the altar. A large pipe organ was on one side. A choir loft was in the center of the platform behind the carved wood pulpit. A piano and two guitars were nearby, ready for use on Sunday. On one wall was a large screen for videos and lyrics to the congregational songs.

The wall on the other side displayed a large picture of Jesus standing in front of a closed door. Le had seen the picture before and it always fascinated him. As he studied the famous painting, he noticed something odd, something he had not noticed before. There was no door handle on the outside of the door where Jesus stood knocking.

Le was startled when a well-dressed man burst into the room. His warm smile instantly gave Le a feeling of serenity.

"Hello. I'm Pastor Murdock. What can I do for you?" The friendly minister extended his hand to Le.

As Le shook his hand, he introduced himself.

The pastor interrupted, "I know who you are. Almost everyone in America knows who you are. I suspect you came to visit a family from our church."

Le nodded in agreement.

"Did they accept what you had to say with a good spirit?" Pastor Murdock inquired.

"Yes, they did. I told them what they already knew in their minds, but were unable to accept in their hearts."

"How many more families do you still have to visit?"

"I would like to visit all 58,000 plus of them, but am only obligated to visit twenty-six. Well, actually twenty-seven. This was my last one. I have completed what I set out to do."

"You look tired and exhausted."

"That I am. It has not been easy."

Le turned back to face the picture, "May I ask you a question, Pastor Murdock?"

"Sure, go right ahead."

"That picture. I've seen it before, but never so close."

"It's a beautiful painting. Holman Hunt was the artist."

"I have two questions. First, why all the vines? Second, why is there no handle on the door? That seems sort of strange."

"The painting is perhaps the most famous one ever painted of Christ, except for "The Last Supper," of course. Hunt painted the original in 1853 and named it "The Light of the World.""

Pastor Murdock pointed to the picture. "It depicts Jesus knocking on a door, which is covered with weeds and vines. The overgrowth suggests the person on the inside has failed to look for truth. I understand it represents a human's conscience."

Le was mesmerized, hanging on to every word the pastor said. "The door does not have a handle on the outside because the human heart must be opened from the inside. Only an individual can ask Jesus into his heart. He will not come in without an invitation, nor will He force Himself into any person's life. The lantern Jesus is holding is a symbol of the light He brings when He enters a life."

The words stirred Le deeply.

"The Scripture that inspired the painting is in Revelation 3, verses 19-21." *Behold, I stand at the door and knock; if anyone hears my voice and opens the door, I will come in to him and will dine with him, and he with me.*

Silence reigned while both men reflected on the meaningful artwork.

The pastor spoke first. "Each person must decide whether to open the door of his heart and ask Christ in, or keep Him on the outside. Jesus still stands outside of the door waiting. Will we invite Him into our lives? Sadly, many leave him on the outside, unwilling to surrender their lives to Him."

"Interesting."

"What do you mean?" the pastor inquired.

Le continued to gaze at the picture; his eyes locked on the image. "When I was a guard at the prison I tried many times to get the prisoners to understand that I was trying to help when I tapped on the wall. They ignored what I told them. I knew freedom was close and yet they would not trust me. One day they finally did. Because they trusted, now they are free."

Le looked at the pastor and added, "I'm not comparing myself to God. I'm just stating the similarities." He sounded defensive; he did not want to be misunderstood.

"I understand."

"In order to be free, we must first trust and then open the door of our hearts."

"Have you invited Jesus into your life?" the wise pastor asked.

"Yes. He changed my life, and now I am able to impact the lives of others."

"That's the way it works. Judging by what I have seen and heard, what happened in your life has helped change the world."

"What do you mean?"

"You have given America a fresh, new hope. Before you stepped forward to help the six prisoners, the world was getting darker. Sin was prevalent everywhere. Many churches were dying. Religion was under attack. Public schools no longer allowed prayer. Even our national motto, *In God We Trust*, was being removed from some of our coins and public places."

He looked directly into Le's brown eyes. He thought carefully before he continued his remarks to the young Vietnamese man. "I can only speak of what I have seen. Since you arrived in America with those six men this congregation has doubled in size. People from all areas of life have come through that door. Giving has doubled and my workload has certainly increased. Trust me, I'm not complaining, I'm just stating a fact."

The pastor took a deep, calming breath. "America is beginning to experience renewal. It seems as though the nation is finally coming to its senses. You sir, have inspired America. I pray that the spiritual interest will continue."

Le nodded his head in agreement and listened intently as the pastor continued. "Many times in the past the same thing happened. The assassination of President Kennedy, Desert Storm, and 9-11 are all American tragedies, which resulted in people filling our churches and altars. However, a few months later, complacency took over. Many stopped attending services. Things went back to the way they were."

"And now?" Le asked.

"God is working—people are still coming. Who would have thought God would use a Vietnamese POW prison guard to lead the way to an American and worldwide spiritual awakening?"

"Who would have thought God would use a poor Jewish girl to bring his Son into the world?" Le added.

Pastor Murdock smiled and nodded his head, "Good point."

Le looked at the picture again. He reached his hand to the pastor. "Thank you for your encouragement. I needed this time with you."

As they shook hands the pastor added, "It was great to meet you in person. Thank you for all you have done. You made my day. It will make a great illustration in Sunday's sermon," he chuckled.

Le laughed.

"May I pray with you before you leave?" Pastor Murdock requested.

"You may. However, would you also pray for my friends; as well as the millions who are imprisoned by something in their lives and do not know God. They desperately need our prayers."

Pastor Murdock looked at Le closely. "Nicely put...Nicely put. I may use that analogy in a sermon, too."

They bowed in prayer. He prayed for Le, the six ex-POWs and their families, and for those who are prisoners of something in their lives—drugs, alcohol, apathy, and other forms of bondage. They are prisoners of a different type, but enslaved nonetheless. Sadly, many do not realize it until they face a disaster in their lives or until they come face-to-face with God.

Le began to walk away deep in thought when the pastor called, "Go with God's blessings, my friend."

Le glanced back. "A few months ago I was a communist guard trapped in a POW prison camp. Today I am a free American. I have my family and a host of new friends. I think His blessings have been abundant."

The pastor lifted his hand in blessing, "Then go in peace, my friend. Go in peace."

Le waved and walked to the waiting automobile. The driver opened the door for him. "Do you feel better now, sir?"

Le paused and turned slightly to face him. "Yes, much better. I feel as if a tremendous weight has been lifted off me."

Le collapsed in the car and looked at his driver. "I feel... feel...free! Yes, that's it. I feel free!"

# TWENTY

# Life Again

---

Arlington, Virginia

As the day ended, there was a chill in the air. The sky was breathtaking. The clouds moved in creating a spectacular sunset with assorted shades of violet, pink, orange, and crimson.

Le sat on the cement bench in front of five grave markers. Buried in these graves in Arlington National Cemetery were brave men Le was proud to call his friends.

Day after day, he typed thoughtfully on his laptop. He was almost finished with the account; it was a saga of freedom and of commitment to a goal.

A generation had passed. He vividly remembered the prison: the sights, smells, and sounds. Le recalled every detail of the frightening escape, and the triumphant return of the prisoners to their homeland and families.

Le kept in touch with all the men through their fascinating lives. After all, he had a special history with them—a unique bond.

Through the years, Le often reflected on the five words. Life…Hope…Faith… Love…Responsibility. He considered how they related to his six friends.

Life. The men lived free again. They appreciated every moment of life. All of them realized they could never recapture their lost years. Forty years stolen from them! The time was gone forever; but the nightmares persisted. Even when asleep they could never forget the horror of their imprisonment.

Hope. During the years of confinement, the prisoners lost all hope. Freedom restored hope to them. Their country's welcome gave them a fresh appreciation and expectation for America—a new hope!

Faith. The men regained faith in their country, people, and God. They realized faith in God is what brought them home. When their own faith was shattered through the long, miserable years, others prayed diligently for their return. It may have been a family member, an unknown veteran, or someone who had lost a loved one in war. The result was answered prayer. God used Le and Sam to fulfill His purpose. Thank God for the people who never lost faith and prayed steadfastly.

Love. Upon their return to America, love was awaiting each of the men. Perhaps it was a wife or child, sibling or friend, grandchild or elderly parent. Love sometimes came from a stranger, a community, or a nation. Love surrounded them and gave them the strength to live again.

Responsibility. The men had a responsibility to survive, which they did. However, their responsibility did not end with their freedom. They desired to share their account with others. Why? Should they not put their horrible experience in the past, and move on with their new life? The answer is simple—they must share their story so that never again an American soldier would be held as a POW, and be forgotten!

---

Le's new life was an adventure; a dream that came true for the former prison guard.

He followed his friend's lives to their end. He attended each funeral with his head held high—confident that he had known a real hero.

## *Thomas Traber*

Following the celebration in Washington, D.C., Sergeant First Class Thomas Traber returned to a gigantic homecoming in his small town in Kansas.

The popular senator, now in his eighties, attended his welcome home festivities. Together they recalled the days of drinking lemonade and lively conversation on the senator's back porch. The well-known politician told Thomas about his political journey, which nearly took him to the White House. Thomas was enthralled with his stories, just as he was as a youngster.

His time in Kansas was a special time to reconnect with family and friends. However, he did not stay there long; nothing was the same as before his military days.

He had enough hot weather in the Vietnam jungle; for a contrast, he moved to Alaska. He operated a commercial fishing boat in Juneau. He enjoyed the beauty and serenity of the area—outdoor activities occupied most of his time.

Thomas enjoyed a celebrity status. Often he would be the guide for Vietnam veterans touring Alaska. He considered that a special privilege.

He married a young, local Alaskan girl. At age sixty-two, his lifelong dream of becoming a father came true when his wife gave birth to twins. They were a close-knit family.

Every year on Memorial Day and Independence Day Thomas spoke at schools and churches around the state. His message was always the same— patriotism and freedom.

Sergeant First Class Thomas Traber was the first of the returning soldiers to die. At the age of sixty-eight, a fishing accident took his life.

A tall, serene mountain overlooking Juneau was his burial place. His grave was nestled under a grove of giant pine trees. The words on his tombstone were simple: Born April 12, 1950. Died August 10, 2018, at the age of twenty-eight. The forty years in captivity erased from his life—as if they never happened. As far as he was concerned those years should be forgotten as the tombstone etching stated.

## Ronald Lomack

Sergeant First Class Ronald Lomack returned to Missouri to help operate the family dairy farm along with his youngest brother, David.

He stayed isolated much of the time enjoying the solitude to which he had grown accustomed.

Every year on Veteran's Day, Ronald would meet the other five men, Le, and Sam in Branson, Missouri. They attended the ceremonies and enjoyed meeting other veterans during Branson's patriotic festivities. Veterans were always welcome in Branson. One year each of the men received a key to that small Ozark city. They seldom had to pay for anything—somebody who recognized them usually picked up the tab. It was an appropriate courtesy for such heroes.

Ron continued to have horrendous nightmares. He never married because of them.

He died in his sleep at the age of seventy-two. Le hoped it was a peaceful death and not a violent one still fighting that war of long ago.

A small cemetery near his farm was his final resting place. His grave was located next to his parents and brother. The tombstone read, "Peace at last." That was fitting for him.

## Anthony Williams

Sergeant First Class Anthony Williams was disenchanted with how much life in America changed while he was away. Nothing seemed to be the same.

His wife, who had been his childhood sweetheart, remarried after he had been gone several years.

He was too old to fulfill his dream of becoming a doctor.

His father died a year after he returned. Only then did he realize his calling was to become a minister. After additional schooling, he accepted the pastorate of a small Vietnamese church in Southern California. His knowledge of the Vietnamese language and customs he gleaned while a prisoner helped to equip him for specialized service for God. His forgiving spirit was a valuable asset and encouragement to others. The church grew in numbers and God blessed his ministry.

In later years, Anthony became a missionary to Thailand. He assisted the people in the villages and shared the gospel with them.

However, he never visited Vietnam again; the wounds were too deep—the pain too real.

He died of malaria at the age of seventy-four in a small village in Thailand.

Le flew to Thailand to bring Anthony's body back to America. He believed his friend deserved that consideration.

Anthony was buried at Arlington National Cemetery. Freeman, McCarter, Pfingston, Le, and former President Nathan Alexander attended his funeral, as well as hundreds of fellow veterans. It was a full military funeral with a twenty-one gun salute—fitting for a man of outstanding valor.

## Brent Pfingston

Sergeant First Class Brent Pfingston readily accepted the offer to be the representative for one of the Indy racecar teams. He married the widow of a famous racecar driver, fifteen years younger than he was. They lived a lively life, promoting racing across the nation.

Ironically, he died doing what he loved most, watching a race on the day of the Indy 500. During the fortieth lap, he lay back in his chair in his private booth, closed his eyes, and entered eternity.

Immediately following the race, his death was announced

over the public address system. The entire crowd stood for a moment of silence. The drivers removed their helmets and joined in the emotional moment. Everyone stood at attention facing the gigantic American flag gracing the center of the racetrack as it lowered to half-mast. It was a memorable scene.

Brent was seventy-seven years old.

His funeral was held at the Indy speedway. The stands were completely full. The former president, Nathan Alexander, delivered the eulogy.

After Brent's funeral, some of his ashes were spread across the speedway using the same helicopter that had brought the six POWs to safety. The rest were buried at Arlington National Cemetery, next to Sergeant First Class Anthony Williams.

## Robert Freeman

Sergeant First Class Robert Freeman lived a remarkable life. The month after they returned from prison camp, he had the opportunity to throw out the first pitch in the World Series. The President of the United States, scheduled to throw the ceremonial first pitch, proudly stepped aside to give the honors to Robert.

The New York Yankees organization offered him a position. His job was public relations. He traveled with the recruiters to check out prospective players. He knew it was not a "real" job, but he enjoyed going to the clubhouse and talking to the team members. They also enjoyed bantering with him. His quick wit and uplifting spirit often encouraged them.

Le became a baseball fan while listening to Thursday talk about it during his captivity. One day James, Anthony, and Robert took Le to his first professional baseball game. Their seats were directly behind the Yankees' dugout.

Everyone stood up for the *National Anthem,* except a nearby group of teenagers who remained in their seats, cutting up and joking with each other. Freeman noticed the teenagers, still seated, had not removed their hats. As the song began, Robert looked at them and politely, but firmly stated, "Show respect for the flag, young men. Stand up and take your hats off."

One kid sarcastically yelled back, "Are you going to make me?"

Robert eyed him and calmly replied, "Yes."

Another boy next to him yelled back the one thing he should not have said, "Hey, old man, you and what army?" With that, the group of teens broke out laughing.

Very quickly, three old, proud veterans and a former Vietnamese guard were standing face-to-face with the four obnoxious, disrespectful teenagers.

People nearby watched, anxious to see how the scene would unfold.

Within seconds, three marines who were sitting a few rows behind the rowdy teens rushed down to confront the boys. One of the marines bellowed, "What army, you ask? I'll tell you what army. It is the United States Army and the United States Marines. Do you really want to continue this?"

It was comical how fast their caps came off. The kids stood at attention trembling as *The Star Spangled Banner* ended.

Unknown to the men, cameras filmed the entire incident. It was shown on the giant screens around the stadium as spectators watched. Every eye focused on a screen as the three marines turned toward America's heroes and saluted them. The men returned the salute, and then they all shook hands.

As the marines headed back to their seats, the entire stadium erupted in a hearty applause. The ball players from both teams walked out of their dugouts clapping hands and cheering in a show of support for the soldiers.

One of the marines turned to the teens. "See those four men. They are real heroes. I hope one day you will be half the men they are."

The young fellows were speechless and embarrassed as they reflected on the whole scenario. During the seventh inning stretch, the announcer introduced the heroes to the crowd. Right after that, the teenagers came to them and apologized for their actions.

Robert smiled at them, pointed to the flag flying high above the stadium, and stated with authority, "That flag is more than merely a flag. To us, it represents life, hope, and freedom."

Le never felt more grateful than at that moment; he was proud to be their friend and even prouder to be an American.

Television networks across America replayed the scene the following days. Spectators at the game would never forget the patriotism displayed.

Robert married a prominent actress. Together, they lived a full life.

He died at the age of eighty-one. His funeral was a massive event with well-known ball players, Hollywood stars, and government officials attending.

James was there, but failing in health.

Robert was buried next to Pfingston and Williams in Arlington National Cemetery.

## James McCarter

An airplane manufacturer offered a prestigious job to Colonel James McCarter. He declined the offer, so he could live in Colorado Springs, near his family. He worked with his son at the insurance company and resumed his old hobby—gliding.

He never turned down an opportunity to speak at a school or church. He shared what God taught him and his fellow prisoners about life and freedom.

James was honored to attend his great-grandson's wedding; his namesake, who was born the day his family received word of the POWs rescue.

In later years, Le and James had memorable times with each other. Often Sam joined them. They fished in the mountains, went to ballgames, and observed holidays together. They reminisced and laughed about some of their unusual experiences. However, they never mentioned their time in the prison camp. It was a closed subject—never discussed.

Le was at James' side the morning he died at age eighty-seven. As his breathing became labored, Le held his hand and thanked him for their enduring relationship.

In a weak voice the old soldier replied, "Thanks again my friend for all you have done."

Le was at a loss for words. He simply smiled back at James. Tears stung his eyes.

"I'll see you on the other side," James whispered.

Le nodded his head and closed his eyes. He took a deep breath, ready to speak, but when he opened his eyes, James was gone.

Death ended an extraordinary life and an incredible chain of events.

Still holding his hand, the former guard stared at the lifeless body of his dear friend and smiled, "Yes my friend, I will see you on the other side." Le looked heavenward and said a silent prayer, then lowered his head and wept.

The funeral was spectacular. There were politicians, dignitaries, and a twenty-one gun salute. Forty jet fighters from four different branches of the military streaked across the sky. One plane represented each year he was a POW. After the sky quieted, four helicopters flew in a V-shape, known as the "Missing Man Formation." One lone chopper soared out of formation, away from the others, a tribute to the deceased. It was a remarkable sight.

Unrecognized, Le sat in the crowd at his dear friend's funeral. Le would miss him immensely.

Le meditated on the lives of the six men. When their government called them to service, they answered the call. They sacrificed their personal freedom for forty years of anguish, so people like Le and Linh could enjoy freedom. For that, all Americans should be grateful.

James' body was laid to rest next to his fellow soldiers, Brent Pfingston, Robert Freeman, and Anthony Williams.

## *Samuel Jefferson*

Samuel Jefferson married. He and his wife raised four children who all served in the U.S. Army Special Forces. He was a proud father, but nothing made him prouder then the day he helped rescue the six POWs.

Sam died a few days after James.

---

Le often wondered what would have happened if he had not met Sam. More appropriately, what would not have happened.

To whom does Le express his gratitude? The One Sam introduced him to at the orphanage, the Man called Jesus. If it were not for Him, Sam would not have been at that orphanage. Le would not have met Sam, nor would he have done the "right thing." Those six men would have died POWs, never returning to America, their families, or freedom.

And Le? He would never have experienced freedom— physically or spiritually.

Now Le sits at Arlington, close to where his friends are buried, putting the final touches on the last chapter of his book. He has recounted the lives of six brave heroes. The details of the hardships they endured, and jubilant return to their homeland will finally be available for the world to read.

The grave markers Le sat in front of day-after-day were inscribed with the names: Sergeant Anthony Williams. Sergeant Brent Pfingston. Sergeant Robert Freeman. Colonel James McCarter.

The fifth tombstone read, "Samuel J. Jefferson. Captain, United States Army, Desert Storm."

His friends were home at last—their final destination. Home in the arms of Jesus. After all, home is where you lay your head.

—————

Le looked skyward as he visualized the events of a night long ago. He clearly recalled every minuscule detail.

Following the incredible homecoming event at the National Mall the night of their return, the six men went to the Vietnam Veteran's Memorial. That snowy night Le followed the men and watched from a discreet distance. He was certain none of the men knew he was observing their activity. They were caught up in the emotion of the moment.

It took a while, but each one of them located his own name on the Wall. Their names had a cross in front of them with a circle recently etched around the cross. The cross represented a missing soldier. The circle—the symbol of life meant the soldier returned home alive.

On that blustery evening, Le observed the men pay humble tribute to their fallen comrades. Later under the cover of darkness, he walked over to the Wall. His friends had left. He was alone; he looked around and made sure no one was watching.

Le stood in awe staring at the black granite wall, overwhelmed by the number of Americans who died fighting for his country's freedom. He searched until he located the name of Corporal Daniel Sparks, the soldier whose identity he assumed for four years, also known as Saturday. He thought about Daniel's parents and the love they had for their son. He rubbed his finger gently over the etching, and whispered a prayer for them.

Then Le bent down and brushed the freshly fallen snow away from the base of the Wall beneath Corporal Daniel Sparks' name. He stood and removed a small box from his coat pocket. His heart beat rapidly. Staring at the box, he reflected on the significance of its contents. Then he knelt and gently laid the box on the newly cleared area—inside it was his "Medal of Freedom."

Le stood to his feet. He looked heavenward. The thousands of names inscribed on the giant monument captured his heart. What an incredible tribute to the brave men, and women who paid the ultimate price for their service; people from all branches of the military who served for the great cause of freedom.

Why would he leave his cherished award at the Vietnam Veteran's Memorial?

He believed he owed a debt of gratitude to Corporal Daniel Sparks, and all the brave heroes whose names were engraved on the Wall. These men and women sacrificed their lives for the cause of freedom for all American and Vietnamese people.

The names on the Wall represent not just one person, but a family—brothers and sisters, sons and daughters, mothers and fathers. Each name symbolized a life, a calling, a future with dreams and goals—all cut short by a tragic death.

Le thought about his friends, the men he originally knew as Sunday, Monday, Tuesday, Wednesday, Thursday, and Friday. They influenced his life enormously.

The lives of the men demonstrated honor...bravery...trust... courage...sacrifice. All for the cause of freedom—freedom is not free!

When Le placed his medal there, it seemed fitting—it was the right thing to do!

*Dear Reader,*

*Many cannot forget the Vietnam War. Others refuse to remember it.*

*As a Vietnam Era Veteran, I experienced firsthand the anti-war sentiment; the protesters who held "Baby Killer" signs, their horrible insults, and the hatred on their faces are difficult images to erase.*

*Our military forces were not to blame then. They are not to blame now. Our courageous troops serve our country—for the great cause of freedom. Our troops deserve our respect, encouragement, support, and admiration for their tireless dedication to keeping us safe and secure.*

*It is our responsibility to support them. Next time you see a soldier, thank him or her for serving our country. If you notice military personnel in a restaurant, offer to pay his or her bill. Express your gratitude to a retired veteran.*

*Teachers, adopt a deployed troop from the community who is separated from his or her family. Perhaps the parent of one of your student's is serving overseas. Gather supplies from the class for a care package. Mail it and save the family the added expense.*

*The families left behind also need our help. There are simple things we can do to assist spouses or parents of our deployed troops.*

- *Provide childcare so the spouse can have needed time to himself or herself*
- *Mow the yard*
- *Help with repairs around the house or on the vehicle*
- *Remove the snow from the driveway or sidewalk*
- *Take the family out to dinner or church*
- *Take the kids to a ballgame or other entertainment*
- *Use your talents to help wherever there is a need*
- *Sometimes a family member just needs a friend—a listening ear*

*Less than one percent of Americans serve in our military. They deserve our support. One day that freedom may be gone.*

*Plan a trip to the Vietnam Veterans Memorial to pay tribute to*

*America's heroes from the Vietnam War. Perhaps "The Moving Wall" will come to your area. Pay your respects. It will touch you deeply.*

*The World Wide Web has hundreds of sites dedicated to POWs/ MIAs. There, you can find many ways to support our troops. Check it out. Become involved.*

*Above all, pray for our military personnel every day. Ask for God's protection on our brave troops and their families left behind. Pray for all POWs, MIAs and their families. "You are not forgotten."*

*John L. Rothdiener*